Solo Goya

Other Books by Jon Manchip White

Mask of Dust
Build Us a Dam
The Girl From Indiana
No Home But Heaven
The Mercenaries
Hour Of The Rat
The Rose In The Brandy Glass
Nightclimber
The Game Of Troy
The Garden Game
Send For Mr. Robinson
The Moscow Papers
Death By Dreaming
The Last Grand Master
Whistling Past The Churchyard
Echoes And Shadows

The Rout Of San Romano
The Mountain Lion

The Journeying Boy—Scenes From A Welsh Childhood
The Land God Made In Anger—South West Africa
A World Elsewhere—The American Southwest

What To Do When The Russians Come (with Robert Conquest)

Marshal Of France: Life and Times of Maurice de Saxe
Diego Velázquez: Painter and Courtier
Hernán Cortés And The Downfall Of The Aztec Empire

Ancient Egypt
Everyday Life In Ancient Egypt
Everyday Life Of The North American Indians
Teach Yourself Anthropology

Solo Goya

Goya and the Duchess of Alba at Sanlúcar

A Novel

Jon Manchip White

Iris Press
Oak Ridge, Tennessee

Copyright © 2007 by Jon Manchip White

All rights reserved. No portion of this book may be reproduced in any form or by any means, including electronic storage and retrieval systems, without explicit, prior written permission of the publisher, except for brief passages excerpted for review and critical purposes.

Iris Press
an imprint of the Iris Publishing Group, Inc

www.irisbooks.com

Cover Painting: "The Duchess of Alba" by Francisco José de Goya y Lucientes
Courtesy of The Hispanic Society of America, New York

Library of Congress Cataloging-in-Publication Data

White, Jon Ewbank Manchip, 1924-
 Solo Goya : Goya and the Duchess of Alba at Sanlúcar : a novel / Jon Manchip White.
   p. cm.
 ISBN-13: 978-0-916078-73-7 (alk. paper)
 ISBN-10: 0-916078-73-6 (alk. paper)
 ISBN-13: 978-0-916078-74-4 (pbk. : alk. paper)
 ISBN-10: 0-916078-74-4 (pbk. : alk. paper)
 1. Goya, Francisco, 1746-1828—Fiction. 2. Alba, María del Pilar Teresa Cayetana de Silva Alvarez de Toledo, duquesa de, 1762-1802—Fiction. I. Title.
 PR6073.H499S66 2006
 823'.914—dc22

2006013730

A la memoria de
Valerie…
Cinco años en Madrid

> Amada, el aura dice
> tu pura veste blanca…
> No te verán mis ojos:
> ¡mi corazón te aguarda!
>
> —Machado

At the ages of 31 and 44, and again at 50, Goya suffered successive bouts of illness. During the last of these, which almost caused his death, he was nursed by his friend, Sebastián Martínez at the latter's home in Cádiz. For a time this illness, which occurred shortly before his historic visit to Sanlúcar de Barrameda, left him paralyzed and without a sense of balance and, when he finally emerged from it, it was to find himself totally and permanently deaf.

This fate he shared with his great contemporary, Beethoven, also stricken by deafness in mid-life and who also surmounted its devastating effect to continue working with magnificent courage.

At the time of their encounter at Sanlúcar de Barrameda in the summer of 1796, Goya was aged 50 and the Duchess of Alba was 34.

Solo Goya

Working, working, always working.

Now again it is raining, just as it was raining that night six years ago when he had watched from a corner of his window the lamps of the coaches as they had flickered down the street and had turned the corner and been lost to sight.

Tonight it is colder, much colder. The charcoal in the brazier in the corner of the studio is cooling to a pale glow. He pulls the thick woolen scarf tighter around his throat and stamps his feet in his felt boots to try and restore the circulation. He puts down his palette and the brushes to blow on his frozen fingers, which even the leather mittens on his hands cannot keep warm.

He has no notion what time it is, only that it must be somewhere towards the middle of the night. He has never bothered to keep track of time when he is engaged on a painting, and it is easy to lose track of time when one is deaf. He is unaware and will always remain oblivious of the occasional passing of a cart or the footsteps of a late pedestrian, the singing and shouting of drunken revelers, or the cry of the night watchman and the jangle of his keys. He cannot and will never hear the beating of the rain on the window pane or the whistle of the wind as it goes prowling around the house.

On that night too, six years ago, he had not heard the arrival of the coaches nor heard the bustle taking place down the street. What had alerted him were the beams of the torches as they begun to play across the walls and ceiling of his studio on the second floor of the house. He glanced up from his easel at the fitful flames as the coaches drew up and halted outside his door. For four nights he had been expecting them, and as he worked he had been holding himself ready for it. He guessed that it might not be long before she would set off after him on the road to Madrid. There had been no lessening of the sense of hurt and humiliation that had made him fling out of the dining room four nights earlier and take horse for Utrera, and from Utrera onwards by post through Seville to the capital. If anything, shut up inside the confines of his house, his anger and bitterness had heightened. If she pursued him, he would refuse to see her.

He remembers how, when the telltale illumination appeared in the street, he had moved around the studio extinguishing the candles and closing the shutters, leaving only a small opening through which to watch the activity in the wet roadway below. He stood to one side to avoid any risk of being seen. He had remained motionless, his arms crossed on his chest, watching as that little Neapolitan mannikin minced his way over the swollen gutters, followed shortly by Cayetana herself. He saw her step down slowly from her carriage, shrinking back a little from his vantage point behind the shutters, telling himself he felt nothing for her but a sharp sense of bitterness and betrayal. And yet, watching her move towards the steps leading to his door, protected by her maid's umbrella, walking with dignity and with her head held high, he had been unable to resist the terrible sense of grief and loss that came sweeping over him. Obeying some obscure prompting, he had found himself abandoning his position at the window and stealing downstairs through the deserted house and along the hallway to the front door. He had tested the locks and bolts as though to make sure it would be impossible for her to enter, but had then put the side of his face against the panel as if, although he couldn't hear her if she was rapping or calling, he could at least feel close to her. And then, his mind in a whirl, he had torn himself loose and gone charging back upstairs, floundering across the studio to post himself again behind the shutters in order to watch the departure of the mud-spattered coach on whose box he recognized the slumped and weary figure of old Esteban and young Pascual.

He had closed his eyes and leaned back against the wall beside the shutters, breathing hard and loosening the buttons on his shirt. Then once more, obeying the same obscure prompting, he had heaved himself upright and dashed again across the studio and rushed down the stairs and run to the front door, clawing back the iron bolts and snatching open the door and bounding on to the top of the steps and staring *frantically along the street as if he wanted to call the carriages back or go hurrying after them. Too late. Too late. And it was then, as he was on the point of darting down into the roadway, that he almost collided with a man who came creeping up the steps with a hand extended to pick up something lying on one side of the doorway. Whereupon he had given the fellow a mighty push that sent him reeling back and scuttling away into the darkness. He glanced down. A letter. He took it up. In the wet glare of the street lamps he could make out the first name written on the outside of the damp cover. He knew that writing well. He had snatched the letter up in his hand, had given a last glance up the empty street, and then had turned and gone back inside the house, slamming the door after him.*

It had been well after noon by the time the Duchess's coach had left Cádiz and was ready to rumble over the causeway joining the city to the mainland and turn north on the highway that led towards Jerez. These days the Duchess, who not so long ago had prided herself on being an early riser, had found herself tending to stay later in bed, so it was only when the morning sun was already growing hot that she had been able to summon enough of her old energy to ring for María Luz to dress her and make her ready for the six-hour journey.

She was not pleased with herself. She had fully intended to start early in the sneaking hope that when her coach arrived at the house of Don Sebastián she would find that Goya was still abroad on one of his all-night absences and had not yet returned. She could not conceal from herself that overnight she had been having second thoughts.

Her guilty wish was not to be satisfied. Goya had risen betimes and was waiting for her coach in the street outside Don Sebastián's house with all his paraphernalia in a great heap around him, while Don Sebastián's servants were scurrying around and bringing out more to add to the pile. As for Don Sebastián and his friend from Seville, they had emerged from the house to take their cordial farewells, without, she noticed, loitering unduly and giving her an opportunity to possibly speak and let them know that she had changed her mind. They were perfectly civil, but pleaded that they didn't want to get under the feet of the servants busy with the loading, and had swiftly made their adieux and taken themselves off.

And what a business the loading turned out to be! It seemed to take an interminable time. Goya was evidently not a man who traveled light: in fact it seemed he had brought half his household goods to Andalucía with him. They weighed down the roofs of two of the four coaches in the Duchess's train that had been intended to carry her baggage and her attendants. Irked by the delay, she let down the window by its leather strap and peered into the street. Goya was standing spraddle-legged in the roadway, gesticulating as he superintended the disposal of his mountain of effects. She hurriedly pulled up the window as she felt the roof of her coach rock as battered trunks and cumbersome packages wrapped in coarse canvas, obviously containing pictures, were heaved up by the grooms and footmen, directed by their owner with strangled and strange-sounding shouts and cries. Some of the boxes clinked and rattled as though they were crammed with the bottles containing his painting materials. She sunk further back on her pile of cushions, her eyes closed, her temples beginning to throb whenever there was an extra loud shout or a heavier thump above her head. Where was her butler, where was Carulli, why wasn't he taking charge of the proceedings? Obviously the broad-shouldered figure, stumping rowdily up and down, had simply shouldered aside the puny Italian, whose venomous sideways glances at Goya indicated that he did not accept such treatment lightly.

This great mass of trappings! She prayed fervently they didn't betoken that the man meant to settle in for a prolonged stay. Why hadn't she thought of providing herself with a larger traveling coach for this visit to Cádiz? And why hadn't she relegated her unwanted guest to one of the coaches in the rear, instead of instructing Carulli that he should be accorded the privilege of traveling with her? She now felt she had been foolish to tell María Luz she wouldn't be needing her services on what would be a relatively short journey, and had sent her to take her place in one of the other coaches with the rest of the servants.

And the trials of loading were by no means over. To her dismay, she heard the door of the coach being roughly thrown open, and opened her eyes to watch more of the painter's personal gear being loaded on to the seat beside her. The coach seemed hardly large enough to accommodate it all, and she had to squeeze back in her corner and draw her skirts aside. What a weird collection it was! First the servants stacked on the seat opposite her a creased and folded gray topcoat, on top of which they placed three large battered boxes of different sizes, covered all over with streaks of dried paint, and a batch of well-used palettes firmly tied with string. Next came a bulbous brass telescope, of a type she recognized from childhood as belonging to her uncle the Grand Admiral Don Leandro de Alba. What on earth could the man want with a telescope? Next appeared an object that disturbed her: a long-barreled hunting gun, its cracked stock roughly bound with copper wire. And finally the servants added to this growing pyramid of possessions a guitar, if one could really call such a pitiable instrument a guitar. Its neck and body were notched and scarred and two of its six strings were cut and raveled, hanging down uselessly across the bridge and sound hole. It was the sight of that cruelly treated guitar that made her wonder again, and not for the first time, what exactly it might be that she was letting herself in for....

Nor were her qualms allayed when her prospective guest now made his appearance, bounding up the iron step into the coach with a force that made the whole vehicle tip to one side. He did at least have the grace to pause awkwardly in the doorway to make her as respectful a bow as the limited space allowed, a bow she acknowledged with a curt nod and a fleeting twitch of the lips. In one hand he held a shabby beaver hat, a high-crowned Bolívar, in the other a tarnished and dented silver flask. Then, his bow completed, he turned back to face the street, presenting his broad back, clapping the Bolívar on his head in order to busy himself unscrewing the cap of the silver flask. Standing there in the open doorway, he proceeded to take a long swig from the flask, wiping the top across his sleeve, then handing it to the servants who had helped him load his belongings and who were crowding around the step of the carriage. They took turns passing it around, lifting it in a toast to him, grinning and making rowdy jokes. Next he produced a scuffed shagreen cigar case and bent down again to offer it around. Again there were eager takers. Finally he fumbled in his pocket again and took out a worn leather purse and slapped into each upstretched palm a big silver coin. She felt a moment of pique, shifting her shoulders under her traveling robe. Handing out gratuities in this way was not Goya's prerogative, but should have been attended to by her butler. It irked her that he had proven so immediately familiar and popular with her servants. They thronged around the door of the carriage and reached up to shake his hand and to utter cries of thanks and farewell to which he replied in harsh, high, squeezed tones, the words blunted and undistinguishable.

He stuffed the flask, the cigar case and the purse back into his pockets. She felt increasingly annoyed by all the dilly-dally and delay. She glimpsed the small green-clad figure of Salvatore Carulli shepherding the flock of servants away and gesticulating with his three-cornered hat and silver-headed cane. She assumed that he was about to give the signal to set off, and expected Goya to close the door, or let Carulli do it for him. Instead, he leaned forward and craned further out, moving his head this way and that and looking anxiously up and down the street. Then he suddenly jumped down out of the coach, clearing the step with a single leap, and she saw him gesturing urgently to someone or something she couldn't see. Carulli and the knot of servants seemed to shrink together and draw back as Goya put two fingers in his mouth and gave a shrill piercing whistle that hurt her ears.

The sound of a rapid pounding of feet. Then a huge dark brown shape came hurtling through the air and vaulted into the carriage. She had never been a timid woman but she shrank back breathless and scared.

In a flash, she realized that the animal had to be the dog Don Sebastián and his friend had spoken of the previous night, the beast that accompanied Goya on his nocturnal ramblings. But what a beast it was! Its big blocky head—its hulking body. A smoky eye raked her with a surly glance as it heaved its great bulk on to the seat opposite her, taking up fully half of it, then swinging around to stick its muzzle against the window in order to gaze through the glass at its master, tongue lolling out and thick tail hammering on her delicate blue velvet cushions. It whined and panted and slavered, and the Duchess, appalled, put up a hand and hastily covered her mouth and nostrils with her traveling mask to prevent herself from being choked by the rank smell that suddenly seemed to fill the carriage.

She stared at the beast with horror, pressing herself back in her corner, having time only to register that, paradoxically, it seemed to be well fed and well looked after, its deep rufous coat sleek and well brushed. Around its neck was a handsome crimson collar, studded with silver spikes and a silver plate on which was engraved its name. What was the name Sebastián had mentioned—Bernabé? Baltasar…? She shuddered, thinking of Conchita, her own pretty Bichon, a tiny creature which this brown monster could have snapped in two with one bite of its massive jaws. What a blessing Conchita was out of harm's way, cradled in the arms of María Luz in the coach behind!

How was it possible to contemplate spending the afternoon's ride to Sanlúcar cooped up with such a brute? It was bad enough to have to make it shut up with its master. She should have banished both of them to a carriage in the rear. What could have possessed the man to inflict this canine monstrosity on her? Insupportable. She must summon Carulli and instruct him that man and dog should be removed immediately.

Too late. She was still tugging at the strap of the window in an attempt to lower it and tell one of the grooms to run and fetch the butler when she felt the iron step being slammed into place and the coach sway violently, Goya swung himself aboard, and banged the door shut and hammered on the roof with his fist and then Esteban and Pascual sprang into action and the vehicle gave a great lurch. She was almost thrown off her seat as the horses gave a heave and the iron rims of the wheels grated on the cobbles. With a crack of the whip, she, Goya and the dog were off on the road to the north.

She let the strap go and lay back. A bad beginning. She would have to endure it. It wouldn't do to give the man the impression that he could dictate the terms of his sojourn at Sanlúcar, however short. King's Painter and Painter to the Court or no, when they reached the palace she would remind him of his place.

She adjusted her traveling mask more closely and leaned back, studying him out of the corner of her eye. He was busy rearranging the heap of his possessions and had laid hold of the dog's collar and was dragging it towards him. He held its head firmly across his thigh, and it wriggled its haunches ecstatically and panted and dribbled and rolled up its bloodshot eyes at him adoringly, drooling over her precious blue upholstery. He gave its thick skull a whack to make it lie still, which only made it slaver and whimper with delight.

The Duchess then realized, with a sense of shock, that the man was attempting to speak to her....

What was he trying to say? She couldn't make it out. Such an odd sound, a muffled bellow, the words jerked out and spaced apart, fitful and erratic, with no control over the pitch or level.

It was the first time he had directly addressed her since the time when she was staying with the family of the Count of Oropesa and he had first painted her. Then, before his illness, his voice must have been quite normal since it had made no impression on her. But what now to make of this hoarse, strident, blurred deaf man's voice, the words tumbling out and all jumbled together? An outlandish, inhuman sound, intimidating and threatening. She strained back in her corner, pressing the black gauze veil harder across her mouth. Fortunately at that moment the wheels were grinding over a particular rough and flinty patch of road so that whatever he was struggling to say was drowned out and after a moment he was forced to give up.

She found herself shaking. She felt under the robe and took out her bottle of smelling salts and inhaled deeply enough to make her eyes water. She produced her bottle of cologne and her handkerchief and dabbed cooling drops freely across her face and forehead. Her cheeks were burning and she hoped she wouldn't develop one of the headaches that had been plaguing her lately. They arrived with a particular force when she had her monthly periods, which were themselves becoming painful and irregular. This one was more than a week overdue. Still, she comforted herself with the reflection that her recent consultation with Doctor Arietta had been reassuring, and had made the visit to Cádiz worthwhile. As Don Sebastián had said, the good Doctor was rather eaten up, like more professional men, with a sense of his own importance, but he had struck her as proficient and thoroughly versed in the most up-to-date medical developments. He had sounded her chest through an ebony tube and made mysterious tappings on her chest with his finger and thumb in a requisite discreet and deferential manner. He hadn't subjected her to an excessive bleeding, only taking a few ounces from the forearm and making no incisions in the backs of the hands or the feet. He had admonished her to be sure and get plenty of rest and had given her medicines which he assured her would take care of the sleeplessness and night sweats and the persistent cough that had been troubling her even before her husband's death. He prophesied improvement as long as she took the medicines regularly and in the prescribed doses. María Luz would take care of that. Even now the African girl was seated in the coach behind with the mahogany box containing the padded vials of medicine supported on her lap, ready to administer the next dose when they halted at Puerto de Santa María for the change of horses. Glancing again at that grim figure hugging the repulsive animal in the opposite corner, she was glad María Luz had persuaded her to gulp down a double dose of the horrid stuff, enough to last her through the first part of the journey . . . .

Why had she let herself succumb to the blandishments of Don Sebastián and his obese friend into having to entertain Goya as a guest? She gave him another sidelong glance, apprehensive that he might break out once more into that incoherent babble. How could she possibly respond? To her relief, she noted that he seemed more aware than Don Sebastián had indicated of the effect of the onslaught of deafness on his speech. For the most part he maintained a stony silence, though now and again, he would whistle softly under his breath, a brief snatch of some popular song she couldn't identify. She was surprised at how sweet and melodious the low whistling sounded. But then, without warning and at unpredictable intervals, he would suddenly start and peer out of the window at something outside that had startled him. He would give a little croaking gasp and one hand would reach for the strap of the window and the other would stretch forward towards the hunting gun, making her heart jump into her mouth. What could he be looking at? What seemed to trouble him? Was it something real and tangible or some shadow, some phantom, the product of a mind clouded by a near fatal illness? But then, to her vast relief, his hand moved away from the window and with a little clicking sound in his throat he sank back in his seat and lapsed into his former silence and immobility. Then he slumped down, staring out of the window as if he was blind as well as deaf, on his face an expression of bafflement and despondency. In other circumstances she might have been moved to pity by an aspect so dazed and so stunned. This was a sick man, who hadn't received from their mutual physician, Doctor Arrieta, a favorable diagnosis as she herself had been given, but had been told that he suffered from a malady that was irreversible and permanent. Mustn't being told one was condemned to be deaf for the rest of one's life only a little short of a death sentence? Sense of smell, sense of taste, even sense of touch, these perhaps one could do without—but to lose, for all the years ahead, the capacity to communicate with one's fellows, with one's friends, with one's family? Again she glanced at him and gave a little shiver. For him, as Don Sebastián had said, only blindness could have been worse....

So there he sat, perfectly still, as the landscape rolled by, a monotonous vista enlivened only by an occasional cottage with its vineyard, its olive grove or cluster of cork trees. He stared at them dully and seemingly without a flicker of interest. He was becoming used, she thought, to being locked into that inaccessible world which he was doomed to inhabit. His only movement was the lingering motion of his hands as he stroked and fondled the neck of the mastiff sprawled across his legs, an occasional low growl sounding from somewhere deep in its cavernous chest.

Apart from the whirring of the wheels on the road, complete silence had fallen inside the carriage. He was unable to converse, and she herself had no wish to, even if she could devise some means of doing so. She was used to encountering blind and crippled beggars on the streets of Madrid, and the freaks and midgets still kept at court as fools and jesters, but she couldn't remember having ever come into contact with a deaf man. Again she asked herself what madness had possessed her to agree to Don Sebastián's preposterous suggestion...?

The sound of the wheels and the swaying of the coach, coupled with the absence of any active communication between the two of them, made her feel more and more sleepy. Not that it was altogether advisable, she felt, to let herself drop off to sleep with that huge evil-smelling dog so close at hand: nor was she entirely trustful of its master. Little by little, however, she found herself nodding off. She hadn't been sleeping well, and a short nap might do her good.... Her nagging headache was becoming more insistent, and there was an ache in her knees and calves caused by the lack of leg room. Her mouth was dry and there was the usual scratchy sensation in her throat. A short sleep would be welcome. Another sniff of the smelling salts, another application of the cologne, and she was ready to pull her lap robe higher and tuck it in and surrender herself to slumber....

The Duchess slept.

IN FACT IT had been her first visit to Andalucía. She had felt she simply had to get away from Madrid. She had been worn out by the interminable services and ceremonials connected with her husband's death which had seemed to go on endlessly. And she was deathly tired of court life, of dancing attendance at the royal palace in Madrid and the summer palace at La Granja as one of the principal ladies-in-waiting on the Queen, whom it was no secret that she had never liked and who had never liked her. And it was more than a mutual dislike—the Duchess was sure the Queen had been plotting with one or other of her loutish lovers for more than a year to do her serious harm.

So was it surprising that she had wanted to get as far away from all that as she possibly could? Even Andalucía had scarcely seemed far enough. She had been feeling for some time that she needed a breathing space to take stock of her life after her husband's death and put her personal affairs in some sort of order. And therefore she had hit upon the idea of Andalucía and had told her secretary

Ramón Flores to write to Don Sebastián Martínez in Cádiz, the man she and her husband had long used as their agent in the west of Spain. Don Sebastián was a director of the Bank of San Carlos and also an influential member of the Council of the Indies. She and Don Sebastián were old friends, and from time to time he had been invited to stay with her at her palace of Buenavista in Madrid when he was visiting the capital on business. She had asked him whether he could find a suitable hideaway for her in Andalucía and so was pleased when he wrote to tell her that the Archbishop of Seville had a palace a few hours north along the coast and would be willing to rent it to her. Apparently the place was somewhat run down, but that didn't matter. It sounded just the sort of place she was looking for, so she had sent some of her people ahead to get it ready. As she wanted peace and privacy, she intended to take only a small staff with her. She had left Ramón Flores behind in Madrid to handle her affairs there and selected only a handful of grooms and footmen and domestic staff, including her personal maid María Luz and her new butler, a Neapolitan named Salvatore Carulli who had a few weeks ago been wished on her by the Queen and her lover, the so-called "Prince of Peace." She regarded it as a stroke of luck that her chaplain Xavier Avalera had fallen ill with a fever and had to be left behind. Since her husband's death she had endured more than enough of sermons and services and cathedrals and confessions. On her arrival at Sanlúcar she had found a letter waiting from the Archbishop, offering to lend her one of his own priests, an offer she had politely declined with a note to say that she had found the palace chapel in a neglected condition and thought it improper to trouble him with the loan of a clergyman until it had been restored to proper order.

So there she was at the estate of Sanlúcar de Barrameda, settling in, and she had to admit that her new butler seemed efficient and had got the place into reasonable order. If it hadn't been for the tiresome cough she couldn't seem to shake off, she would never have bothered to have driven all the way to Cádiz this morning to see Doctor Arrieta. Her physician in Madrid, Doctor Bonells, had not been happy about letting her travel, though he thought the climate of Andalucía would have a beneficial effect on her lungs. He had given her the name of Doctor Arrieta, his colleague in Cádiz, who was reputed to be one of the finest doctors in the west of Spain and who was thoroughly conversant with conditions like hers—she had always had a delicate chest.

All the same, although good old King Carlos had much improved the roads of Spain and for the most part freed them from the scourge of highwaymen, the relatively short ride south had not been an easy one. An hour north of Cádiz a rough patch of road had almost torn a wheel off and by the time her old coachman Esteban had put it right the delay had meant that it was already mid-afternoon by the time that she reached Doctor Arrieta's house. She had then had to submit to a lengthy session in his consulting room. He obviously knew his business and had poked and prodded her very thoroughly, and at the end of the session had written out prescriptions for a whole new list of medicines. One of them had just been introduced to Spain from Bavaria and had called for ingredients that were not on hand in the doctor's surgery. He had to send out one of his assistants to obtain them, and by the time the medicines had been made up it had been too late to start the journey back to Sanlúcar and she had been forced to spend the night in Cádiz.

Fortunately, there was no question of her having to spend the night in some pestilential inn. A number of her friends in Madrid who had establishments in Andalucía had been urging her to visit them, and she had sent a message around to the home of the Marquis del Valle. Enrique del Valle was a celebrated bore and his wife Hortensia was a chatterbox and featherbrain, and although they were a good-hearted pair she dreaded the prospect of having to spend an entire evening in their company. However, she hadn't been there for more than an hour or so, listening to Hortensia prattling away about her dreadful children, when quite suddenly the situation was saved and she received a reprieve. A note arrived from Don Sebastián Martínez, no less, to say that he had heard she was in Cádiz and enquiring whether she would care to step around to his house for dinner? She would indeed. Trencha del Valle's twittering had already threatened to bring on one of her headaches and although she and her husband had pulled long faces, she had managed to convince them that seeing Don Sebastián was really an urgent matter of business connected with the tidying up of some of her late husband's financial affairs.

It came as no surprise to her, aware as she was of her friend Don Sebastián's skills and reputation as a man of business, to discover that his house in Cádiz put her little retreat in Sanlúcar and even of one or two of her own Alba palaces to shame. It was magnificently situated, standing on a hill outside the town with a splendid view of the sea. A house? A mansion, rather. Very grand, perched up high with a breathtaking vista across the town and the harbor. Below, in what she had heard was known as the celebrated "Silver Bowl", rocked a crowd of tall-masted ships, some of them no doubt belonging or on charter to Don Sebastián himself, their crews bustling about as night was falling. Don Sebastián had been waiting to receive her with a band of servants as her carriage drove up the steeply winding approach that led to the house, and after an interval to allow her to refresh herself had ceremoniously conducted her into the high-ceilinged dining room, long and spacious, with the dining table set in the window overlooking the harbor and the darkening ocean, where a crescent moon was high above the Atlantic horizon.

She noticed, as she was being ushered to her place, that although the table had been laid for four, there were only three people sitting down to dine. The table itself was of modest size, obviously intended to provide an intimate setting, and situated on a low platform so that the diners could fully enjoy the sweeping view of the sea. Don Sebastián seated her with a little flourish that was very restrained and charming. As she had when he had been her guest in Madrid, she found herself warming immediately to him. He was already showing himself to be an attentive and practiced host and the movements of his footmen and servants were deft and quick. He may have been a merchant, a man engaged in trade, but he nevertheless had the air and manners of a gentleman. She would guess that he was about forty-five, very suave and assured. He was tall and well set up, lean and with a graceful carriage. The impression he gave was one of courtliness. She could wish that there were more men in trade and indeed more persons in court with the bearing of Don Sebastián. He was wearing a simple black velvet frock coat, a buff waistcoat of fine-grained leather with small gold buttons, a plain white shirt and a white stock. His skin was lightly tanned and his long chin smoothly shaven. He was a calm and soothing presence after her earlier and somewhat stressful session with Doctor Arrieta, and she found herself looking forward to what would certainly be a more agreeable evening than the one she was likely to spend with Enrique and Hortensia del Valle.

As she settled into her chair, she eyed the third person at the dining table with curiosity. It struck her at once that there could hardly have been a greater contrast between two men than there was between Don Sebastián and the person who was introduced to her as Señor Juan Agustín Ceán Bermúdez, who Don Sebastián explained was a fellow lawyer and businessman from Seville who was staying with him while they settled the terms of some complicated contract concerning mineral rights in New Spain. This Ceán Bermúdez was small and squat, with a pear-shaped head on top of a spherical and sack-like body. He had little plump white hands that, when he wasn't swilling wine and stuffing food into his mouth, he liked to fold over a large round belly which rested like a quivering mass on the top edge of the table. Notwithstanding his lamentable looks, he seemed a jolly little man, and palpably well-intentioned, if dismayingly vulgar. There was a penetrating shrewdness in the small eyes sunk in the fleshy face that suggested he was an astute man of business, and explained why he was a welcome guest in Don Sebastián's house.

Of the wonderful food that had been painstakingly prepared and placed before her she remembered little. To tell the truth, even the rich smell of the food and the fatty smell of the candles that the footmen had now lighted made her feel distinctly queasy. She managed to sip a few spoonsful of soup and a mouthful of fish and picked at a wing of some species of fowl garnished with a vegetable of a sweetish taste and a yellowish color that Don Sebastián said was native to New Spain, but of the sugared cakes and custards and other confections she took none, though she was glad to accept a cup of the wholly delicious coffee brewed from a bean that Don Sebastián had recently introduced into Spain from some distant corner of Arabia.

What they talked about during the meal, Don Sebastián dealing with his food slowly and methodically, his friend slobbering and guzzling, the Duchess dabbing sporadically at her plate, was not of any great consequence. All the same, although too polite and good mannered to be obvious about it, she had been aware that Don Sebastián had been studying her closely throughout the meal. His expression was quizzical and guardedly questioning. She began to ask herself what was the meaning of that coolly appraising yet sympathetic gaze? What exactly was a clever and experienced man seeing when he looked at the Duchess of Alba? She turned fully towards him in her chair and tilted up her head directly to meet his gaze. Firstly, of course, he must be conscious that he and his companion were in the presence of no less a personage than María del Pilar Teresa Cayetana de Silva y Alvarez de Toledo, thirteenth Duchess of Alba, one of the premier grandees of Spain. They were in the presence of the descendant, among others, of the great Count Duke of Alba, old Blood and Iron, conqueror of Portugal and Viceroy of Flanders, executioner of Counts Egmont and Horn. No doubt Don Sebastián was asking himself what could have brought the Duchess to Cádiz in the first place, and why she had chosen this particular moment to bury herself in Andalucía? Here was a woman accustomed to living in a regal state, very much a woman of the city and not of the country, yet when he had handed her down from the coach she had seen him looking around inquiringly for her customary entourage and discovering to his surprise that she had been traveling with only a minimal number of servitors.

Why could that be? Where was her secretary, her chaplain, her treasurer, all the crowd of stewards and servants with whom he was used to seeing her surrounded at court or at one of her palaces? Where was old Gabriela Gómez, her nurse and *dueña*, who had been with her since infancy and from whom she had been inseparable? He had immediately recognized, of course, her maid María Luz, and had returned her little curtsy with a broad smile of welcome and a clasp of the hand. María Luz was a general favorite, and since the young woman was black-skinned and slender and appealing there was no danger of anyone overlooking her. Presumably, like many others, he was familiar with the peculiar history of this striking young woman who, together with Gabriela Gómez, was seen in constant attendance on their mistress. The Duchess had bestowed on her the affectionate pet name of María Luz—María Light—because her coloring was so black it seemed to absorb the light. She was tall, a little taller than her mistress, aged no more than twenty, shy and somewhat timid yet carrying herself with a regal bearing that rivaled her mistress's, making one wonder whether she might not possess royal blood herself. In spite of her dusky coloring her features were not Negroid but well-defined, suggesting a North African origin, Moorish or Berber, her hair set close to her head in a cap of tight curls in contrast to the Duchess's loosely flowing and luxuriant locks. She had been captured as a girl of fourteen or fifteen by the Duchess's uncle Grand Admiral Montalbán, in the course of one of the raids by the Spanish fleet on the African coast, and had been presented by him to the Duchess who had quickly taken a fancy to the girl.

Lamenting her own childlessness, she had adopted and become godmother to the baby girl Estrellita—Little Star—who had been born four months after the girl had been taken captive. The Duchess's critics, of course, of whom there were many, circulated a rumor that she had trained María Luz to be her personal maid out of vanity and to gratify her whims. The girl certainly added a touch of the exotic to the Duchess's appearance at Court or while riding through the streets of the capital, throwing the Duchess's riper and more luminous charms into brilliant contrast.

Of course, it was no secret to the Duchess that even friends like Don Sebastián could not prevent themselves from harboring certain reservations about her. Nevertheless, if she enjoyed something of a dubious reputation, and could be said to have courted some minor disasters, no one could deny that she had become highly popular in recent years. Everyone in the kingdom knew that the Queen and the Duchess of Alba detested one another and how the Duchess was one of the few persons in Spain who had shown the courage to stand up to the despised foreign woman and not infrequently face her down. The country loved her for it—how could Spaniards not admire someone who has nerve enough to play a dangerous game? In spite of some detractors, she had become the people's champion, and when she rode abroad men ran beside her carriage and threw their hats in the air, their cheers rattling the windows. When she shared her seat in her carriage with one or other of her presumptive lovers, she was admired for that too. What red-blooded Spanish female would not aspire to be the lover of a great *torero* like Costillares or Pepe Hillo who had been privileged to ride beside her in her outings, or more particularly of the *torero* rumored to be her current favorite, the incomparable young Pedro Romero?

And yet it seemed to her that there was something more than these abstract speculations in the way Don Sebastián was looking at her, after the servants had withdrawn and they sat sipping their coffee as the light above the ocean faded in a haze of purple and the candles began to brighten and the moonlight strengthened over the masts of the ships in the harbor. She took it for granted, and yet found room for regret, that many people whose attachment she valued must view her as an inordinately wealthy and willful woman who had been too much indulged by her dead parents. She hoped that Don Sebastián, at least, could make allowances for what he surely knew had been an excruciatingly long and loveless marriage.

She sat up straighter and smoothed a hand over her hair and pinched her cheeks a little, unable to prevent herself wondering, as a woman will, what sort of impression her physical appearance was making on him, a handsome male, a man of intelligence and experience—a man of the world. She felt herself giving him a coquettish and encouraging smile.

Well, finally he must register, mustn't he, the acknowledged beauty of her creamy skin, its olive glow enhanced by what she had heard described as the exquisite oval of her face? Admittedly the face might be held to be a trifle fleshy and a little marred by a slightly too full and too determined chin, evidence of what the world considered that pampered upbringing. However, could her mirror lie about the brilliant effect of those enormous eyes of an intense black-brown, surrounded by their clear white ring around each pupil? Was it perhaps those date-colored eyes that gave the face, in spite of the faint dark bruising beneath them that was the result of recent indisposition and fatigue, its wayward look even in repose, a look accentuated by the somewhat intimidating stare habitual with women of her class? The lashes were curled and feathery and the eyebrows, slanting across the forehead with hardly any division between them, were bold and thick even for a Spanish woman. And what of the nose? The nose was adorable, surely, arched and narrowly molded at the nostrils and still without a trace of a line running down between it and the mouth? And the small but delicately sculpted mouth with its full lower lip? Could anyone deny it was an appetizing mouth, so crimson and so wine-colored, the upper lip a little short, perhaps, but the lower lip so plump and rounded? Admittedly, she had to acknowledge that from time to time she had harbored reservations about her voice and manner of speaking. She suspected that her voice might tend to sound rather too slow and surprisingly deep for someone of such small stature, the phrases enunciated a little too deliberately even in moments of stress or anger, and each word spaced out so that it might often seem detached and somewhat affected. Of course, great ladies were schooled not to talk too loudly so she was never called upon to raise her voice. Castilians are notorious for mumbling when they talk, and she had also caught the habit of drawling in the favored fashion cultivated by the Court. Moreover, in addition to the closeness of her lips when she spoke, she had developed a marked reluctance to part her lips while smiling. True, high-born Spanish women were seldom seen to smile and were taught from childhood not to do so. King Philip the Second was said to have smiled only twice in his life, though admittedly that unfortunate monarch never had much to smile about. In the case of the Duchess, the reluctance to smile, though adding to her aura of mystery, may have been due to the fact that she could not claim to possess perfect teeth. Not that they resembled the teeth of her mistress the Queen, who was given to grinning hideously with teeth visibly rotting, the gaps between them filled with false teeth manufactured from diamonds, which gave her false and tight-lipped smile a grotesque resemblance to a death's head.

This frank appraisal of her own deficiencies was starting to make her restless, and she was glad to rouse herself from the reverie into which she had fallen, realizing that Don Sebastián had been speaking to her.

"I'm sorry, Don Sebastián." she said. "What were you saying?"

Waiting until the last of the servants had been dismissed, he listened for the closing of the door. Then he waved his hand at the empty fourth place at the table.

"I'm sure you've noticed, Duchess," he said, "that tonight I was hoping that we'd be joined by an extra guest?"

She collected her thoughts.

"An extra guest, Don Sebastián?"

Señor Ceán Bermúdez had stopped chewing and was sitting with his hands on his bulging stomach. Like his friend he too was now regarding her intently.

Don Sebastián's tone was carefully judged.

"I really must apologize for my guest's absence, Duchess. I most particularly wanted him to be here to meet you this evening. I regret that we may have to give up expecting him to make an appearance here tonight. He has been a guest in my house for several weeks, but often absents himself for a day, or for several days and nights at a time."

"Is that so?" the Duchess asked rather lazily in her drawling voice. "And who exactly is this slippery guest who hasn't chosen to honor us with his company?"

Don Sebastián put a hand to his mouth and gave a little cough. A slight pause before he spoke again, a little more loudly.

"Señor Francisco Goya."

He took note of the cloud that passed across the Duchess's face at the mention of the artist's name. He provided a temporary diversion by lifting the decanter at his elbow and insisting they sample a dessert wine he had obtained from a fellow shipping magnate in Málaga, the owner of one of the choicest vineyards in the high hills above Antequera. He poured each of them a glass and made a little ceremony of tasting it. His friend Bermúdez licked a fat finger to chase the last crumbs of Manchego around his plate and lounged back in his chair, loosening another button on his baggy coat and stifling a belch. From the recesses of his ill-fitted jacket he produced a bulging cigar case, holding it out across the table with a pudgy hand.

Don Sebastián did not return to the matter in hand until the two men had completed the ritual of passing a candlestick to one another to light their cigars.

"My old friend Francisco," he begun, "has been staying with me here in my house for the past six weeks. I have known him for many years, and admired him as an artist long before he became famous as Court Painter and Director of Painting to the Royal Academy." He twisted a little in his chair and pointed with his cigar at the wall behind him. "In this light it is difficult to make out, but if I ask you to kindly turn your head a little, Duchess, you will see a far too flattering portrait of me that he painted on one of his previous visits to Cádiz. And I have several other works of his in other rooms of the house. There are many people in Cádiz and Jerez and Huelva who are eager to be painted by him. He also wanted to tour around our churches and cathedrals, for here in Cádiz we have paintings by Murillo, El Greco, Zurbarán and Alonso Cano for him to study or reacquaint himself with. We had plans afoot to engage him to paint a series of murals in the Oratorio de la Cueva. But then he had only been here a day or two before he fell ill."

He took a long pull at his cigar. He now spoke softly.

"Ill, Duchess, very ill. So ill, in fact, that our esteemed Doctor Arrieta quite despaired of his life. I believe you have just had dealings with the good doctor yourself? He came to this house to attend to my friend three times a day for three weeks. That's how long Francisco was confined to his bed. We all believed he was going to die."

"Goya was a patient of Arrieta too? He never mentioned that to me, but then doctors do not discuss their patients with others... So he is here now—upstairs in bed?" The Duchess was not thrilled at the idea of an invalid painter suddenly appearing in his nightshirt, unwashed and reeking of medicaments.

"No, no Duchess." She couldn't help noticing his manner was becoming increasingly guarded. "He isn't in the house at the moment. He left his chamber three weeks ago—he has the constitution of a horse. It was a miracle he somehow managed to struggle back to almost complete recovery." He slowly twirled the glass of wine in his hand. "*Almost* complete, that is."

His friend Juan Agustín spoke next and the Duchess could not help but be touched by the note of genuine distress in the plummy voice of the lubberly man as he slowly tapped the ash off his cigar.

"He is deaf, Duchess. He is totally deaf."

"Deaf?"

"Absolutely stone deaf."

She frowned. "But what sort of an illness results in total deafness? A mental illness, perhaps?"

Don Sebastián shook his head and said quickly. "No, no Duchess. That is, not so far as we can tell."

"So what has caused it?"

"Yellow fever? Typhoid? Some form of poisoning? Dr. Arrieta couldn't form a definite opinion. Evidently it had been threatening for some time."

He paused with another shake of the head, until after a moment the Duchess ended the silence.

"But if he's deaf, how have you and Doctor Arrieta been communicating with him?"

"That has been difficult. We try to make signs. Or he writes down what he wants to say in one of those notebooks he carries around with him. Part of the problem is that he won't yet admit how deaf he is. He won't come to terms with it. The servants clap their hands and drop things behind his back. Nothing. There is no doubt he is absolutely stone deaf."

He then said what struck the Duchess as a strange thing.

"Of course, in one way we have to regard it as a blessing."

"A blessing, Don Sebastián? How could deafness possibly be a blessing?"

'Just think, Duchess, what it would have meant if he'd gone blind instead of deaf? Think what blindness would mean to an artist."

"But will he be able to go on working? I mean, hasn't it been a very great shock?"

"A good question, Duchess. It was a huge relief to us when

he started sketching again." He drew on his cigar. "It's just such damnable luck that he was hit by this appalling illness just when he'd already suffered what he probably considers is something more devastating than simply becoming deaf…."

"Oh?"

He gave a sad little shrug. "The death of two of his sons. What were their names, Juan?"

"Vicente and Eusebio."

"Vicente and Eusebio, yes. His wife Josefa nearly went out of her mind. Her mother had to travel to Madrid to take charge of her and take her back with her to Zaragoza."

"And what did the boys die of?"

"Who knows? Contagion from playing around in filthy sewers? The curse of all our cities. Whatever it was it only leaves Francisco a single son, Javier. The boy's about twelve, I believe, and not very robust either. God knows what Francisco would do if word came from Zaragoza that Javier had died too. I asked Doctor Arrieta whether he thought such suffering might have helped to bring on his terrible illness. He said it was more than likely."

"But why didn't Goya go with his family to Zaragoza?"

"He wanted to, but the family in Aragón will have its hands full coping with Josefa and Javier without having to look after Francisco too." He gave a low laugh. "Not that he has been the easiest man to deal with, has he Juan…?"

The fat man licked the end of his cigar with a liver-colored tongue and laughed in turn.

"Easy, Sebastián? Oh no, I'd hardly say that…!"

Don Sebastián poured himself another glass of Málaga while he gathered his thoughts. He gave the Duchess a reflective glance before he spoke.

"No, Duchess, we'd be bound to admit that Francisco's behavior has become, shall we say, rather difficult…?"

"But you had already said, hadn't you," the Duchess said, "that he was a difficult man to deal with? All the same, I must say that I hadn't noticed that his behavior was particularly difficult when I encountered him previously, when he painted my portrait a year or two ago at the Osunas. Nor whenever I have glimpsed him around Court."

"I'm afraid you would find his behavior rather changed now, Duchess."

She accepted another glass and cast an uneasy glance at the chair beside her.

"Oh—how changed?"

Don Sebastián pursed his lips, sipped his wine, taking his time.

"Well, to start with Duchess," he said speaking slowly, "he has taken to shutting himself up and locking the door of his room. We hear him pacing up and down, groaning and cursing and talking to himself. The servants leave his meals outside in the corridor, then come and report that the food hasn't been touched. He mostly comes out at night in the small hours and goes crashing around the house, still groaning and cursing and frightening the servants to death. Some nights he'll leave the house and go roaming around the countryside. He doesn't return until dawn, sometimes not for the whole of the next day. He carries a big knife, one of those ugly knives that gypsies call a *navaja* or "razor" and uses his hunting gun to shoot into the dark at heaven knows what. He's also got a pocket pistol that he fires out of his window in the middle of the night."

Juan Agustín pointed his cigar at him. "The dog, Sebastián, don't forget the dog."

"Ah, yes, the dog. That big ugly dog he keeps in his room that scares all the servants."

"Scares us too, Sebastián!"

"It goes roaming around the town and countryside with him. He's inordinately fond of the brute, for some unfathomable reason."

"Pestilential creature!" said Juan Agustín.

"Before he fell ill, he insisted the dog eat all his meals with us here!" added Don Sebastián.

"Greedy beast!." Juan Agustín sounded as if the dog had been snatching the food from his own mouth.

They were becoming increasingly worked up. And Don Sebastián was only just warming to his subject.

"One night he tried to harness up one of the carriages and was going to take the dog on a midnight ride. The grooms had a devil of a job restraining him. Everyone in Madrid has heard of the crazy way he drives those lightweight carriages he's fond of buying and which he's always tipping over. One night he wound up in Chipiani, notorious for gambling and brawling, and got involved in a knife fight!"

Juan Agustín nodded. "He's always been known for indulging in that kind of lark. Climbing cathedral roofs when he was young, taking outrageous risks in the bullring in the days when he fancied himself as an amateur *torero*."

He dipped the frayed and chewed end of his cigar in his Málaga and drew on it furiously.

Then, as if by an unspoken accord, they both broke off. Evidently they had been saying more than they meant to.

It was the Duchess, speaking dryly, who broke the silence.

"It rather sounds to me, gentlemen, as if your friend Francisco, illness or no illness, has succeeded in making a somewhat spectacular recovery?"

Don Sebastián shook his head.

"No, Duchess, I wish it were." He gave a wry little smile. "I know we've given you the impression he has been a troublesome guest and that we are anxious to get rid of him, but Juan and I are deeply worried about him. We've been putting our heads together and discussing what the next step in his recovery should be. We've been trying to decide what would be in his best interests…."

"Then why not send him back to Madrid? There are people there who know how to look after him. I can recommend Doctor Bonells."

He shook his head again. "No, Duchess. That is not a good idea. Plunging him into the hurly-burly of the capital might easily bring on another attack. What he really needs is somewhere quiet where he can rest. He'll scarcely find that in Madrid or Cádiz."

The Duchess felt a sudden chill. She began to sense what it was that Don Sebastián and his friend had been so stealthily and painstakingly leading up to….

"I think I've got a better suggestion, Duchess." He cleared his throat. "And this brings me, if I might presume to say so, to the favor which I would like to ask you? "

He saw the look on her face.

"You don't look happy, Duchess. But you have met Goya before, I believe, and you found his behavior quite normal and acceptable?"

"My dear Don Sebastián," she protested, "at the time I wasn't called upon to pay much attention."

Surely he could see she was speaking faintly, without enthusiasm?

"But when he was painting your portrait, Duchess, I'm sure his attitude and demeanor were perfectly respectful?"

"The man was employed to paint a picture. Why should he want to make himself unpleasant? As the Court Painter I hope he'll long ago have learned the proper way to conduct himself?"

Don Sebastián was growing assertive. His companion was eyeing her and stirring his wine with a thick finger.

"You see, Duchess," said Don Sebastián, "it's like this. We honestly think that the best course is to get him away from Cádiz. So Juan and I politely suggest that your residence in Sanlúcar would be an ideal place for him. The news of your arrival in Cádiz this afternoon immediately struck us as nothing less than providential. A perfect solution."

Though he could see her attitude was distinctly unencouraging, he pressed on.

"I have driven past the palace at Sanlúcar so many times, Duchess. It would be an ideal place to keep Francisco out of mischief for a while so his mind can heal and until he's fit to return to society. It stands far from town and is surrounded by scrub land, salt flats and marshes, virtually isolated. And when he's fit to return to Madrid, he'll be that much further along the path to recovery, not to mention that Sanlúcar is further along the road to Madrid."

The Duchess sat up straighter.

"Don Sebastián. Please. Hasn't it occurred to you why I've chosen to travel so far from the capital and the Court in order to bury myself in such an obscure little place? It's not as if I don't have other bigger and better furnished palaces. I could have gone to Liria, Piedrahita, Villafranca. Even if my health is not as bad as your painter friend's, I assure you I feel just as much in need of some solitary place where I too can heal and escape from the pressures that have plagued me since the death of my husband. I have met Señor Goya, true, I have had dealings with him. But I do not *know* the man and feel no obligation toward him. At the moment I've too many responsibilities and obligations of my own. And if your friend is such a trouble to you, don't you think he will prove to be even more of a trouble to *me*? I have my own troubles, Don Sebastián."

It was a long speech and it had provoked the obstinate tickling sensation in her chest and throat that had disturbed Doctor Arrieta and Doctor Bonells. She drank a mouthful of wine.

Silence fell around the table. From where they sat their faces were becoming obscure as the darkness deepened and the tips of their cigars burned brighter. Above the roofs of the town the sky had melted into soft hues of primrose and lavender, a darker line of violet resting on the rim of the ocean beyond the harbor. The silence of the two men and the pale gleam of their eyes served to irritate the Duchess further. She smoldered. She resented the sensation that she was somehow being selfish and being put in the wrong. After waiting for a moment to let the tingling in her throat die down, she began to speak again, trying not only to control her mounting indignation but a growing foreboding that her carefully planned seclusion at Sanlúcar might be coming under threat.

"Besides, there is another consideration. Has it crossed your minds that it would hardly be prudent for me to entertain a solitary male guest at Sanlúcar so soon after I've been widowed? As you've pointed out, the palace there is very isolated. Tongues wag. I don't know much about your painter, but I know enough about what is said about him in Madrid to know he has a very dubious reputation."

She was annoyed to hear Don Sebastián's chubby friend greet her last words with a high-pitched cackle.

Angrier still, she said, "I haven't brought my secretary, or my chaplain, or my treasurer, or my *dueña* here to Andalucía. Apart from a handful of footmen, grooms, kitchen maids, laundry maids and so on, I have only retained my butler Carulli and my personal maid, María Luz. If Goya came I would be virtually alone with him. Don Sebastián has mentioned his long suffering wife but he has not mentioned all the other women whom I gather everyone in Madrid whispers and snickers about. Not to mention the people in court circles and in the Paseo and in the Puerta del Sol. We don't miss much in the way of salty stories, you know. Isn't it true that his name has been linked to a score of well-known dancers and actresses? For a start, isn't it common knowledge that he has been involved for many years with La Tirana, the leading actress at the Maravillas?"

She felt flushed and slightly out of breath, the rasp in her throat lending an edge to her speech. She was vexed with herself for being provoked to speak so vehemently. Women of her rank did not do that. Nor was her vexation lightened by the sound of a fruity chuckle from Don Sebastián's fat friend at the mention of the voluptuous María del Rosario Fernández, the celebrated "La Tirana."

"Well, Don Sebastián?"

Don Sebastián had moved further back into the shadows. He spoke in a detached and measured tone.

"Yes, Duchess, Juan and I will have to concede that Francisco may have a somewhat questionable reputation. He is, after all, what one may call a full-blooded man. However, I can assure you that he is truly devoted to his family, even though like so many marriages here in Spain his marriage was not a love match but one that was arranged." Was he aware that in speaking of arranged marriages to the Duchess of Alba he was treading on dangerous ground? Nonetheless he pressed on. "The marriage was arranged by his father-in-law, the painter Bayeu, to whom he was apprenticed as a young man. It was entered into on both sides for professional reasons. Nevertheless he has always treated his wife with the greatest respect. She has her own servants and her own carriage. In his own fashion he is a man of integrity. Otherwise would he have been entrusted to paint the portraits of such important and illustrious men as our recent Prime Minister, the Count of Floridablanca? Or of Count Cabarrús, or that great man whom we all revere, Gaspar Melchor de Jovellanos—soon to be our Minister of Justice?"

He leaned forward so that she could see his features more clearly in the light of the candles. He put his elbows on the table and made a steeple beneath his chin with his fingers. He studied the Duchess's face for a moment and when he spoke gave weight to his words.

"Duchess," he said, "What we are talking about here isn't just a simple act of Christian charity. We are talking about a man, still barely fifty years of age, who is widely acknowledged to be the most important painter in Spain. We are talking, Juan and I, not just about a friend of many years' standing whose sanity we wish to save and whose life we want to prolong, but…" his voice wavered. "As you can see, I have many paintings and drawings"—there was a pale flash as he pointed a finger to the walls around him—

"by such artists as Correggio and Veronese, and by Rubens and Titian. I believe that he could come to rival not only Correggio and Veronese but Rubens and Titian as well. I believe he could become almost the equal of the artist he himself worships as the greatest of our Spanish painters, I mean Diego Velázquez himself." He waited in order to allow his invocation of the name Velázquez properly to sink in and then, after what he judged to be a suitable pause, he continued. "And so, Duchess, could we possibly let this superbly gifted man, who at this very moment is wandering about somewhere out there in the night, go down deaf and despairing to death and defeat? It would be a tragedy for him, for us—and for Spain. Surely, Duchess, you can find it in your heart to help us to try and rescue this unhappy man by bringing him to a place of safety, a place of seclusion, where his mind and body may have at least some slender chance of recovery?"

His friend Juan had not uttered so much as a squeak or titter during the course of this long impassioned speech.

What was the Duchess to say in reply? She was disconcerted. In the society to which she was accustomed, speakers seldom gave way to such high seriousness and lofty sentiment. To express oneself in such an outspoken manner was a breach of good taste. And was Don Sebastián really speaking so fervently about that provincial and rather peasantish figure she dimly remembered from years ago? And what did she profess to know about *art* for heaven's sake? All she was conscious of was that she was in danger of being wheedled and cajoled into doing something she didn't want to do and didn't see why she should. She wished bitterly now that she hadn't so eagerly accepted Don Sebastián's invitation to dinner. Much better to have spent the evening enduring Enrique's tedious monologues and pretending to listen to Hortensia's aimless babble.

She was still collecting her thoughts in order to frame a polite but stinging response when Don Sebastián once more leaned forward into the candlelight and began to speak.

"So, Duchess, Francisco had painted your portrait a little time ago…?"

"Yes, Don Sebastián," she replied, and this time there was no mistaking the tart inflection in her reply. "He did. He painted me."

"And, Duchess?"

"And, Don Sebastián, I didn't like it."

"You didn't like it?"

"I didn't like it."

"Might I be permitted to ask why?"

"Because I *did not like it*, Don Sebastián. That is why."

She saw no reason why it should be necessary for her to explain herself, and certainly not with his snuffling companion present. She had only agreed to Goya painting her portrait to please her husband, who had wanted it done because he had already felt his death to be imminent. After it was finished he had hung it on the wall at the foot of his bed, where he could look at it as he lay dying. Poor man, he thought the painting was marvelous! Mercifully, Goya had painted the thing rapidly, which her husband assured her was his usual practice. She hadn't paid much attention to Goya while he was painting her and he hadn't made much impression on her. She remembered that she had chosen the costume for it hastily and without taking much care. She recalled that the whole time she had been fretting about cutting the sittings as short as possible in order to get back quickly to the Osunas' house party.

She had realized afterwards that she should have taken more trouble over her costume and makeup. As it was, Goya had made her pose in the ridiculously stiff attitude thought appropriate for women of her class when they had their likenesses painted. In the picture she was wearing altogether too much red. Floppy red silk bows in her hair and on her bosom. A chunky red coral necklace. An oversized red sash. Scarlet cheeks. He had made her look like a silly schoolgirl all dolled up to go to her first ball. He had even painted a bright red bow on the hind leg of her little dog Conchita, standing there looking miserably unhappy, poor little creature.... Anyway, there she was, in that wooden posture, staring with a vacant look at nothing in particular, with her right hand pointing vaguely at some non-existent object outside the left-hand frame. And Don Sebastián had asked her why she hadn't liked it. How many women would enjoy going down in posterity looking like a vapid milk-and-water little ninny?

She felt so exasperated at the thought of the picture that she wasn't prepared for what Don Sebastián said next.

He spoke softly, making the words sound almost off-hand.

"If his first portrait failed to please you, Duchess, then why not engage him to paint a second one?"

"A second?"

"At Sanlúcar."

She was startled. Or had she, she asked herself, been half prepared for it? Don Sebastián was a shrewd and tenacious advocate, and she realized that this further suggestion, as he called it, had been cleverly devised to seal his argument.

"A new portrait, Duchess, and one that hopefully will please you better. A fitting tribute and testimony to the nobility and surpassing beauty of our Duchess of Alba!"

How could she resist such charm? *The nobility and surpassing beauty of our Duchess of Alba...!*

Well, well. A second portrait... Not that she still wasn't irked by the thought of the wretched first one. After her husband's death she had had it taken down and removed to an attic. A second portrait. Perhaps this time, if she saw fit to agree, Goya would take more care and make a better job of it. She would pay more attention to her makeup and costume. And at the same time another thought crossed her mind. During those first few days at Sanlúcar she had certainly come to feel that the days were dragging by somewhat slowly. True she had found the longed-for rest and peace she had been seeking, but she had also begun to sense that in the little palace among the salt flats and the marshes she had been growing rather lonely. If Goya's physical deficits didn't prove intolerable, and if as Sebastián promised, he would behave himself, then might it not perhaps provide her with company of a sort, provided she took prudent precautions? And posing for a new portrait might give her something to occupy the empty hours, might help to fill up the three or four weeks that would have to elapse before Miguel de Altolaguirre finished up his family business in Galicia and traveled south to join her at Sanlúcar. And then came another thought—surely an inspiration! This new and splendid portrait, executed by Spain's foremost master and in his finest manner, would it not be a marvelous surprise gift for Miguel, at some tender moment during their dalliance at Sanlúcar…?

She still had reservations, of course, but after reminding herself that she was, after all, indebted to Don Sebastián for the hire of the palace, she finally contrived to give way with an air of good grace. She gave a resigned little smile and shrugged.

"Very well then, Don Sebastián. You may inform Señor Goya, wherever he is and whenever he decides to favor you with his presence, that I shall be pleased to welcome him to my palace at Sanlúcar for a stay of a reasonable length, during which time he will be engaged to paint for me a new portrait."

Don Sebastián's thanks came floating towards her across the shadowed table, his friend joining in with a fulsome contribution of his own. She cut them short.

"I am sure you will remind Señor Goya, Don Sebastián, that my invitation is provisional and subject to sufferance? He will be expected to conduct himself, during that time, in a correct and seemly fashion. And perhaps you would be so kind as to settle whatever terms are customary with Señor Goya, and afterwards communicate them to my treasurer Manuel Molina in Madrid? Tell Molina that I would wish to be generous."

How long had she been asleep? Half an hour? At first she seemed to be floating on a thin sheet of water, trying to force her limbs to sink deeper into the darker and more peaceful depths below. Odd slivers of dream drifted through her consciousness. The shape of her dead husband went floating limply past, then the flickering form of a bullfighter she thought may have been Pedro Romero, executing one of his elegant passes with his cape. Then, more distinctly, she saw close up and staring at her the leering, raddled face of the Queen, María Luisa. One of her nurses had had *gitana* or gypsy blood, and from childhood she had been interested in dreams, spending many hours with the nurse seeking to unravel the meaning of her dreams before her religious grandmother had found out and put a stop to it. Vague and disjointed images were gliding through her brain, and she was seeking to make sense of them when suddenly and shockingly, as if she had been struck an unexpected blow, she was jolted brutally awake. She gave a little shriek and jerked upright. The robe slid from her shoulders and the traveling mask slipped from her mouth.

Her first thought was that the coach was overturning and was being furiously reined in by the drivers.

It came as a thunderclap to her to realize that what had roused her was the sound of Goya's dog barking. A thunderous bark, a pulverizing bark, a bark that in that confined space shattered her eardrums. She stared wide-eyed across the carriage, where of course Goya was sublimely unaware of the terrible racket that the dog was making. He could only guess what it was doing from the gnashing of its jaws and the quaking of its body, and sought to quiet it with a couple of hard but indulgent cuffs across the muzzle. He snapped shut the flask from which he had been taking a swallow. He grinned at the animal affectionately, unaware of the devastating effect its mad baying was having on his fellow traveler.

She thought it must have started howling at the sight of something outside the window, a flock of sheep, or a wild animal, or a peasant tending his fields. Then she saw that while she was sleeping, Goya had taken two other objects out of his capacious pockets and was occupying himself with them. The first was a pinkish cake of some sort of sticky foodstuff. The second was a knife, the knife Don Sebastián had mentioned the night before, the broad-bladed *navaja* used by the gypsies, the blade folding back into an ebony sheath inlaid with silver coins. The fearsome object sent a tremor through her as she watched Goya slicing off chunks of the sweetmeat and giving it to the dog, teasing it by waving them in the air before letting them drop into its slobbering chops. Goya was laughing a little, a piercing sound as discordant as the yelping of the dog. She couldn't prevent herself from putting up her hands to cover her ears.

Goya, arms raised high, a slab of sweetmeat in one hand and the *navaja* in the other, was laughing as the dog pushed him back in the corner with its great paws on his chest, snapping and slavering as it licked his face with its huge purplish tongue. It was some moments before he took notice of the Duchess and realized from her anguished attitude what effect all this pandemonium was having on her. He gave the dog another couple of wallops, then two more, before he could get it to desist and lie down.

That done, he gave the Duchess a look, not of mute apology, as she might have expected, but a sullen almost truculent glance that betrayed the hurt and perplexity his newfound handicap had created in him. He put the knife and the block of sweetmeat back in his pocket, then took from inside his coat a flat oblong sketchbook and, using the dog's back as a desk, turned to a blank page and attempted to divert himself by drawing with swift, slashing strokes. After a moment he broke off to snatch his beaver hat from the pile of luggage and clap it on his head, pulling it down over his forehead. He rummaged in his coat for his cigar case and shook out a black cigar and clamped it in his mouth. She was alarmed that he would light it, but he only chewed on it and rolled it around from one side of his mouth to the other as his charcoal pencil swept over the page. His attitude seemed to her more clenched and grim than ever.

 She seized the opportunity to take a really close look at him, feeling she should size him up before they arrived at Sanlúcar. She would have to decide, among other things, in what part of the palace to tell the butler to put him, and whether to invite him to eat with her at her own table or take his meals alone in his quarters. The more she studied him the less prepossessing he appeared. It was difficult to associate this figure, running so badly to seed, with the painter who was the favorite of royalty and the protégé of families like the Osunas, the Benaventes, the Solanas, the Chinchóns, the Carpios and Altamiras, not to mention gaining the approbation of someone with tastes as finicky as her late husband. True, his clothes seemed smartly cut, but they were spotted with grease and paint-stains and the fur of his beaver hat was ratty and unbrushed. The musty smell coming from his neglected clothing was heightened by the nasty reek emanating from his body, prompting her to further recourse to her *eau de cologne*. He gave the impression of a man facing defeat, a middle aged matador or *picador* down on his luck, and though he could only be barely fifty, the black hair straggling down from under the brim of his Bolívar was heavily streaked with grey, and the shoulders as he worked over his sketchbook were slumped and sagging. In the obstinate droop of the wide thin lips and the deep channels running down the side of his nose to the outthrust chin there was the hint of a man fighting a desperate and losing battle, and she noticed that there was a red line on the protruding lower lip that appeared to be the result of a slip of the razor.

It was the eyes, she saw, that were remarkable. This was the salient thing she remembered from the time when he was painting her first portrait, though then she seemed to recall that his features had appeared milder and his whole demeanor more accommodating. She would surely have remembered it had it been otherwise. But that was before his deafness had lent a savage edge to his character. But it was the eyes, yes, the eyes that she mainly remembered, the small black eyes flickering from side to side behind the easel. She looked at them now as he squinted at the sketchbook, cigar tilted at the corner of his mouth. Animal eyes. Not the hot rounded eyes of the mastiff doing its best to lie still, but hooded eyes, cold and sharp, sheathed by the downward slanting lids. They disturbed her. Since his illness the peculiarity and the penetration of his eyes seemed to have grown doubly powerful and unsettling. They were like the eyes of one of the big cats in its cage in her private menagerie at Moncloa. They kept darting backwards and forwards between the window of the carriage and the sketchbook, and she realized that he was using the glass in the window as a mirror in order to execute a self-portrait. He glanced across at her. He opened his mouth as if to speak. Immediately she averted her face and turned away.

For the moment she had seen all she wanted of this uncouth and shabby man in the grubby clothing. How could she help contrasting this lumpish commoner with her Miguel, her Miguelito, the sparkling figure who for so many months had been in her thoughts? Miguel! What a contrast between her Count of Altolaguirre, so smooth and poised, and this plebeian personage with whom she had been compelled to share this tedious journey. Or, for that matter, between Miguel and the Duke of Villafranca, her dead husband, who had been required to take her name in order to become the Duke of Alba. Drawing the robe around her, she slid her hand into the bodice and felt for the locket on the violet cord around her neck that bore Miguel's likeness. She stroked it with the tip of a finger. Then she moved her hand down her skirt until it reached the secret pocket that María Luz had sewn into it. She smoothed the square shape of the packet of letters tied up with a black velvet ribbon. She carried them everywhere. She had read them in bed last night at the house of the Del Valles. She had read them this morning before she dressed for the return journey. She knew them by heart.

Miguel's image came dancing into her mind, effacing the displeasing reality of the figure seated from her. She saw the lively laughing young man with the light coloring of the North, she saw the smooth light skin and straw colored hair, the soft blond lashes and the hazel eyes. She remembered their early meetings at court, when she had been immediately taken with him, even though she had had qualms about him because he was the favorite of the Queen and her lover, the Prince of the Peace. Nor had she been entirely reassured when his first notes and letters and the locket with his portrait had been surreptitiously delivered to her by her future butler, Carulli, shortly to be wished on her during her vulnerable first days of widowhood by the Queen and that same Prince of the Peace. But how could she fail to have become captured by his polite and discreet attentions, his exquisite manners, his smiling and unfailing charm? Admittedly his title was not a noteworthy one, and neither was he wealthy. His estates in the far north, one of the barest and stoniest stretches of distant Galicia, were said to be deteriorating and paying poor rents. His only assets were social ones. He was an outstanding horseman and adept with weapons. What woman wouldn't find it flattering to be singled out by this twenty-five year old young man, whose letters were so ardent and whose reputation around the court was that of a dexterous lady-killer and accomplished lover?

Of course, she was well aware of what was said about him by his enemies at court. But who did not have enemies at court? His detractors whispered it about that he was a popinjay, a *señorito*, lazy even by the standards of a Spanish *hidalgo* to whom any kind of practical work was deemed dishonorable. It wasn't hard to guess what Don Sebastián and his liberal friends would think of him. It was probably true that he had had more than a hand in squandering the last of the family substance, and no doubt at all that he was a confirmed gambler. People said he was a fortune hunter who battened on women for their money, and that he was only scouting around for some silly heiress or dowager whom he could reduce to ruin and beggary....

Ah yes. But what of the yellow hair, the fair skin and the hazel eyes? What of the slender legs of the dancer? What of the slim thighs of the horseman...?

And the passion? The grand passion? Heaven knows the name of Cayetana de Alba had been linked often enough to a whole string of suitors and *cavalieri sirventi* and famous matadors. But apart from her husband, in all the nineteen miserable years of her marriage, she had actually only surrendered herself on three unsatisfying occasions. Her husband? Impotent. Literally a dry stick. His one true love had been his music, sawing away on his violoncello. After barely a score, if that, of humiliating efforts to provide the House of Alba with an heir, he had given up and admitted defeat. Married at fourteen, she had had to endure her enforced chastity until she was eighteen. She could then hold out no longer and took the first of her so-called lovers, a bland and elderly *roué*. Then came a chilly Englishman. And finally a callow stripling....

But why should she dwell on such woeful muddles and messes? It was for Miguel, as well as for her health and a refuge from Madrid that she had sought the secrecy of Sanlúcar, that she had departed from court without obtaining royal leave and leased an obscure little palace in a distant province. It was here, in far-away Andalucía, that she would step out of her widow's weeds and find the passion, the delight, the tumult of the senses she had always sought.

When would Miguel come? This month? Next month? She must write once more to tell him to hurry....

She came to herself with an abrupt jerk, her reverie brought to a sudden end by the shrill grating of the wheels. The coachman was braking the coach and bringing it to a stop.

A yelp from the dog. She shook herself awake. She saw Goya's eyes fastened on her. How long had be been staring at her with pencil poised, with that unwavering gaze?

From outside the carriage came shouts and the tramp of feet.

Puerto de Santa María. Time to change the horses and light the lamps. Dusk would soon be falling.

One more stage to Sanlúcar. A drearier landscape now. Bare sandy plains and salt flats laced with stagnant pools and meager stands of straggly pines.

Goya's eyes were still fixed on her unblinkingly. Those small unnerving eyes. Was he thinking of her new portrait, studying how he would paint her?

She must make him do it quickly. She needed time to make her preparations to receive Miguel.

If the portrait is good, if she likes it, she will put it in her bedchamber in order to please and stimulate Miguel....

She felt again for the packet of letters that lay warm against her thigh.

She touched the locket that nestled between her breasts.

At Sanlúcar, when María Luz and Salvatore Carulli had hastened to help her from the coach, she was overcome with such a brief but acute spell of dizziness that the household staff lined up to greet her were alarmed, and she had to be hurried inside the main entrance by a flock of maids and conducted straight to her bedchamber. There she was put to bed, but when María Luz suggested that she send to Cádiz for Doctor Arrieta, she declared that the dizziness was only the aftermath of the long journey to Andalucía and the journeys between Cádiz and Sanlúcar. In a few hours it would pass.

All the same, for the rest of the day and the following day she was glad to lie abed, cosseted by María Luz and diverted at intervals by the young Arab woman's little daughter Estrellita and by her little white lapdog, both of whom she allowed to frisk around her on the bed. At intervals María Luz brought her a little nourishment and dosed her with the drugs Doctor Arrieta had prescribed.

By early the next morning she pronounced herself sufficiently recovered to rise and sit herself in a chair by the window. She spent the morning reading through Miguel's letters, now locked in a tortoiseshell case on her dressing-table next to her box of medicines. She had had her chair placed in the wide window of her bedchamber where she could enjoy the view of the lawns sloping down to the far horizon, beyond which she could just obtain a glimpse of the silver band of the ocean. It dismayed her a little that, in contrast to the magnificent gardens of her own palaces, with their battalions of gardeners, the lawns of this little palace in which she intended to recuperate and to receive Miguel were sparse and neglected, its single fountain cracked and dry.

The September morning was fine and warm and she had ordered the windows to be opened. Angling a little sideways in her chair, she saw that Goya was seated beside a small table that had been brought out and put in the shade of one of the few spindly trees. He was leaning back in a chair that seemed too fragile for his weight, its rear legs tilted at a perilous angle, his legs propped up on the table. He was seated with his back to her, but as far as she could judge at that distance, he seemed to have taken advantage of the previous twenty-four hours to make himself more presentable than he had appeared on the journey down. The high-topped boots had been polished and a smarter coat substituted for the shabby one. The black mane of his hair appeared to have received some attention from a brush and comb. Even the hat on the table at his elbow, not the high-crowned Bolívar but a small one with a rounded top, possessed a fresh gleam, and she thought she could detect a new crispness in the cuffs and collar of his shirt. On the table beside the hat she could see the glint of his flask and his brass telescope, together with his painting and sketching materials, though she wasn't happy to note his hunting gun leaning against the end of the table and his pistol lying next to the inkpot and the box of paints. However, this morning he looked much more at ease, much more the Painter to the Court and the Director of the Royal Academy. Altogether a distinct improvement.

She couldn't see his right hand, but in his left he held a lighted cigar that at intervals he raised to his lips in a leisurely manner. Occasionally she thought she could see the movement of a pen or pencil across the page of the leather-bound sketchbook he balanced on his lap. She wondered what he was sketching. The landscape, the fountain, the parched lawns meandering down to the sea? From the little she knew about his art, he seemed less a painter of nature than a painter of people. And indeed, following the direction in which he kept glancing, she was just able to make out that he was sketching a group of young female servants who were working near a corner of the palace, folding and spreading out on the grass a heap of newly washed sheets and household linens.

All innocent enough. And yet all of a sudden, at some moment when he had seemed completely absorbed in the lively spectacle of the girls, he dropped his pen or pencil, the sketchbook slid to the turf and he twisted around, staring behind him, first over one shoulder then the other. She could see the sudden darkening of his face. He bent forward and put his hand on the pistol, peering around this way and that. His brown brute of a dog, which had been sleeping out of sight beneath the table, woke up and came crawling out, gazing around with its ears pricked up and its teeth bared. Then, just as unexpectedly, its master's shoulders slackened and after a moment he leaned down and picked up his sketchbook and went on sketching the scene in front of him as if nothing had happened.

Intrigued, she had half-risen from her seat to watch him more closely. What had alarmed him? There had been no sign of an intruder or anyone approaching across the lawn. The girls had gone on laughing and skipping around as they folded the linens. Again she felt a sense of unease at having installed him at her palace. Was he really in danger? Was he being pursued? Was he being spied upon? By whom? She'd have to instruct her servants to stay alert, to watch for and report any peculiar antics on his part. She was glad she had had him lodged in a separate and distant wing of the palace....

It wasn't until noon that she felt ready to leave her bedchamber. She sensed that the climate of Andalucía was already beginning to do her good. Her urge to cough had lessened. She stretched her limbs, feeling that the ache in her legs and thighs of which she had complained to Doctor Arrieta had largely subsided. Her menses had finally started and her cramps and the flow of blood were proving not painful at all. She was feeling stronger than she had for several weeks.

She sat by the window, enjoying the soft breezes wafting through the window from a cloudless sky. Doctor Arrieta had made a point of prescribing fresh air. With half-closed eyes she listened to the birdsong drifting in from the distant trees. At noon she rang her bell to summon María Luz and ordered her to prepare her for the day. She felt alert, suffused now with energy. She found herself in a mood to begin the sittings for her portrait and had word sent down to Goya to tell him she was making herself ready.

Before María Luz had begun to dress her and when the Arab girl had drawn off her nightdress, she was visited by a sudden impulse to step across the bedchamber and look at herself in her great carved mirror in its carved oaken frame. She walked across the room to study her body with a lack of concern for her nakedness in the presence of personal attendants characteristic of the great ladies of her time, and while María Luz was laying out her clothes she stood still, regarding herself critically in the glass. After her recent indisposition, and with the prospect of Miguel's arrival, it was important to take an impartial look at herself. She smiled coquettishly, twisting herself this way and that. She cupped her hands beneath her breasts and squeezed the nipples between thumb and forefinger. She placed her hands on her hips and rotated them, raising her hands behind her neck and letting her head drop onto her left shoulder. What she saw pleased her. Her small compact body was as shapely as any woman of twenty or any of those young girls Goya had been sketching on the lawn. What man would not be gratified by the sight of those small firm breasts with their damson aureolas and their pert nipples, by the tiny waist she could almost span with her two hands? She moved closer to the glass and leaned forward and could detect on her features only the faintest, almost invisible, marks of her recent malady. And what about that magnificent mane of black hair, so assiduously brushed and tended by María Luz, flowing over her shoulders and halfway down her back? Not a single trace of gray. She combed it with her fingers, admiring at the same time the gossamery tangle in her armpits and the delicate black hairs curling up over the flat belly from the dark triangle below, over the edge of the bandage tied by María Luz around her loins. She caressed the hairs in her armpit and her inner thigh lightly. The date-colored eyes of the woman in the mirror stared back approvingly into her own. Oh yes, a prodigious improvement on those other finicky high-bred women Goya had been called on to paint, and to whom, according to gossip, he had made love. She thrust her breasts out further and swivelled her hips. The Marquess of Pontecorvo? Pockmarked. The Duchess of Benavente? Thin as a rail. The Duchess of Osuna? Another beanpole. Yes indeed, Cayetana de Alba was altogether a more sumptuous and opulent female proposition than the pitiable marquesses and countesses and duchesses Goya was used to....

María Luz was already bustling back and forth, bringing out the clothing the Duchess had selected for her first sitting. While sitting in her chair in the window she had given the matter careful consideration and had given María Luz precise instructions. She was determined not to give Goya an excuse to depict her in the way he had done before. Why had she humored her husband and let herself be got up in that ridiculous red and silver costume with big silly bows all over it? And her makeup—what had she been thinking of? Oh no, she wasn't going to make that same mistake twice. She would tell María Luz to be more careful with the rouge and the powder. She meant to present Miguel with a likeness of herself as a vital, alluring woman, radiant and robust....

She moved across to fondle the rich and lustrous stuffs draped on the bed and on the backs of the chairs. At first she had hesitated between her *robe d'anglaise* and her Polonaise, two special favorites in which she thought she looked particularly well. But then she was visited by an altogether brilliant idea. She had remembered the costume of the *majas*, those gaudy lower-class hussies of doubtful morals, many of them simply shop girls out for a good time, while others were ladies of the evening, brazen and bedizened, insolently soliciting the passers-by with their pimps lurking in nearby alleyways, yet all of them, artless and childlike or sinful and shady, eager to drink and dally and sing and dance the night away. It was in the guise of one of these that the Duchess had often elected to flaunt herself for the approval of the crowds when she went riding through the streets with Pedro Romero and his friends. She was glad that on some impulse she had told María

Luz to pack her *maja* costume when leaving Madrid. She had even worn it earlier in the year to a fancy dress ball at court, thoroughly enjoying the general disapproval. It was the perfect contrast to the foolish costume in which Goya had previously painted her. Moreover to be painted in *maja* costume would make manifest to the world her new independence as a single woman, her new sense of freedom. She would banish the dismal widow's weeds she had been compelled to wear in the poisoned atmosphere of the court. Hadn't she played the grieving widow long enough? Hadn't she earned the right to indulge herself in at least a little of her former glory and gaiety?

She closed her eyes and let herself sink into a kind of trance, giving herself up to the rustle and whisper of the silks and satins as María Luz began to dress her. First came the white silk stockings and white cambric slip, then the silken blouse, its color a startling burnt orange. Over its sleeves, shot through with gold and silver thread, María Luz drew a pair of glistening armlets heavily embroidered with gold and scarlet. Then came the ceremony of wrapping around the waist the amplitude of the layered black skirt, its folds reaching to the ankles and covered by an apron of Mechlin lace tufted with black rosettes. With the languorous pirouette of the bullfighter being readied for the ring, she lifted her arms high and twirled around as María Luz tightly encircled her waist with the bright crimson sash, then lowered them and stood still while the Arab girl deftly inserted in her hair the jeweled comb on which to arrange the lacy black scarf enfolding her head and bosom. When she opened her eyes and turned to regard herself in the mirror, she was a shimmer of gold and silver, of crimson and burnt orange, all heightened by the black froth and foam of the Flanders lace. What then remained? Only for María Luz to lead her to a chair at the dressing table and impart a last practiced pat and primp to the hair before darkening the brows and applying a light touch of rouge to her cheeks and mouth. A light sprinkle of violet scented perfume to hands, wrists, bosom, neck and temples, and finally the placing on the small shapely feet the gilt and silver Turkish slippers of soft Córdoba leather, sparkling with sequins and with high vermilion heels.

The Duchess rose. A brief pause to pluck out of the jewel case on the dressing table the huge topaz encrusted with diamonds and boldly incised in black letters with the name of ALBA that had been given to her as a wedding gift by her great uncle, the Captain General of New Granada.

It was not a ring she wore often. And never, of course, at court. At court the Queen was too fond of sidling up to her and fingering her earrings, her necklaces, her bracelets, her rings. The Duchess fancied she could feel on her cheeks the sourness of the breath which the Queen tried to disguise with scented pastilles. She could feel on her flesh the lingering touch of those stringy fingers with their sharply pointed nails. How dearly the Queen would love to adorn her bony fingers with the celebrated jewels of the House of Alba! With what avidity she was plotting and scheming for the chance to do so.

She slid the big topaz onto her middle finger.

"Are you ready, María Luz? Then let us go down."

THE VOICE WAS hoarse, like the breathless bellow of a wounded bull when its forces are spent and it can only manage a gasping wheeze of the lungs. But yes. She realized that that was what it actually was. It was singing—or an attempt at it.

Her immediate reaction was a feeling of annoyance, of indignation, even. How could he have been permitted to encroach on what she had set aside as her private music room? The liveried footman on duty outside the door sprang to open it, and as she entered the first thing she saw was an easel, on which was propped a blank canvas coated with an even layer of terra cotta pigment. On one side of the easel stood a chair over the back of which was thrown a long brown smock with turquoise edging, badly splattered with paint, and on the other side stood a large table on which, in meticulous order, were laid out the artist's palette and palette knives, brushes and spatulas and bowls of paint. Behind this table were two smaller tables on which were arranged, in a tidy and methodical fashion, row upon row of small flasks and vials containing ground-up colors and pigments. She remembered the sounds of sloshing and rattling when he was loading his precious trunks and boxes on top of the coach. No doubt in his studio in Madrid he had an assistant to grind up his colors for him and to stretch and prime his canvases, but, like her, he had come to Andalucía determined to travel lightly and had left his assistant behind. Nevertheless he had taken no chances, and had provided himself with an ample supply of paints, and on the big table she remarked the presence of a mortar and pestle. He would attend to the grinding of his own paints. She was interested to notice that on the small table to the left were ranged the bottles containing his bright colors, his reds and greens and yellows and whites, while on the table to the right stood his dark colors, his browns and grays and blacks.

All this she took in quickly, at a glance, her throat already becoming irritated by the acrid fumes of the Seville cigars that were floating around the room in spite the fact that the double doors at the far end of the room stood wide open to a view of the lawns beyond. She wished María Luz had reminded her to bring her fan. She had not enjoyed being at close quarters with him in the carriage, nor was the atmosphere of the room improved by the pungent smells of the linseed oils and turpentines and the fatty odor of his paints.

She saw that he was sitting half-turned towards her on the music stool in front of the harpsichord in the far corner of the room. As she had already noticed when she had been watching him from her bedroom window, he appeared freshly shaved and barbered, his hair newly trimmed, no doubt by one of the female servants with whom he seemed to be on such familiar terms. His linen was clean and his plum-colored velvet jacket newly sponged and pressed. She could make out the lighted end of his cigar in the corner of his mouth and made a resolution to request him to refrain from smoking while their sittings were in progress. At least the odor of his dog wouldn't be added to the stink of his cigars, since she could now make out the form of the massive beast sprawled on the flagstones outside the double doors, tethered by a stout rope.

All such thoughts were immediately swept away by the sight and sound of the painter himself. It was from Goya's throat that the blustery noise was coming, as he sat huddled on the small stool in front of the harpsichord, making her feel again a sharp sting of irritation. This was *her* music room. That was *her* harpsichord. She had a particular fondness for the pretty instrument from the workshop of Dutilleux, its case elaborately decorated with scenes of a *fête galante*. A liking for music had been the one thing she had shared with her husband, almost the only thing. She was by no means an expert performer, but she had liked to accompany him when he played on his baryton or his violoncello. As a girl she had been a tomboy, given to outdoor pursuits, riding horses, scrambling among the mountains, not a great reader of books. But she had a sympathetic music teacher who had persisted with his unruly pupil and had encouraged her, and she had brought her harpsichord to Sanlúcar to while away the time. Salvatore Carulli had been instructed to pack plenty of music by the composers she and her husband had especially admired, such as Puente, Terradellas and Nebra, and by such Italian masters as Cimarosa, Galuppi, Porpora, Giardini, and by Scarlatti and Boccherini, both of whom had lived out their lives in Madrid. They had helped her get through many a dull evening with her husband at one or another of their palaces. There was a fandango by Antonio Soler that she had planned to make her own, and which she was sure would touch Miguel's heart and thrill his senses.

By moving a little to one side, she could see that Goya was holding the sorry-looking guitar he had brought into the coach with him. Holding it? He was trying to *play* it. With two of the broken strings trailing down towards the floor, with his right hand moving across the frets, he was trying to accompany himself as he droned out a tuneless song. She stood still, trying to make it out. Was he making a grotesque attempt to sing a *tonadilla*? A *sevillana*? Or something slower and sadder? Behind her she heard María Luz give a little sob of distress, and when she turned she saw that the young Arab woman was staring at the deranged figure sitting in front of the harpsichord with a petrified expression, supporting herself by leaning against the wall. The Duchess herself could not help feeling shaken in her turn, as she listened to that sinister-sounding dirge and watched those hands roving crazily across the severed strings.

Without warning he suddenly sprang up from the music stool and hurled the guitar violently away from him so that it flew across the polished floor. María Luz gave a little shriek. Still unaware that he was being watched, he crossed rapidly to the open double doors behind him. He approached them obliquely, as if he was fearful of being watched from the outside. He pressed himself back against the open doors and peered around them cautiously at the parched lawns beyond. As far as she could make out they were deserted. So who did he imagine might be watching him? And why? Or was it merely some hallucination, some fit of internal panic caused because the outside world was blocked off from him?

She was anything but a nervous woman, but her heart gave a flutter when she saw his hunting rifle propped against the wall beside the window. She took a step backwards before walking quickly towards him, holding up a hand and calling to him.

"*Señor Goya!*"

She kept moving forward and called a second time, more loudly:

"*Señor Goya!*"

Then, annoyed with herself at having forgotten that he was unable to hear her, she nerved herself to approach him. She meant to lay a hand on his arm. But when she had reached halfway across the room something, some disturbance in the air, caused him to swing around and the wild-eyed and ugly expression on his face made her stop dead. Then he recognized who she was, and she was relieved to see the hostile fire in his eyes fade quickly away. His face lit up. He gave an admiring little grunt. He smiled. He was plainly enchanted by the sight of the figure that confronted him.

"*Duchess!*"

He stepped towards her, his hands extended as if he wished to take hold of this woman in her bold and enthralling costume in order to study her more closely. It was only the second time that she had heard him speak at close range. She noticed again that his voice was loud and thick-tongued and hardly sounded human.

He halted in front of her, making what she had to admit was a very presentable bow, and spoke again in that peculiarly gruff and tuneless voice.

"Good morning, Duchess!"

With a polite inclination of his head he motioned her towards a chair he had positioned in the center of the room.

"If the Duchess would kindly…?"

He had a habit of not completing his sentences, another mannerism resulting from his deafness. It was something to which she would have to accustom herself.

The chair was low-backed, of gilt and blue velvet. María Luz knelt down and arranged the folds of the long skirt before rising and retreating to a chair near the door. As she sat down, she cast a doubtful glance at Goya's brown mastiff, tethered on the flagstones.

She had expected him to begin the business of painting without undue preliminaries, as she seemed to remember he had done the time before. Instead, he began stroking his chin and walking slowly and thoughtfully around her. She sighed inwardly, surrendering herself with as good a grace as possible. But what happened next made her open her eyes in a hurry and gave rise to a loud gasp from the young Arab girl in the corner. The Duchess felt her chin grasped by a strong square hand and turned vigorously this way and that. Then the hand transferred itself to the back of her head, exploring in a deliberate fashion the conformation of her skull, easing back the *mantilla* and pressing down firmly through the thick mane of hair. She felt him adjusting the high tortoiseshell comb. Then suddenly he was squatting at her feet, rearranging the folds of the skirt in order to display more of her white silk stockings and her jeweled shoes. Next came a plucking at the sleeves of the orange bodice and a pinching up of the edges of the scarlet sash. Not content with this, after stepping back for a moment, his next move produced an even louder gasp from the girl in the corner and even provoked an exclamation of surprise from the Duchess herself. She felt herself stiffen under the *maja* costume as he moved in closer and put his hands on her shoulders in order to twist her upper body into the pose he wanted. He lifted her hands one after the other and positioned them in her lap, right after left, bringing his wrists close to his eyes to study the bracelets and rubbing his thumb slowly over the great topaz ring. Nor was he yet finished, for while she was still quivering with indignation at the familiarity of his touch, he turned his back and stepped quickly across to his tables. And before she knew it, he was once more advancing towards her holding two pots of paint, one red and one black. She almost passed out from shock as, stooping over her, he dipped his middle finger in the pot of black paint and whisked it with two quick sure strokes along the length of each eyebrow, darkening and thickening them. He then applied a smear of red to the tip of a forefinger and drew it swiftly across each of her cheekbones. It was done so quickly and his touch was so adept she scarcely felt it. Moreover, before she could protest, he had retreated again to his work table, put down the pots of paint and taken up a charcoal pencil and one of his sketchbooks. He took a plain wooden chair and placed it squarely in front of her, then leaned forward and regarded her intently, screwing up his hooded and penetrating eyes.

Usually when he spoke it was in a strange and strident voice she could hardly catch. The two words he uttered as he crossed his legs, resting his sketchbook on his knee and beginning to ply his pencil, were pronounced softly and distinctly. He took a long deep breath and exhaled it slowly, the words floating across the room with an inflexion that sounded strangely rapt and reverential for such a blunt, rough-natured sort of man.

"*Now*, Duchess."

He raised the hand that held the pencil high and let it descend upon the paper.

After a few quivering moments, now that there seemed no further danger of him prodding her or pulling her about, she let her body slacken a little. She willed herself to keep still, telling herself that nothing must distract him from getting on with his specific assignment as speedily as possible. She compelled herself to remain as motionless as she could. Indeed, after fifteen or twenty minutes, she found herself sinking into a mild trance, a not unpleasing mood in which she began to follow the movements of the artist's hand in a kind of hypnotic haze, seemingly unable to move her limbs even when he began to shift around so he could take her likeness from different angles, first on this side and then on that, finally scraping his chair completely around so that he vanished completely from her line of vision and was sketching her both from the rear and in profile. When he came back into view, he had risen from his chair, and she noted out of the corner of her eye that he moved remarkably nimbly for so brawny a man, stealing around her as light on his feet as a dancer or the *torero* he was once reputed to be. She became dreamily conscious of the sleepy silence of the sunlit room. For the first time for what seemed many weeks she was filled with a sense of surrender to that feeling of repose and quietude she had come to Sanlúcar in the hope of finding.

She had no idea, later, how long she remained in this somnolent state. She only knew it had been pleasant to let herself drift into a state in which she was only aware of the motes of dust twisting lazily in the mellow late summer sunlight. She heard the occasional distant shout or burst of laughter from the servants in the stables or from the lawns. She felt at peace. Sitting for this new portrait was turning out to be oddly soothing. She was congratulating herself on behaving so well and sitting so still, she had quite forgotten the tickling sensation in her throat that was starting to make her cough. She was thinking vaguely of summoning María Luz to bring her smelling salts to prevent her from sinking completely into slumber, when all at once she felt herself being lifted. Goya's hands were shifting to her shoulders to steady her. Blearily she became aware of a brown smock reeking of paint and perspiration, of cigars and pomade. She staggered and fell forward, her face pressing against the coarse texture of the smock. She had the sensation of being precipitously snatched up by a pair of powerful hands, whirled around like a doll, and deposited on a wooden footstool that had been placed on one side of the easel.

Her first impulse had been to slap his hands away, but then, stunned into compliance, she swayed and tottered on the high stool until his hands were transferred from her waist to her hips, holding her clamped in a painful grip. She heard the Arab girl give a little shriek and opened her eyes to see that María Luz had run forward and was pummeling at the artist's back as he growled out something incomprehensible and seized the girl and bustled her back to her chair in the corner, plumping her down with a guttural sound that was obviously a command for her to stay put. Frantically the girl wrestled with him, trying to squirm away and run for help to the footman outside the door, but he jammed her roughly into a chair and kept her there until she gave up the struggle and sagged back with a little whimper.

He turned his attention once more to the Duchess. He prowled around her, assessing her. Again her clothing was subjected to a prolonged pulling and tweaking. Nor did it stop with her clothing. He disappeared behind her and she heard him mumbling to himself, and then her left wrist was suddenly grasped and twisted behind her and pressed against her left hip in the characteristic attitude of a Madrid *maja*. He wrenched her around so that her bosom was slanted sideways and upward, her breasts straining against her bodice. None too gently, he jerked her right arm in its embroidered sleeve so that her beringed forefinger pointed directly down at her silver slippers with their long tapering gold points. He forced her feet apart and drew her left foot forward so brusquely that if he had not gripped her around the top of her thighs she would have toppled off the stool. Finally he released her, standing back to study the overall effect of the pose, then shifting his gaze to study her face. She was afraid he was going to fiddle with her makeup again, but he only stretched out a finger up to her chin, tilting her head back to impart the haughty bearing that was shared alike by Spanish *majas* and Spanish duchesses.

He walked back until he was standing beside his easel, contemplating her for a long time, the eyes beneath the low broad forehead narrowed and searching. The corners of his hard mouth, flanked by deep furrows, dragged grimly down. He cocked his chin and cupped it in his hand, propping one elbow with the other, all the time remaining still while she stood unsteadily on her stool, fuming inwardly and striving to maintain her balance. Was this the way all his women allowed themselves to be treated? Serve him right if she tumbled off the stool and went crashing to the ground. The stool felt none too stable. She now regretted donning the *maja* costume. She might have done better after all to wear the schoolgirl white dress with the red bows and the chunky coral necklace. A Duchess of Alba—letting herself be hoisted onto a silly stool like a wretched puppet! How the Queen and her toadies would split their sides with mirth! So what if this man Goya seemed to like positioning his subjects at an angle sloping up from the eye of the viewer? He could hardly expect to please the sitter, see-sawing about in mid-air, even if that sitter was a Duchess of Alba. She put up with it, staring indignantly above his head with as much dignity as she could muster, for the sooner he did it the sooner it would be over, and the sooner he could pack up his bags and leave Sanlúcar and the sooner she could look forward to the arrival of Miguel....

In any event, the session passed more swiftly and uneventfully than she anticipated. It was not, of course, easy to endure, but it was mercifully short. Once he had taken up his stance, whistling tunelessly but mellifluously beneath his breath, his shoulders square to the canvas and legs widely sprawled, he scarcely moved, apart from recharging his palette with blobs of paint from the pots arranged neatly beside him. She noted the paints on the palette were placed in order, the lighter colors at the front, close to the thumb, shading down through the darker colors towards the grays and the blacks at the rear. He picked up or exchanged one brush for another with a precise and economical movement, frequently substituting for the brush a knife, a spatula or a length of split cane. Sometimes he would abandon the brush altogether, dabbing his thumb or his forefinger in the paint and smoothing it on to the canvas with a little flick of the wrist, after which he would pause for a moment and wipe his finger with a rag, his head on one side as he studied the progress of his work. Or instead of using a rag, he would suck the remaining paint off his finger or off the brush—a very nasty habit, surely, and one that could scarcely be conducive to his health? The habit was instinctive, since his concentration was absolute. He had withdrawn deeply into himself, though she sensed that behind the black eyes a bright cold fire was burning.

At any rate, almost before she knew it, before she needed to ask for a break or have recourse to her smelling salts, he was licking the paint from the last of his brushes and stripping off his brown smock. Then he was giving her a little bow and, as she was stiff and unsteady, handing her ceremoniously and courteously down from the stool. His manner was very correct. When he spoke he enunciated the words slowly, pitching them in what was obviously intended to resemble an agreeable tone.

"*Will you forgive me, I—? I hope I haven't—?*"

And then, looking at the Arab girl who had risen from her chair and come hurrying across the room to join her mistress, his smile was frank and radiant. He lifted the young woman's hand to his lips, bending over it and kissing it as solemnly as if she, and not her mistress, were the Duchess of Alba.

"*Forgive—?*"

In response the girl could only gasp and giggle and put the back of her hand where he had kissed it to her cheek causing him to throw back his shaggy head, utter a raucous guffaw and plant a resounding kiss on her dark-skinned forehead.

The Duchess was not amused at this display of familiarity. When he went to the door and opened it for her, she swept out of the studio with a disapproving frown and a curt toss of the head to María Luz to follow her.

Yet why, she asked herself, should she have felt flustered and discomfited by this petty exchange of casual affection between the painter and her maid?

Some mornings later, guided once more by María Luz, she stepped out with rather more confidence on her way to the makeshift studio.

The early sittings had gone well enough, in spite of the discomfort of posing. She had been encouraged by the energetic way he had set about painting this second portrait—surely the determined manner in which he was going about it suggested that he intended it to be a more striking and mature piece of work than its unfortunate predecessor?

Sanlúcar was starting to do her good. She was sleeping soundly. There had been no recurrence of the nightly sweats of early spring and midsummer in the capital. If she had dreams, they were pleasant, and she had the impression that the main character who had begun threading his way through them would turn out to be Miguel. Doctor Arrieta's medicines seemed to be working. There was less soreness in her throat and chest and she breathed more easily. Her monthly discomfort was now passing. No headaches. No queasy stomach. The autumn days were warm. The nights were cool. If she had any doubts about her decision to quit Madrid and cloister herself in Andalucía, they were evaporating. She had done well to come to Sanlúcar.

It was in a good mood and with heightened expectations that she entered the studio. She swept past the footmen and through the double doors with her head held high, intent on presenting an imposing appearance. She had shed her misgivings regarding the *maja* costume. Such a costume would inspire any artist to render a woman's looks and coloring splendidly. Goya had realized this was no ordinary woman he was painting—not one of his every day countesses or singers or actresses.

As it happened, her imposing entrance was wasted. When the doors had closed behind her and María Luz she saw the studio was empty. She stopped short and looked around. Goya was not there.

This was a surprise. His behavior during the previous sessions had proved reassuringly natural and normal. He had given way to none of those sudden fits of panic, which she had likened in her mind to those fits called frights or *espantos* which will sometimes unaccountably seize *toreros* and make them flee from the bull and leap over the barrier. At no time had he broken off the sitting to make a crazed dash and snatch up his hunting gun and peer out of the window. He hadn't even uncapped his flask to gulp down a mouthful of spirits. He hadn't even stuck a cigar in his mouth, let alone light one.

All the same, this morning the studio stank of stale smoke and the fatty reek of candles, of the rank smell of dog and of paints and perspiration. The high widows were still shuttered so that the whole room was so heavily steeped in shadow she could barely make out the outline of the easel, its canvas covered with the white cloth.

Where was he?

She straightened her back and took a deep breath.

"Open the shutters, María Luz. Open the windows."

The Arab girl ran to the windows and then to the double doors in the far corner. She fumbled with the catches and fastenings and the morning light poured in, together with a welcome draft of fresh air.

The Duchess blinked and took another breath and tried to prevent herself from inhaling more of the fouled atmosphere until the morning air could sweeten it. She felt it rasp her lungs. Then, when she beheld the state of the room she let out one great indignant gasp.

It was a mess. She had assumed from the tidy way in which he normally laid out his painting materials and from his recent exemplary behavior that, despite his slovenly appearance on the journey from Cádiz, his everyday habits might prove after all to be more or less orderly. So why had he reduced her music room to such a shambles? She now saw that the canvas on the easel had been knocked half sideways and that the floor beneath it was spattered with blobs of paint. His smock lay in a tangled heap on one side of the easel, and the chair on which he had been sitting had been capsized on the other. For a moment she was tempted to draw aside the cloth over the canvas, but shrank from handling the paint-smeared cloth. His rags and spatulas and brushes and pots of paint were scattered across the tops of all three tables and on the larger table was a mound-like object she had to move closer to identify. Approaching the table she saw it was a hat, not the high-crowned Bolívar he wore in the coach, or the hat he was wearing when he was sketching on the lawn beneath her window, but a peculiar low-topped hat with a wide brim. What made it look odd and sinister, beside its filthy condition, was the ring of small metal candleholders screwed around the brim, eight or nine of them, containing the melted stumps of burned down candles. It roused in her one of those vague tremors of disquiet associated with so many things belonging to this singular man. She put out a hesitant finger to touch it and quickly drew it back.

She rounded on María Luz.

"*Why has this room not been put in order?*"

Goya's absence and the state of the room provoked her. She had been looking forward to another productive session, since tomorrow they would be forfeiting an entire day because she and her household had been invited to participate in the *vendimia* or annual grape festival dedicated to Nuestra Señora del Rocío in the local village. It was an invitation that she and her people could scarcely refuse, and since the village was some distance away it would be necessary to start soon after dawn and the festival would last at least until sunset.

All the same, she shouldn't have spoken so sharply to María

Luz whose duties, after all, did not include these particular domestic arrangements. She softened her tone a little when she saw the girl's top lip trembling and her eyes filling with tears.

"The butler. Why hasn't he seen to it?"

The girl could only stammer.

"Señor Francisco—I mean Señor Goya—has given special instructions that no one, no one at all, is ever to enter any of the rooms he is using, not the studio and especially not his private room."

The Duchess raised her eyebrows.

"Oh? And since when have Señor Goya's instructions been permitted to override the authority of my butler?"

"Oh, Señora, Signor Carulli tried to send two men to clean his room, and Señor Goya threatened them and told them he'd kick them out and knock them down if he ever found any of his possessions had been so much as touched!"

"Knock them down?"

"Señor Goya is very obstinate, Señora. He insists on having his own way."

"Does he indeed!"

"He attends to his own needs and makes his own bed. The servants have to leave his trays of food and bowls for washing outside his door. Often they take them away without his eating his food or touching his wine. And he always keeps his door locked."

The Duchess frowned at the notion of the painter offering to knock down her servants.

"Is Señor Goya in his room now?"

"No, Señora. Since he is deaf it is no use tapping on the door. We sent Esteban your coachman, with whom he's particularly friendly, to go around and peer in the window. But he is not there."

"Then where *is* he?"

"We have no idea, Señora. Last night after supper he came into our hall wearing his funny hat, the one on the table over there, and made us laugh by parading around the table with all the candles lit—he is very fond of his little jokes. Then he said he was coming to the studio to spend the night working. There is never any point in waiting up for him since he never seems to sleep at night, at least not until the small hours. I expect that when he'd finished working in here, he did what he usually does."

"And what is that, exactly?"

"Go roaming around with his dog, Señora."

"Oh, and where, pray, does he go roaming around?"

"Heaven only knows, Señora. All over the countryside. He sometimes doesn't come back until sunrise. He seems to prefer night to day, Señora…."

The Duchess remembered similar stories related to her by Don Sebastián and Señor Bermúdez.

"And does his roaming around disturb the household?"

"Well, Señora, to be honest, we'd rather have him outside the house than inside it. When he doesn't go out we hear him pacing up and down, or wandering along the corridors moaning and cursing in that loud voice of his. And sometimes he fires his gun or pistol out of the window"

The Duchess laughed.

"Then I'm glad that Señor Goya's room isn't close to mine!"

"Ah, yes indeed, Señora."

The Duchess was curious though.

"And who or what is he shooting at, do you suppose?"

"I do not know, Señora. When we hear it we send a party out to search. They come back saying there's been no sight or sound of prowlers or bandits. We think it is something in the poor gentleman's imagination. Naturally, we do not like to ask him straight out. It would not be polite and besides he is deaf and we do not like to have to shout at him. So we cannot say what it is he shoots at. We only know that when the fit comes upon him he'll go out, mainly at dusk or after dark. Some of us think, Señora, that it might be the bats."

"The *bats*, María Luz?"

María Luz nodded. "Yes, Señora. Señor Goya really seems to hate bats. There is a whole swarm of them out in the stables. They are always trying to get into the house." She gave a little shudder. "Naturally, many of us are frightened of the nasty things ourselves. All the same, it does seem rather strange that a big and strong man like Señor Goya should be so afraid of them. He is always on the lookout for them, even when it is broad daylight. He is always dodging and ducking as if he can see them fluttering about. Even when there's no sign of them he seems to be on the lookout."

The Duchess laughed again and more heartily this time.

"Well, María Luz, surely letting off his pistol or his hunting gun doesn't make our guest very popular with the servants?"

Her maid's answer surprised her.

"Oh no, Señora. He is *very* popular! We are getting used to his odd ways. When he comes in early in the morning he will often bring us a hare or a brace of birds for the pot. He is very fond of shooting. The only person who really can't abide him is Signor Carulli. Even young Pascual the coachman, who got a beating from Señor Goya for taking a liberty, soon made friends with him. He and Esteban and Señor Goya are as thick as thieves. Señor Goya likes horses too. And in spite of his deafness he is very good company and appreciates everything we do for him. He loves to watch us while we're working or while we're singing or dancing in the servants' hall—he does his best to join in! And he is very generous and shares his last drop of brandy and his last cigars with us. After he sketches us he give us some of the drawings. He's done several of Estrellita and me. The sketches are lovely, Señora, I'll always treasure them. And of course, he loves dogs. Conchita is always pawing him and licking his face and jumping into his lap. And I mentioned the horses—he spends hours in the stables talking to them. Neither we nor the animals mind him being deaf!"

She saw the frown on the Duchess's face and broke off, rather breathless.

Indeed the Duchess was struggling with foolish feelings of what she had to admit was something close to jealousy at this recital of Goya's success with her domestics, and couldn't help resenting the idea of all those sketches of her pretty personal maid and her daughter. She resented him capturing the attentions of her pet dog. She was surprised by the sharpness of her gesture of dismissal.

"Go then, María Luz. Perhaps by now your Señor Goya will have done me the favor of returning to the palace. If not, take the footmen and some of the servants and search for him. And when you find him, tell him the Duchess is waiting."

María Luz curtsied.

"Yes, Señora."

"Go!"

The girl gave another quick bob and sped away, leaving the Duchess standing decidedly ill-tempered and irresolute. It seemed to her that Goya might at least have shown her the courtesy of leaving her a note of apology for his absence, or some excuse for the delay.

She scanned the tables with their distasteful clutter of objects, the queer hat with the dead circle of candles, the sprawls of pots and brushes. She could see no note. Perhaps, then, he had left it elsewhere?

She looked around.

The harpsichord.

She crossed the room, alarmed that she might see the fine-grained wood of the closed lid with its delicate inlay strewn with the artist's possessions. She was thankful the lid was closed and the shepherds and shepherdesses of the *fête galante* were not exposed to any damage. She could see no sign of scratches on the pale wood. Only the forlorn and ill-treated guitar was propped up against one of the harpsichord's legs. She was glad that except for his heap of sketchbooks there was none of his usual collection of paraphernalia, the pistol, the gypsy knife, the telescope, the flask and the cigar case. Presumably he had taken all those with him on his midnight ramble.

But neither was there any sign of the note, only his sketchbooks surrounded by a miscellaneous assortment of pencils and pens and sticks of charcoal.

Earlier she had fought back the temptation to lift the cloth on the canvas to see how the portrait was progressing. Now, alone and loitering aimlessly, her eye lingered on the sketchbooks and she felt an urge to leaf through them. Surely she must pass the time somehow? Was she merely to hang around and twiddle her thumbs? Did he expect her to traipse about this smelly room he had appropriated as his studio until such time as he condescended to show up? No, she told herself petulantly, she would sit down on this bench in front of the harpsichord and entertain herself by glancing through the sketchbooks. As his patron and employer, surely she could make herself familiar with his artistic abilities and procedures? Nevertheless, as she seated herself down and reached up to take the topmost sketchbook from the pile, she couldn't repress a faint pang of guilt as she opened it.

The sketches in the beginning of the first book were for the most part rendered lightly, in black ink. There were several studies of the same woman, a woman with a plain, sad and sensitive face, dressed in mourning. The Duchess guessed these might be studies of Josefa, his wife, who was now at Zaragoza.

There were more sketches of the same woman, surrounded now by a group of children. Several pages were devoted to a pair of small boys, one about ten and the other about eight, drawn with great tenderness and with their smiling faces brimming with mischief. And there was a page consisting of sketches of a large dog, probably the brute she should have insisted should be left behind in Cádiz.

She turned more pages. More sketches of women. There were women of the town tricked out in *maja* costumes like the one she was now wearing, chaperoned by bent and toothless crones.

There were women who by their dress and extravagant attitudes she took to be dancers or singers. She and her late husband had been devotees of the opera and the theater and she thought she recognized one of them as Narcisa Zárate, the popular singer that the people of Madrid flocked to see at the Ateneo. And that surely was the actress Rita Luna? And who could possibly mistake that big and bosomy woman with the florid complexion and blatant bearing? Who could that be but the high and mighty La Tirana of the Maravillas? La Tirana whom all the males of the capital lusted after. La Tirana whose husband was so comically jealous of her. Oh, yes, it wasn't difficult to appreciate the appeal a brassy piece of goods like La Tirana would have for a man with the reputation of Francisco Goya. He certainly seemed to favor bouncing and busty females! She frowned. She had half expected there to be some trial sketches of herself, made for that first portrait that had been painted not such a long time ago, and was surprised to feel quite put out when she failed to find any.

The next pages came as a shock. She was shaken by their dark, unpleasant content and found herself running through them hurriedly. Here were witches and wizards, with their attendant trains of misshapen cats and owls and other denizens of the night. Here were men and women wearing the tall conical white hats called *sambenitos* being herded through the streets or being interrogated and tortured by the officers of La Santa Casa. The drawings made her tremble. They were in such marked contrast with what had come before. It therefore came as a breath of relief when she came upon to a sequence of drawings that had obviously been executed since his arrival in Sanlúcar. These were altogether lighter and carried out in a flowing carefree manner with pale washes and colored chalks. She was surprised to see two likenesses of María Luz, one of them capturing that lost and wistful expression that so often saddened the Duchess, but the other depicting her laughing and playing with her little daughter Estrellita. These were followed by a charming and cheerful series of sketches showing the servant girls romping on the lawns and laying out the linens. All these were a pleasant change after the disagreeable scenes she had just been looking at.

Nevertheless the final series of drawings brought her up short again, even though they were in the same blithe vein as their predecessors. Only now the same girls were shown bathing in the meager little streamlet that flowed through the downward slope on the far edge of the lawn. And they were naked.

It wasn't as if she had not seen pictures of naked women before, although to own one or to be found with one in one's possession was exceedingly dangerous. Yet many of the people at court, herself among them, had at one time or another been accorded a peek at the secret hoard of forbidden pictures that over the course of several reigns had been tucked away in the royal collections. All the same, the sketches produced in her a strange and unexpected mixture of queasiness, mingled with an odd but distinct feeling of excitement.

She came to the end of the first book and opened a second. And now, turning the pages, she was pleased to discover that it appeared to be entirely devoted to a single subject, the *corrida de toros*.

She brightened. She herself was a great devotee of the *toros* and Goya was reputed to be an expert. It would be fascinating to discover his impressions.

The initial pages were given over to a series of truly enchanting sketches of *toreros*, clearly done on the spot and demonstrating the basic passes with the cape and the cloth. They twisted and pirouetted and flourished the cape and *muleta* high and low in graceful passes to the left and right. The faces were mostly blank or casually rendered, but she could identify several of the *toreros* from their individual styles. Her guesses were confirmed by the series of portraits of leading *toreros* that followed. This one must be José Cándido, and that one another old-time matador, Juan de los Santos. And there could be no mistaking the likenesses of the bullfighters who were her personal friends, with whom she liked to hobnob in Madrid. Here was dear old Costillares, now retired, who was said to have invented not only the *volapié* but the *verónica* itself. And this one was Costillares' fellow Sevillean, José Delgado—"*Pepe-Hillo*"—now at the height of his powers. And there were no less than a dozen pages given over to progressive studies of the rival of "*Pepe-Hillo*" in the art of the *fiesta brava*, her own especial friend Pedro Romero, the grandson, son and brother of the dynasty from Ronda who had battled the bulls for a hundred years. There was a wonderful study of that celebrated afternoon in the bullring at Madrid when "*Pepe-Hillo*" had fought a bull using only his hat as a lure and young Pedro Romero, not to be outdone, had snatched the comb from his hair and used that. Outside the ring the two men were firm friends and often rode together with the Duchess in her carriage, to the frenzied plaudits of the crowd and the biting disapproval of the court and the Queen's sycophants. She had even let herself be seen holding hands with the handsome Pedro and whispering to him behind her fan. It amused her to encourage rumors that the popular young hero might be the Duchess of Alba's lover. Of course, Goya was a close friend of Pedro Romero too, and would know all about those rumors.

    She smiled, she glowed as she turned over these airy pages. She almost forgot about her exasperation with their author, almost forgave him his offense at keeping her waiting. By the time she had reached the mid-point of the book, she was in a sunny mood.

    But then, without warning, as she turned to another page, her mood was dashed as if she had suddenly been doused with icy water. She was confronted with a two-page spread that was so brutal it was like a slap in the face.

    It was an incident from the *fiesta brava* depicted with appalling savagery. The left-hand side of the sketch was almost completely empty, rendering more ghastly the spectacle of horror on the opposing side. The right-hand of the drawing was dominated by the figure of a gigantic bull that had leaped the barrier and was standing motionless and with a massive indifference. On its horn was impaled the drooping body of a dead spectator, and other dead and trampled figures littered the foreground.

She shuddered and quickly turned the page, only to find that the drawing on the next was even more repulsive. Again the artist had made lavish employment of chalk and crayon to heighten the bloody overtones. A gang of ruffians was tormenting a proud young bull with a bristling variety of weapons, including darts, swords, spears and an array of agricultural implements. What made the drawing especially repellent was that the young bull was white, white and beautiful, a bull of the purest white. And down its perfect flanks poured a cruel stream of scarlet. That fine young creature—so white and innocent, wantonly torn and tortured by a pack of gleeful savages!

Again she hurriedly turned the page. And here were more gruesome studies of horses being upended and disemboweled, of bulls being harried by hounds, of *toreros* being gashed and slashed with ferocious wounds. The entire emphasis seemed to be on the anguish of the *corrida*. The Duchess loved the *corrida*. Although her husband had found it abhorrent, her grandparents had been the founders of a *ganadería* celebrated for the quality of its fighting bulls. Since childhood she had been a regular attendant at the *fiesta*, basking in those unforgettable moments when a *"Pepe-Hillo"* or a Pedro Romero would come swaggering across the ring to dedicate the bull to her and toss up his *montera* for her to catch. What young woman in the ripe flush of her beauty would not be flattered to receive the homage of those dashing men in their glittering uniforms? What young woman would not be intoxicated by the rapturous crowds? But where in these sketches was the sun, the spectacle, the dazzle of the *fiesta* as she had known it? Yes, of course, there were distressing moments—the screams of the horses, the shouts and oaths of the *mozos* and *picadores*, the brutish yells of the crowd, the agonized belling of the bull as it choked in its own blood. But this was Spain. Blood was an essential part of the drama. Where in these sketches was the grandeur and the glory of it? They expressed nothing of the joy and delirium of it. Why emphasize only the ripping, the tearing, the jabbing and the slashing? Where was the gallantry? Where was the pride? Where was the hard-won beauty? There was only an insistence on its ugliness, an ugliness rendered even more ghastly by being shown so close up to the eye and from the dead level of the bloodied sand. Was it really possible that in his youth this man had been a bullfighter? Was this all he saw in it…?

And yet, was it possible that there might be something else here, something more? Looking at the drawings she realized that at the *fiesta brava* her own perspective had always been a remote one, an elevated one, ensconced as she had been in her private box, above the uproar and the tumult, shielded from the heat and the blare by a silken parasol, reclining in her padded chair, waving her fan and sniffing at her perfumed handkerchief. Goya on the other hand had taken his stance down there in the very center of the action, exposing himself to the stink, to the blood and snot, to the sweat and the slobber. Why did she and Goya see the world in such different ways? Why did he see a world that was not the world of others? The longer she knew him the more baffling he seemed to become….

She grimaced and shut the book with a snap and reached out to open another one.

What was this? Worse and worse! What now? A drawing of a young woman, her features distorted with dread and loathing, balancing on top of a wall and pressing a white kerchief to her face as she reached around in order to tug a tooth from the slack jaws of a hanged man. The hanging man, in a dirty white shirt, dangled with bound and stiffened arms, his neck broken, the whites of his eyes fastened on the viewer with a winking leer. And beneath the drawing were the words "*Hunting for teeth, for the teeth of a hanged man are a useful ingredient for sorceries, and without them there is not much you can do."* And then came pages filled with drawings of the sorcerers themselves. Sorcerers and witches. Witches young and witches beautiful, witches ancient and witches haggard, witches clothed and witches nude, witches straddling broomsticks and witches perched in rows on the branches of moon-blanched trees. And there were pages of processions of dwarfs, midgets, misshapen homunculi, babies starved and babies half-witted, babies more like fetuses than living children. Pages of men and women sick and dying. Pages of rag-wrapped corpses being shoveled into graves with great stone slabs waiting to be dropped on them.

She felt nauseated. The sketchbook was heavy in her hands. The room swam before her eyes. Freaks and demons. Her head fell forward and she swayed on the bench and felt the sketchbook falling to the floor.

And then she realized the book was being taken from her. She heard it being softly laid back on the top of the harpsichord. A gentle pair of hands closed around her upper arms to steady her. She opened her eyes to see María Luz kneeling in front of her, holding her, her dark face filled with concern.

She heard the girl speaking in a hesitant voice.

"Señora! Signor Carulli has sent me to tell you that Señor Goya has returned to the palace. He has gone to his room and locked himself in. Esteban can see through the window that he is lying on the bed with his dog Baltasar on the rug beside him. Shall I instruct Signor Carulli to rouse him and tell him you are waiting here for him?"

The Duchess put her hands on María Luz's shoulders and rose slowly to her feet. The giddiness was passing.

"Señora?"

María Luz spoke in the same tentative tone.

The Duchess's eye fell on the sketchbook on the harpsichord. She edged it away with the tip of her finger. She felt suddenly sickened by the smells of turpentine and linseed oil and cigars.

She shook her head.

"No, María Luz. It is too late for a sitting today. Please take me to my bedchamber."

She was not sorry that there would be no sitting today. She was not sorry there would be no sitting tomorrow, when they would all attend the celebration of the grape harvest.

Nevertheless, when she had returned to her bedchamber and María Luz had prepared her for a *siesta* she did not immediately retire to her bed.

When María Luz had left and she was alone, she went to her dressing table and took out her writing materials. She then scribbled a brief note to the Count of Altolaguirre. Her pen flew across the sheet. She wrote furiously, impetuously, the pen digging into the paper.

"*Come soon, Miguel. Come soon. Come soon....*"

She rang for María Luz and bade her send her butler to her. When he came in she gave him the letter while the ink and seal were still wet.

"See this gets off at once, Carulli."

The white-wigged Neapolitan gave her an obsequious smile and a little bow.

"Of course, Señora. Immediately."

"At once, Carulli. At once!"

"I understand, Señora. At once."

With a gloved hand the butler tucked the letter slowly and carefully into the pocket of his green velvet jacket and turned and left the chamber.

It would be a two hour drive along the road that led northward to Nuestra Señora del Rocío. After the tedium and travails of the journey from Cádiz, she feared it might prove physically fatiguing and that the painter's presence, after the revelations of his sketchbooks, might prove embarrassing.

On the contrary, the drive to the little river called the Guadalimar turned out to be invigorating. Ever since her arrival at Sanlúcar the weather had been kind, one flawless day succeeding another. The sky today was cloudless, the temperature mild, and she had no qualms about ordering up an open carriage, wearing a light green gown of filmy cotton and seeking no more protection from the sun than a shawl and a parasol. Indeed, the autumn breeze was still warm enough for her to bring a fan.

In spite of yesterday's doubts and discomfiture concerning Goya, she had slept soundly. There were no sweats or headaches, no dreams about the butchery of bulls or the slaughter of spectators or *toreros*, of hanged men or covens of witches. Doctor Arrieta's medicines tasted less rank and seemed to be taking hold. Her message to Miguel was speeding on its way. She could surely expect his arrival within a few days of Goya completing his commission and taking his departure for Madrid.

She could go as far as describing her mood as serene. She was looking forward to the festival, ready to lose herself in the laughter and bustle of country folk as she had been ready to lose herself in the mirth and revelry of the streets of Madrid. Not even the roughness of the road dampened her growing feeling of anticipation, nor the unappealing appearance of the landscape as their little cavalcade wound its way across the Coto de Doñana before turning east along the track that would take them away from the dreary vista of salt flats and stagnant pools towards the bank of the tiny tributary of the Guadalquivir. She had to hold fast to the leather strap inside the carriage door to stop herself being thrown about as they lurched along the narrow track, though she couldn't prevent herself from almost laughing out loud at the shrieks of merriment coming from the wagons behind them as the men and women of her household were hurled against each other as they bounced over the ruts in the trail. Their shouts of laughter mingled pleasantly with the ringing and jingling of the bells on the bright holiday harnesses of the mules and horses.

She braced herself and gripped her parasol more firmly. In front of her Esteban and young Pascual seemed about to topple off the box as they wrestled with the reins, while behind on the step she could hear the grunts and gasps of the poor footman as he hung on desperately to prevent himself being flung off his perch and thrown down the slope beside the track.

A good start to a stimulating outing! This would restore the color to her cheeks after those miserable months in Madrid and bring back a sparkle to her eyes for Miguel....

And what of Goya, seated once more in the opposite corner of the carriage? She saw that Goya was laughing too. A Goya bareheaded and shirt-sleeved, a muscled arm thrust through the strap on the other door, who was altogether different from the clenched and withdrawn figure she had known until now. The sight and feeling, if not the sound of the commotion in the open wagons behind them, somehow communicated itself to him as he faced backwards in the carriage, each roll and tilt making him throw back his head with its thick mane of hair and utter hoarse braying shouts, his teeth glinting in the sun.

Glancing sideways at him between jolts, the Duchess was glad that she hadn't decided to suggest, after his capricious behavior regarding the previous day's sitting, that he should travel in one of the wagons with his friends the servants. If his manner still seemed a little rough and rowdy, his attitude and bearing were improved. Perhaps today's jaunt would prove as beneficial for him as it promised to be for her. Perhaps it would make a further improvement, perhaps even a turning point in what was after all a difficult relationship. She hoped so. And at least he had done her the favor, before handing her with a gallant little flourish into the carriage, of consigning his awful dog to a wagon in the rear. Nor was there any evidence of the pistol, the hunting gun, or his fearful gypsy knife.

When they reached the gently sloping banks of the winding little Guadalimar, a lush burst of green in an otherwise arid landscape, they found that the advance party had already pitched and pegged out for them a pretty little Turkish tent of peach colored silk. The tent was open on three sides, its rear wall affording welcome protection from the steadily increasing heat of the sun. It was furnished with tables, an oriental carpet and two well-padded armchairs and afforded a charming view down the valley with its meandering streamlet. Goya's chair had been positioned a little below hers, since though he was the King's Painter she, after all, was the Duchess of Alba. The arrangement of the chairs had been superintended by Salvatore Carulli, who had taken up his station at the rear of the tent and whose manner indicated that he disapproved of a mere painter being invited to sit with the Duchess. It was with a certain air of hauteur that he directed the footmen who served them the food and wine from silver plates and goblets as they watched the people from Sanlúcar joining in the festivities with the farmers, shepherds and vineyard workers from Nuestra Señora del Rocío and all the estates around.

And a lovely sight it was, with every man, woman and child arrayed in their best and brightest costumes. There was much laughter and handing about of flagons of the local wine that had been put into the stream to cool, accompanied by shrieks and shouts as some of the men lost their balance and fell or were tipped into the water.

The music had already started. The picnickers lounged in groups on the grass, eating and drinking, one group playing cards, another flying kites, others throwing wooden balls at a post, and some trying to stagger about on stilts. A male singer with a fine baritone voice was regaling them with *seguidillas, sevillanas* and romances from popular *tonadillas* and *zarzuelas*. As the notes came floating up the slope the Duchess thought she recognized an aria from the comic opera *Clementina* which she recalled had been such a success when that bedizened creature La Tirana sang and danced in it a few seasons ago in Madrid.

The sky was filled with stately clouds. The turf in the well-watered valley still retained its brilliant summer green. On the slope on the far side of the stream the black flanks of a herd of bulls gleamed in the sun. Yesterday the sight of a herd of fighting bulls would have brought to the Duchess's mind the bloody sketches in Goya's notebooks and would have struck a menacing note, but on this happy day they seemed to provide a pleasing dab of color. The Duchess leaned back in her chair letting the brisk little breeze cool her cheeks as it rippled against the silken sides of the little tent. She watched the bulls through half-closed eyes as they cropped their way placidly along, fanning herself lazily and telling herself that she felt better and stronger than she had for many weeks.

As for Goya, he too seemed settled and relaxed. He was attacking the cold fowl and tartlets and tucking into the local wine with gusto. Seated only a little behind him and barely an arm's length away, picking at her food, the Duchess studied him. The dense black hair on his round Aragonese head was streaked with grey, though there was only a hint of thinning around the crown. The hair was freshly barbered and his linen freshly laundered, he was wearing a smartly cut coat of dark blue velvet with gilt buttons. True that from time to time the breeze wafted a scent of his rather overemphatic pomade, but at least it masked the odor of those noxious cigars. It would be pleasant to be able to report to Don Sebastián that, under the benign influence of Sanlúcar, both of Dr. Arrieta's patients were making steady progress.

Suddenly he craned forward, spilling wine from his goblet, which he set on the grass beside him. He took up his plate on which he had left some scraps of meat and pushed himself to his feet. He removed his velvet coat and draped it over the back of the chair. The Duchess thought he looked a little unsteady and recalled he had been signaling rather too frequently for the footman to replenish his cup. Not that he could be described as seriously tipsy, so reminding herself this was after all a festival, she smiled indulgently to herself as she watched him leave the tent at a shambling trot, raising his arm with the silver plate to retain his balance as he set off down the grassy slope. She watched him shouldering his way through the clumps of picnickers, then fetch up with a bump against the side of the wagon, decorated with ribbons and streamers, to the wheel of which his dog Baltasar had been tethered. The huge hound bounded madly from side to side as it saw its master approach, its frantic barking clearly audible above the rising clamor of the music. Steadying himself against the wagon, Goya fed the scraps of meat to the dog, laughing as the beast snapped and slavered as he teased it by throwing the scraps high in the air. The Duchess shuddered when she saw the diminutive white flash of her own little pet dog as it scampered to and fro among the villagers, daintily begging for tidbits in its turn, and was glad to see it swerving away from the wagon with the captive mastiff.

 The musicians were standing up now, wiping their lips and brushing the crumbs from their costumes as they came together to form a regular band. There were guitars, drums and the shrill Andalusian flutes called *pitos* and a hefty fellow was providing the bass by blowing lustily into a *cántaro* or big earthen jug. They launched into a lively *fandango malagueño* wherein the dancers joined hands in a circle and were soon stamping and swirling around in joyful abandon.

 The braying and the twanging and the shouts of the dancers quickly rose to such a fever of intensity that the Duchess wanted to cover her ears. Certainly the bulls on the opposite hillside were roused. She saw their blocky shapes blundering restlessly about. Yet Goya, kneeling with his back to the revelers and fondling his dog with touching tenderness, was totally unaware of the people gamboling behind him, the men clapping and cheering, the women twisting and turning as they clicked their little Andalusian *castañuelas* and *chinchines* and jingled their *panderetas,* their little tambourines. It was only when the dancers in one of the circles accidently bumped into him that he turned around and saw the whole meadow bouncing and seething.

For a moment the Duchess lost sight of him behind a billowing skein of dancers. Then, when they moved aside, she saw him sitting on the ground with his back against a wheel and on his face an expression of amazement and delight. He had brought up his hands and was trying to clap in time to the rhythm of the high-stepping dancers, their arms lifted above their heads as they smacked their palms together. He clapped doggedly, but however hard he tried he couldn't follow the beat of the music or capture the elusive, shifting motions of the dance. It was a pathetic sight, and she couldn't stop the spectacle of his jerky, tardy movements from tearing at her heart. What seemed to make it even more pitiful was that he went on smiling and laughing, yearning to join in and merge with the happy throng of merrymakers.

A pair of girls from the nearest circle of dancers broke away and came tripping across the grass towards him, holding out their hands. They caught hold of him and pulled him, laughing and struggling, to his feet. The Duchess assumed they were two of his female friends from the servant's hall and was surprised to see that one of them was María Luz. Only minutes before she had waved a hand to allow the Arab girl to dart out from her place behind her chair and run down the slope to join her comrades. Now the Arab girl and her companion were hauling Goya upright and lugging him forward and, although the Duchess had been aware that the girl was pretty, she now realized her personal maid was not merely pretty, but beautiful. The dark glowing face, the bare heaving black shoulders—this was no girl but an exotic and mature woman. They both dragged Goya into the middle of a circle of dancers and María Luz's little daughter Estrellita rushed forward to hang onto her skirt, hopping and skipping around her. Watching them, the Duchess felt a sudden pang of loneliness, a sudden impulse to throw down her fan and run down the slope and lose herself in the surging throng where Goya was being turned and twisted about by his admiring females. Only a short while ago, before the dreary requirements of widowhood, Cayetana de Alba would have done just that.

It was not an impulse easily stifled. And her sense of resentment grew at the sight of Goya jiggling about foolishly with the Arab girl. He was hopping from one foot to the other as the dancers snatched him and spun him around to the strains of the *fandango*. Capering crazily to keep his balance, and laughing uproariously, he seized Estrellita and swung the little black girl up onto his shoulders, prancing about with her as she pummeled the top of his head in delight. It was like watching a bear in leading strings, except that for so solidly built a man who had drunk too much wine and couldn't even hear the music, he seemed surprisingly light on his feet, making her recall the stories of his being a bullfighter in his younger days. There was about him, she realized, a palpable air of virility, no doubt not unattractive to a certain sort of women, such as actresses and singers and servant girls or, if the rumors were true, even to certain grand ladies of title who had sat to him for their portraits. What a pity, that as Painter to the Court, he thought so little of his dignity as to romp around in the company of lackeys and peasants! And was it really necessary for him and María Luz to display such a distinctly free and easy manner towards each other? She would have to have a word with the girl when they got back to the palace.

And what was the pair of them up to now? Why, the woman had taken off her colored shawl and was flicking and flirting it at him like a matador. He was encouraging her by stooping and rushing at the shawl. Little Estrellita slid off his back on to the grass as he raised his fists to his forehead and pointed up his fingers to imitate the horns of a bull, while all the while the silly crowd was pressing around and urging them on with cheers and cries.

Nor, to her disgust, did these antics end there. María Luz was now flourishing an imaginary sword as Goya went down on all fours in front of her, his head lowered like an exhausted bull. And then, when she had darted in to deliver the *estocada*, and after he had given an exaggerated shudder and rolled over as if he were dead, she suddenly flung the shawl aside and snatched a handkerchief from a nearby spectator. Falling to her knees beside him, she jerked his head up and swiftly bound the handkerchief over his eyes and knotted it behind his neck. Willing hands tugged him to his feet, and in another moment he was being whirled this way and that in a game of *gallina ciega*, blind hen, or blind man's bluff. He staggered around, arms outstretched, playing a helpless blind man to amuse the crowd as he had previously amused them by pretending to be a helpless bull. He swayed this way and that, stumbling on the rough grass, grabbing at the men who dashed towards him, or to deliver a playful twirl or slap at the women and children who dodged him and ran away shrieking.

The music was drowned out. Everyone was milling around and shouting with laughter. Everyone was applauding him, egging him on. He seemed to be laughing as hard as they were, so she was shocked to see him suddenly catch hold of one of the men and shake him violently and pitch him to one side with such violence that the man lay dazed and spreadeagled full-length on the ground.

The crowd moved back, suddenly silent, and the Duchess saw Goya tear the bandage from his eyes and run up the slope towards the tent. He floundered up the slope and when he raised his head she could see his face and neck were flushed and that tears were pouring down his cheeks. He flung himself into his chair with such force that it rocked and almost fell. She could see the sweat shining through his thick hair and on the back of his neck. Behind her, Signor Carulli, who had been tending to her needs and watching the antics of the country folk with an ironic eye, leaned forward to offer the painter a napkin, a half-smile on his face. Goya took it and without glancing back began to wipe his face which she could plainly see was wet with tears.

Her first impression was that he was exhausted after his ill-conceived exertions. He was no longer a young man and was recuperating from a nearly fatal illness. But the anguished expression on his face seemed to be caused by more than simple exertion. He seemed to be in the grip of some black emotion that had swept over him in the middle of all that childish horseplay. He sat with his forearms planted on his thighs, his white shirt a wet rag, his rounded back shaking. He let his head sag between his knees and she could hear a deep raucous sobbing coming from deep within his chest.

Her first instinct was to draw away from him, her fan fluttering faster in her hand. Then, looking at his huddled form, she could not repress a sense of pity. All that music, all that laughter, all the rich sounds of this beautiful day could never fully reach him. He would never henceforward communicate with his fellow beings except through his solitary craft. It was all very well for Don Sebastián to say that he had been spared the ultimate catastrophe of blindness. Wasn't it possible that in spite of what was commonly assumed, deafness might be a greater affliction than blindness? Blind people can hear laughter and music, they can share in banter and chatter. But the deaf? People may be kind to deaf persons, try to draw them in and include them in their groups, but soon surely their presence would become an encumbrance, an embarrassment? Hence the deaf are excluded, disregarded, overlooked, banished to the outer fringes of the company. She had heard that when one loses one sense the other senses become more acute. But what sort of compensation would that be to a man like Goya? Even if there were increased sharpness in his sense of sight, would that lead to any added intensity in the pleasure of seeing? Would it restore the feeling of pure gaiety that had been such a feature of his earlier paintings, like the designs for the royal tapestries which had done so much to lighten the gloomy confines of the royal palace in Madrid? On the contrary, deafness seemed to have led to the horrible drawings in his sketchbooks. Could it be that the drawings were horrible because he couldn't actually *hear* the sounds associated with the frightful subjects he was portraying? Surely sound would provide some sort of release, might even render the dreadful scenes more human? Those bulls bellowing in their death agony, the men and women screaming as they were being strangled in the cellars of the Holy Office, weren't they the more appalling because Goya couldn't actually hear the bellows and the screams, could only see the agonized lips and jaws senselessly opening and shutting, could only watch these abominations taking place as if they were taking place on the other side of a sheet of thick glass? Was it his deafness that heightened his sense of the cruelty of the world, that had driven him to concentrate with such single-minded intensity on its barbarity? The Duchess thought that the silence of his depictions was what made these horrible scenes doubly strange and terrifying.

Seated behind him as he sat bowed, his head in his hands and his shoulders shaking, it swept over her what an abnormal afternoon this gifted and tormented man was experiencing. For the first time she understood more fully what an alien world Goya had been condemned to live in. For him there was no whisper of the breeze as it ruffled the silk of the tent, no chuckle of the river as it wound its way through the valley, no lazy lowing of the bulls on the distant slope. Never would he hear the clack of the *castañuelas*, ringing voices lifted in song, or the thrumming of a guitar. He would never even hear the barking of his own dog.

Was it any wonder his sketches hinted at madness? Was it any wonder that such a man might feel he was trapped in some kind of asylum? Or worse than an asylum, a place of measureless fear, a labyrinth of endless horror? How can a man retain his sanity when he cannot hear and make sense of the simplest things around him, when a friend or an enemy could creep up behind him and clap him suddenly on the back making his heart stop beating and the blood freeze in his veins…?

In a surge of sympathy, before she knew what she was doing, she leaned forward and placed a hand on the wet sleeve of his shirt and pressed her fingers softly into his arm. It was the first time she had deliberately touched him and she was taken aback by the hardness of his arm, its roundness and tightness against the sweat-soaked cloth.

Immediately collecting herself, she pulled her hand away. But suddenly he reached around, still staring ahead, and put his hand over hers.

She looked down, startled, at the square hand with its knotted sinews and paint-blotched skin, feeling a queer little thrill as his fingers closed on hers with a painful pressure.

She tried to remove her hand but felt such a spasm of trembling go through his fingers she let it lie still.

She sat with him, sharing his deafness, oblivious to the sound of the flutes, the drums and guitars as they started up again.

Oblivious too, not caring whether Signor Carulli, standing behind her, noticed or not, she put her fan in her lap and took out her handkerchief and began to wipe Goya's forehead.

SHE REALLY DIDN'T know why, but after the picnic she found herself thinking differently about Goya. Perhaps it was seeing him so helpless and vulnerable at the close of the festivities that had aroused her sympathy. At any rate, he had started to seem more human, less tousled and unkempt, less like a shaggy ogre, if one had to put it like that.

Much of this beneficent feeling, of course, was attributable to this unusual spell of delightful weather. They had already entered the early days of October but it seemed that this delightful Indian summer was destined to last forever. Increasingly Sanlúcar seemed to her to be a little paradise, an oasis set among the sandy wastes between Cádiz and Huelva and sufficiently remote from both. No rumors of civil broils or news of the progress of the war against England seeped through to this remote corner of Andalucía. She would have ignored them if they had. She luxuriated in the absence of the pressures and obligations that had been weighing on her in Madrid. She was free of the strain and falsity of the court, with its incessant play-acting and striking of attitudes. Here there were no responsibilities, no social life, no Father Xavier Valera to pull long faces and shake his head over her shortcomings and peccadilloes. Not that she didn't have occasional qualms about having left poor sick Father Valera behind her in Madrid. Again she reminded herself how woefully she had fallen behind in her religious observances. Even as a girl, to the distress of her family, she had never shown herself to be unduly pious. In any case, piety had fallen out of fashion in recent years. Since the recent revolution in France, skepticism had taken hold among such people as her husband and Don Sebastián, who prided themselves on their advanced views, although, of course, they expressed them with suitable caution. As for the court, it was a subject of scandal that so few of them there now took religion seriously. All the same, she had been bred in the faith, and was not a scoffer. She reminded herself to write to the Archbishop of Seville to assure him that she intended to pay more attention to her religious duties, and would give instructions without delay for repairs to be carried out to the palace chapel.

And she was glad that she had told Carulli to send a carriage for the priest from the local village to visit Sanlúcar on Sundays and holy days to attend to the religious needs of the servants.

Still, putting these solemn thoughts aside and getting back to the more immediate matter of her portrait, she was glad that work on it was going well. In the week since the picnic, there had been no less than five sittings and she had the impression that Goya was taking particular pains with it. All to the good. Naturally, she was dying to take a peek at it to see what he was making of it, to learn in what light he saw and represented her. But at the end of every session he arranged his damp cloth carefully over the canvas, and she felt she must respect his wish to shield his efforts from view until the moment came for the unveiling. María Luz had described for her the way he had chosen to lock himself in his room and in his studio, so presumably it was his regular practice to work, after hours and mostly at night, in this secretive fashion. Remembering the hat with the candles and the crepuscular drawings she had seen at the end of his sketchbook, she felt he certainly seemed to have a special predilection for darkness. But he seemed to be growing more at ease in the studio. He had started to smile, to hum discordantly and whistle tunelessly as he applied the brush to the canvas, or smeared on paint with his thumb, or gave way to his awful habit of sucking the paint off his fingers and even off the brushes before putting the latter into a jar of turpentine. Indeed, during these last few days they had become so comfortable with each other that she had sent Carulli to invite him to take his evening meals with her in her dining room. True, she had seated him at the far end of the table, for what was the point of sitting him any closer when there was no possibility of conversation? Luckily there was no need of it, as the servants were kept very busy attending to their needs, and she felt that they had settled down in a suitably comradely manner in which to eat their food and drink their wine.

Nor was it only a question of the evening meal. Yesterday

she had ordered a place to be laid for him at the table in the courtyard where she was accustomed to take her breakfast. His friend Esteban the coachman had routed him out of his lair in the depths of the palace and now, blinking in the early morning sunlight and leaning back easily in his chair, he sat sipping his chocolate and nibbling at his sweet roll with an air as placid as her own. This morning he was dressed simply in a long-sleeved white shirt and white breeches, looking quite the courtier for a change, a white scarf drawn through a silver ring at his throat and his black hair neatly combed and curling over his collar. She too was dressed all in white, in a long loosely-flowing morning gown of sprigged muslin. Eventually they would stir themselves and move indoors to the studio, but in the meantime there was nothing to do but dawdle together over the breakfast table in companionable silence.

The courtyard, approached by a pair of double doors at the end of the palace close to her private suite, was a pretty little enclave, the walls covered with *azulejos* or blue and white tiles and its floor paved with white tiles from Tarifa. On one wall was an image of the Virgen del Rocío executed in Triana tiles and overhead were strung wires from which hung bunches of grapes that would be left there until the time came to harvest them for a special late pressing. Their leaves stippled the courtyard with patches of shade and lent it an agreeable coolness. True, due to neglect during the time the palace had been left unoccupied, many of the tiles with their pattern of bluebirds had cracked and some of the wires were now slack and sagging, but until the sun became too hot and drove its occupants inside it was a pleasant spot in which to linger.

At first when the servants were bringing out the fine china service and her precious French *chocolatière* and María Luz was supervising the laying of the table, the Duchess fussed over her little white dog Conchita while Goya amused himself playing with Estrellita. The little dog, the silver bells on its collar tinkling as it frisked around, had been picked up and placed on the Duchess's lap, while Goya, whose own dog was confined somewhere in the distant recesses of the palace, had taken the little black girl and placed her on his knees, tickling her until the tears streamed from her eyes. In fact he was tickling her too roughly and, as he was deaf, could not recognize the point at which the shrieks of pleasure were turning into those of pain. María Luz had to run forward and fairly wrestle the child from him in order to pacify her.

As María Luz was withdrawing, holding her child, the Duchess signaled to her to come close. To her surprise she found herself telling her maid not to return until she was summoned by the Duchess's bell, which she always kept on the table by her glass. Until then she was to remain out of sight, although within call.

Why had she said that? She told herself it was for María Luz's own good—she had been paying too much attention to Goya at the picnic and perhaps Goya had been paying too much attention to her. Not that she had any serious doubts about the young woman's virtue. After all, she had successfully rebuffed the attentions of a number of young bloods who had come sniffing around and had been very skillful in fending off the overtures of the young coachman Pascual, who the Duchess knew had been pestering her. No, the Duchess had nothing to complain about regarding the young woman's conduct. But what of Goya's? On the evidence of his notebooks alone, crammed with images of women, he clearly represented more of a danger than the callow young coachman or the importunate puppies at court. And what about his reputation in Madrid, which had spread as far as Cádiz and Seville? How well had he known the actresses and dancers skipping about on the pages of his sketchbooks? And quite apart from his reputation as a seducer, how could she expose a trusting young woman to the possible attentions of a man capable of executing such black and horrific drawings? The images lingered hauntingly in her mind, refusing to go away, and the more she thought about them the more she was becoming convinced that there must be a strong vein of cruelty in Goya's character. Why would one assume that his macabre outpourings were simply a protest at life's atrocities? Didn't they contain an undertone of something like furtive glee? Wasn't there some secret relish in the relentless rendering of accidents and torments, of deaths and disasters? Would he have bothered to have drawn them in the first place unless, underlying the cries of so-called indignation, there weren't some lurking spirit of positive enjoyment…?

Gazing across at him over the breakfast table on this beatific morning, he didn't seem unduly dangerous or sinister. On the contrary, his features seemed to have softened and lightened. She fancied she could see what it was in his manner and appearance that would appeal to impressionable young women and to raffish theater people. He gave off a palpable air of strength and vitality. She was reminded of the bulls she had seen at the picnic….

She lifted the silver *chocolatière*.

"More chocolate, Señor Goya?"

He did not answer and she repeated herself snappishly.

"I said, Señor Goya, will you have more chocolate?"

She particularly prided herself on the quality of her chocolate and was accustomed to being complimented on it. She had made sure that generous supplies had been brought from Madrid. She loved to vary her chocolate from day to day. One day it might be her musky Sonosco, another her bitter Guayaquil. This morning it was the deliciously smooth and fragrant Moxos chocolate from Bolivia and she had rather hoped Goya would comment favorably on it.

As he sat immobile staring into his cup she again remembered his deafness. There would be no comment this or any other morning. She put out a hand, moved it into his line of vision and rapped with a knuckle on the tablecloth in front of him.

His head came up with a jerk and he stared at her foolishly, his jaw slack, his eyes out of focus.

"Eh—did you say—? What did you—?"

She held out the *chocolatière* and, staring into his eyes, spoke very slowly and distinctly.

"I asked if you wanted me to refill your cup?"

Again, she didn't know exactly why she had spoken since he was unable to hear. She had done so automatically. So she gestured with the *chocolatière*, pointing it at his empty cup.

He gave a start and came to himself, speaking once more in the broken garbled phrases that were, since his deafness, so habitual with him.

"Oh yes, Duchess. That would be very—"

And when she had refilled his cup he raised it to her in a little salute and gave her an apologetic little smile.

She sighed as she poured more of the Moxos for herself and set down the pot. Breakfasting *à deux* with Goya was not going to be easy…. But that little smile on his face? Was it the sadness behind it, the hint of insecurity she had not until now detected that gave a small wrench to her heart? And suddenly she had a novel idea. He could interpret the motion she had made with the *chocolatière* even if he could not understand the accompanying words. He had been deaf for too short a time to enable him to decipher the movement of a person's lips. But if he was to be sentenced to a lifetime of deafness, as both Doctor Arrieta and Don Sebastián had indicated, surely it would be essential for him to acquire that skill as soon as possible?

Looking at the doleful figure opposite her, his head bowed and his shoulders slumped like a bull subdued and resigned to its fate, she made an effort to dismiss the memory of the contents of the gruesome notebooks and was filled with a desire to help him.

Her first thought was of Doctor Arrieta. Could he be asked to draw up a course of treatment? Or would he know of some other doctor, or one of the clever doctors in France or Germany, who might be devoting special attention to this problem? There must be some medical books and pamphlets that the doctor could send her? She would dispatch a rider to Cádiz. But there would be delays, delays in acquiring the books, delays in fetching them. All at once she was fired with an urgency to begin. After all, she was an intelligent woman, he an intelligent man. In the course of each day they spent hours in the studio, at the dining table, and would spend hours in the courtyard. They must work on this problem together. Why couldn't she be his teacher…?

She determined to make an immediate start. She leaned over the table and began to mouth sentences at him, speaking very slowly and searching for words with only one syllable.

She pointed at her lips.

"*Can. You. See. My. Lips?*"

He scowled and slouched in his chair.

She persisted.

"*I. Want. You. To. Watch. My. Lips.*"

She was sure he guessed what she was trying to do. Stubbornness, mixed with pride and perhaps a feeling of shame at his predicament, made him disinclined to participate.

He folded his arms and turned his head away. He gazed up at the swags of grapes above him.

She waited until his eyes moved back in her direction. She spoke more emphatically.

"*You. Must. Watch. My. Lips.*"

But again, like a sulking schoolboy, he frowned and looked away.

She took a minute to collect herself. This particular approach was meeting with no success. Perhaps the trouble was that, except for the word "lips" all the other words had been abstract?

Between them on the table lay a silver dish filled with an assortment of fruit. She began to pick them out one by one, leaning forward to wave each of them slowly in front of him.

"*Orange. Lemon. Peach. Grapes.*" And again. "*Orange. Lemon. Peach. Grapes.*"

He gaped at her, not taking it in. Then he got the idea. He

rocked forward and uttered a shout. The shattering sound made the little dog snoozing in her lap wake up with a squeal and leap down and scuttle away through the French windows to safety.

"*Orange! Lemon! Peach!*"

He snatched an orange out of the silver dish and tossed it high in the air, so high she feared he wouldn't catch it and it would land on the table among her glass and china. He caught it with an adroit turn of the wrist while still continuing to chant triumphantly in a discordant voice:

"*Orange! Lemon! Peach!*"

She began to point to a succession of objects on the tablecloth, taking care to keep her face close to his and shaping each word distinctly.

"*Cup. Knife. Spoon.*"

Immediately he understood, and shouted the word as she touched each object and called out its name.

She went further still. She folded her arms and spoke the names of all the different articles on the table so he had to recognize them without her touching or pointing at them, spacing out her words even more slowly and clearly.

He craned forward, his eyes fixed on her moving lips, jabbing at each article violently with his forefinger and proclaiming its name violently in a sound between a shout and a splutter whenever he identified it.

"*Spoon! Knife! Cup! Plate! Jug! Fork! Napkin!*"

He frequently got the name of the object wrong, but he was quick, and after two or three attempts she seldom had to repeat the name.

She relaxed and lay back with a sigh. She smiled. Of course it was only a minor victory. He would not be able to comprehend any word spoken to him unless you pushed your face directly into his. He would never be able to understand any complicated sentence, if he ever managed to get the hang of any sentence at all. He would be confined to the most simple and primitive exchanges. Yet it was a breakthrough, surely, if only a limited one? She had made a tiny hole in that wall of silence. And perhaps through that tiny hole some of the foul juices that found expression in his hideous sketches might begin to trickle through, relieving some of the terrible pressure in his head? Had she created some small measure of hope? Was she bringing him into some tangible contact with the world? She felt a thrill of pride that she, Cayetana de Alba, was the first person to communicate with this suffering and gifted man since the onset of his illness, with this man of genius, as Don Sebastián had called him. She had reached out and touched him through the bars of his prison! Don Sebastián would be proud of her.

They both rested easily in their chairs, the Duchess smiling at Goya and Goya smiling back at her. She felt the slight but obstinate tingle in her throat that always returned whenever she disobeyed Doctor Arrieta's orders and over-exerted herself. Yet having got so far she was reluctant to bring this first lesson to a close. They would take a few minutes more to drive the lesson home before she had to rouse herself and move inside and start putting on her costume and painting her face in readiness for the morning sitting.

They seemed to have run out of objects on the table, so she turned her head and looked around the courtyard for something suitable. She frowned, puzzled, then had an idea.

With an intake of breath, fighting down the prickle in her throat, she sat on the edge of her seat and slanted her upper body across the table.

For a moment he looked perplexed and remained leaning in his chair. Then he pushed himself upright and set himself squarely opposite her.

She pointed to her forehead.
"Forehead."
He gaped.
She pointed to each eye in turn.
"Eye."

He still looked befuddled.

She tapped her cheek

"*Cheek.*"

She sat quite still, looking at him steadily. When she spoke, she made not the slightest movement to betray what part of her face or head to which she was referring.

She opened her jaws wide and mouthed silently.

"*Hair. Hair. Hair. Hair.*"

He stared.

"*Hair. Hair. Hair. Hair.*"

Then he understood.

She jerked her head back as his face cleared and he uttered a booming, jarring laugh.

"*Hair! Hair! Hair!*"

And then without moving her head, she went on slowly articulating feature after feature.

"*Nose. Chin. Neck.*"

Carried away, he bent forward and touched her nose and chin and neck as he named them.

"*Nose! Chin! Neck!*"

She swayed back, trying to evade his finger, aware of the fierceness of his gestures. But his touch was unexpectedly gentle, as if he were applying a delicate stroke to a canvas.

He remained silent for a moment, his finger on his chin. Then he mouthed each word over again, slowly and in a guttural whisper.

She had seen him weep at the picnic and fancied she again saw tears in his eyes.

She sat upright, half-flinching, half-frozen, and he suddenly did something unexpected. He leaned forward and reached out and slowly wrapped one hand around the back of her neck, while the other slowly brushed back the dark hair tumbling about her shoulders. He stroked it back from her forehead.

Too surprised to move, she could only stare as he lightly stroked her hair.

He spoke in what she took to be an attempt to whisper.
"*Thank—. Thank—.*"
He shifted his hands and cupped them on either side of her face.
She shivered.
And he said in a slow and marveling tone, mouthing the words carefully as she herself had done.
"*Mouth. Lips.*"
He began to pass his thumbs, faintly smelling of paint, deliberately and tenderly down her cheeks and across her quivering mouth.
Then he collected himself and let his hands drop.
She felt an irksome tightening sensation in her chest but couldn't resist an impulse to lean forward and put a hand on his arm.
"Well done, Francisco. Well done indeed!"
He beamed and gave a vigorous nod. Then, as it had in the silken tent during the picnic at Nuestra Señora del Rocío, his hand closed tightly over hers.
They were elated. Carried away. And much to their surprise they simultaneously leaned across the table and felt their lips brush lightly across each other's cheek, then travel down to fasten on each other's mouth….

How HAD IT begun? She had the feeling when it started that she was conscious only of a kind of shifting veil through which she could glimpse vague whirling figures, which slowly dissipated.

But when the veil gradually dissolved, she found herself back once more in the valley of the Guadalimar, now bathed in a warm late-evening light. She realized that it must be the aftermath of the picnic, though the valley was deserted and she was no longer seated in the Turkish tent but lying on the grass on the other side of the valley, high up the slope. The tent itself seemed far away and the little stream below her seemed wider than she remembered, flowing more smoothly and giving a hint of darker depths.

It did not occur to her, at first, that she might not be alone in the dream. She lay with her eyes half-open, lapped contentedly in the soft sunlight. The sun itself, round and luscious as a piece of fruit, was sinking slowly toward the rim of the valley, its rays caressing the surface of the river. The scene filled her with a sense of calm. Then, in such a natural way that she felt not the slightest feeling of unease, an arm in a white sleeve reached across her from behind, holding an object which she recognized with the sense of inevitability with which one accepts such happenings in dreams.

It was a telescope. But not bulbous and battered, but a shining instrument polished as if newly purchased. And the hand that held it above her and motioned for her to take it was not paint-stained and middle-aged, but youthful and unblemished, and as she took it and guided it towards her eye, she saw her own hand was white and flawless too, the hand of a young girl.

She sat up and took the instrument in both hands and through the smooth warm barrel she could see the far side of the valley with sharper clarity. She saw the empty tent with its two brocade chairs, its peach-colored silk bright against the evening green of the grass, its sides undisturbed by any breath of breeze. There was no sign of a living being but she could see that the slopes around the tent were strewn with skirts and blouses, with stockings and shoes, as if the dancers had divested themselves of their festive raiment and gone skipping over the crest of the hill and out of sight. The slopes were empty, though she could make out a smattering of abandoned drums and guitars and tambourines. Away to one side were the black rectangular shapes of a line of deserted coaches and wagons, their shafts resting on the ground. There were no mules or horses. The only sign of life she could discern was some kind of a dark brown shape that appeared to be padding about between the wheels of one of the wagons.

It was while she was scanning this deserted landscape that she grew aware of the sound of music. At first she was conscious of a low sweet whistling, a scrap of melody she was unable to recognize. And then the sound of a guitar crept in. It was being played close at hand and the playing was plangent and languorous. She sat up straighter and turned her head. The player was seated on the grass a short distance above her and to her right. For a moment her sight was blurred, but when she put down the telescope and was able to focus, she saw that the person serenading her was Goya and that he was playing the same guitar on which she had seen him flogging away that first morning in the studio. But now it was not the broken and sorry-looking instrument with the snapped and trailing strings which he used to belabor, but a guitar with taut new strings, its varnish slick and shiny. The piece he was playing was so captivating and bewitching that she listened to it as if she were double dreaming, as if it came to her in a dream wrapped within a dream. And then she recognized it was an accompaniment and that she was hearing the words of a song.

Singing. Goya was singing. Not the raucous baying she had heard in the studio, but tuneful, melodious singing, the singing one hears in a dream....

> *Guadalquivir*
> *Beautiful river*
> *White ships sailing*
> *Branches of green*

Leaving Sanlúcar
    Rippling water
        Silver boats sighting
            Tower of gold

Many-oared vessel
    Bound for Triana
        First in the fleet
            Bearing my heart

It was clear and strong. It was the voice of a young man. And his face and body were those of a young man, the sullen slouch gone, gone too the scowling mask and the bitter lines running down either side of his mouth.

He set the guitar down and reached into the back pocket of his breeches and produced his silver flask. With one of the magical motions typical of dreams, there appeared in his hand two silver goblets, into each of which he poured a generous measure of red wine. He held one out for her to take and raised his goblet to his lips:

"To your good health, Duchess!"

And again it struck her that it was perfectly natural for him to speak to her like this, in an easy tone of voice, different from the maimed mutterings she heard while he stamped around his studio.

She let herself fall back onto the warm grass and allowed her senses to sink into a drowse, at intervals raising her head to take a sip of the delicious wine. And then, without being in the least surprised at how the conjuring trick had been effected, the dream made another magical shift. At one moment they were lying side by side, the telescope, the guitar, the flask and goblets scattered around them, and the next moment she was lying with her head cradled on the white sleeve of his outstretched arm. All was utterly still. The shadows crept down the slope and across the river where the rim of the setting sun was touching the ridge of a distant hill.

She was settling her head down deeper into the crook of her companion's arm when she opened her half closed eyes and glanced downwards along the entire length of her body.

Instead of the light green summer gown she was wearing on the afternoon of the picnic, she saw she was swathed in a garish and flamboyant costume—more flamboyant than the *maja* costume she was wearing for her sittings. What she saw, as she squinted down at herself, was so outlandish and unexpected she nuzzled closer to her companion's flank and surrendered herself to a fit of silent laughter, of the sort to which one can only give utterance to in dreams.

Even in her wildest attempts to be provocative she would never have dared in waking life to look so like a woman of the streets. She was enfolded from neck to toe in a gauzy white silken shift, so transparent she could see through it not only the pink of her flesh, but the purple thrust of her nipples and the black triangle of the down between her thighs. Around her waist was a broad rose-colored sash, bound tightly in order to emphasize the bulge of the belly below and the curves of the breasts above. And topping off the flimsy shift was a flashy and flimsy yellow jacket lavishly sprinkled with gold sequins, and on her feet a pair of pointed golden slippers.

And it was at this point in the dream, when she seemed to be slipping willingly into the role of wanton and courtesan, of an actress such as La Tirana or a dancer like Zárate, that the dream suddenly turned in on itself and skewed itself sideways and slithered unexpectedly and without warning into an unnerving final phase.

First came a blackness. The radiant sky darkened. She heard a sound she couldn't describe, so close it seemed to be coming from her head—a low dull sound, not human. She rolled over and lay flat on her back, rigid and quivering. She knew one wasn't supposed to have the sensation of smell in dreams but her nostrils were suddenly assailed by a suffocatingly foul odor. At the same time she felt as if a damp cloth was being clamped over the lower part of her face, a cloth soaked with a substance giving off a slimy reek. Then it lifted and its place was taken by something thick and leathery that began scraping its way across her jaw and cheek. The skin of her face and neck was rasped with something wet and rough.

The bulls. She had forgotten the bulls. While she was admiring herself and her gaudy finery, the bulls had wandered down the slope and were sniffing them, nudging and shoving them with their heavy muzzles.

Eyes squeezed shut, she felt a huge furry mass was hovering above her, obliterating the dying glare of the sun, butting her recumbent body this way and that. From the stink and the snorting she sensed a huge herd of bulls must be huddled around them, their shaggy sides jostling against each other as they rummaged at the meaty creatures below them. She was terrified at the thought of their hoofs. She was terrified by the thought of their horns. Did the fear of being crushed and mangled by those hoofs and horns prompt the next freakish twist of the dream?

She raised her hands across her body in a pathetic attempt to save her breasts and belly from the beasts. But what defense could her hands and her gossamer silks and gauzes provide against the slicing horns and crunching hoofs? And when she risked opening her eyes she saw, gazing fearfully along the length of her body and expecting the plunge of a horn, that there were no more silks and gauzes, no more white shift or rose-colored sash. She was completely naked. The dream had stripped her bare and laid her wide open to the bulls....

She lay there quaking, believing that another minute would end it all. Above her hung the massive weight of a bull. And then, as she waited for the thrust of the horn, the white-sleeved arm slid gently across her naked body and the calm voice of Goya spoke softly in her ear.

"*Lie still!*"

A gritty tongue nibbled at her neck and covered her belly and thighs with a coat of drool.

"*Keep still!* They won't attack while they are with the herd. Then they are harmless."

The voice was the voice of a practiced *torero* who knows that a bull will become puzzled and lose interest when confronted with a *torero* lying on the sand. One last disgusted poke with its nose and it will walk away.

Her eyes ran upwards along her belly and flanks to the thick swinging pizzle of the bull that was straddling her, its lips dropping foam on her cheeks and neck. But she didn't see the deep ebony hide of the bulls which had been grazing across the valley, she saw the gleaming hide of a pure white bull, a beautiful ethereal bull, a bull of an immaculate and milky purity. Its pale and lustrous eyes were staring unblinkingly into hers. It lowered its head and its fringed lashes brushed across her forehead. She could feel its peppery breath as it shifted a cud of grass in its jaws. The drool from its spongy tongue dripped warm on her neck….

As she was waking, she first remembered her terror, then amazement at the fleeting memory of the lack of any trace of ferocity in the bull's final gaze. She had expected to see a raging flame in its eye as a horn thrust deep into her belly. Instead, she was imbued with an impression of mildness, almost of benevolence, as the great glistening head dropped down again and the rough tongue drew itself in light lingering strokes along the length of her naked body.

She could not move or breathe. And as she came fully awake she felt the arm that had been pressing her down on the tussocky grass lighten its grip, while a hand moved up slowly to fondle each of her breasts in turn. At the same time she seemed to hear the bump and swish of the huge white animal as it slowly withdrew, its hoofs dragging along the turf.

When she came fully to herself and found herself laying warm and safe in her wide high-canopied bed, she was amazed at how content she felt, how unexpectedly light of heart….

FOR SOME DAYS after that spontaneous and unpremeditated kiss across the breakfast table, a kiss that had taken them both aback, Goya and the Duchess acted towards each other with a certain constraint verging on mutual embarrassment. For two days they found an excuse to politely avoid each other, the Duchess finding it necessary to devote herself to domestic matters within the palace, Goya needing to be driven by Esteban to Cádiz to purchase fresh supplies of paint and pay a routine visit to Doctor Arrieta. It was three days later that they came together again in the studio to continue the sittings which now seemed to be taking an uncharacteristically long time.

She walked rapidly into the studio in her *maja* costume and went directly to the stool on which she was to take her pose. Goya was already in his painter's smock and put a hand out to help her onto the stool as they exchanged a quick glance and a diffident smile. She looked down to adjust her dress and he turned and began to busy himself with his pots and brushes. María Luz, who had witnessed the intimate exchange between them in the courtyard and had been perturbed by it, stole quietly over to sit at her place in the corner.

For half and hour or so, just before the Duchess made the small signal they had agreed upon for her to take a short break from the strain of posing, the minutes passed in unbroken silence. The Duchess fixed her gaze above Goya's head in the direction of the French windows and Goya seemed more absorbed in rendering the details of the black lace *mantilla* than working on the nuances of her face. He uttered no word of prompting or suggestion in his gravelly voice and the Duchess expelled a soft and stifled sigh to indicate a growing discomfort with her pose, but otherwise the only sounds were the dab of the brush on the palette and the tap of the brush on the canvas.

There was no warning whatever of the imminent crisis that would overtake them in the next few minutes.

All at once, the Duchess gave a sudden cough and as her hand involuntarily flew to her mouth to cover it, she swayed dangerously on her stool, threatening to topple over as another and fiercer cough racked her body. Precipitately, Goya flung down his brush and palette and ran towards her just as María Luz came rushing from her corner. He reached the Duchess just in time to catch her as she crumpled in his arms, now overcome by a fit of violent coughing.

He held her in his arms, his face alight with concern while María Luz hovered behind them uttering little gasps of fright. The coughing went on and on. Goya looked around as if for a chair on which to lay her down. He made up his mind. Carrying the Duchess, he strode across the room and gave a hard peremptory kick at the double doors, accompanying this with a loud bellow. He then kicked the doors again to summon the footman on duty to open them and when they were flung open marched through them and headed down the corridor.

María Luz realized what he intended to do and darted around him and scampered ahead to lead the way through the maze of corridors which led to the Duchess's bedchamber.

The Duchess, half-conscious, her chest heaving, her throat

constricted, let herself go slack. Goya's grip was strong and reassuring. She heard him shouting, clearing the footmen and servants out of the way, but the words were blurred and she failed to take them in. She was conscious of the rough texture of his smock against her cheek and of a male odor potently different than that of the powdered and perfumed courtiers she was used to in Madrid.

Cradled in his arms, she willed the paroxysm to stop before it could take hold. She hadn't had a serious attack of coughing for several days. After the visit to Doctor Arrieta in Cádiz and after experiencing the sunny weather in Sanlúcar, she had assumed that she had shaken off the worst of her indisposition. But this present attack was the most distressing yet. She fought for breath. Her sight dimmed. She could hear herself giving way to a spasm of choking and strangling. Once it had seized her, it went on and on. She gagged and felt a sickening taste of what might be blood or bile in her throat. Her body heaved and she felt herself falling into blackness. She arched her body and threw her head back in an effort to breathe and leaned back against his chest.

She felt his hands loosen and feared she was about to fall, but his grip then tightened as he carried her across the bedchamber. She saw the room tilting and the ceiling canting above her as she was laid on the bed. She was dimly aware of being alone in the room with him. He must have shooed María Luz away and dismissed the footmen and any other servants who had formed part of the small procession in the corridors between the studio and the bedchamber and had come crowding around the chamber doorway. In this emergency he trusted only himself to tend to her.

The constriction in her throat and chest eased a little. The coughing began to slow. She was aware of a pillow being placed beneath her neck and a small bottle being pressed to her lips. She twisted her head away, still coughing, but the hands were insistent and forced the medicine between her teeth. She spluttered and dribbled until the grip on her neck was loosened and her head fell back and a napkin was gently wiping her mouth. Then hands were reaching for her, taking her beneath the arms, drawing her body firmly up the coverlet towards the nymphs and Cupids on the headboard until her head and shoulders were lying on the pillows at a comfortable angle.

She felt a downward pressure on the mattress as he seated himself beside her on the bed. He put down the napkin and stroked her face with the back of his hand. María Luz's touch could not have been more solicitous. She felt drowsy. She wondered if he had snatched the wrong bottle and given her a sleeping draft by mistake. No matter. Its sour flavor was preferable to the slippery sweet taste of whatever it was that had surged up and blocked her throat. She sank back more deeply into the soft mattress.

He had taken up the napkin again and was placing an arm across her body to make it easier to wipe her face. She smiled tremulously, nestling her head into the pillow. For some reason there came into her head the memory of the dream, when she had been lying with her head cradled in his arm, of the approach of the white bull. She remembered how, in the dream, when he had done his magic with the bulls and they had gone away, he kept holding her close to him.

She took a deep breath, letting it out slowly, feeling the rawness ebbing from her lungs. She put up a quavering finger and, smiling at this moody, earthy man, drew a finger down the side of his cheek.

She saw that his forehead, like hers, was coated with perspiration. She took the napkin from him and gently wiped it away.

She let the napkin fall, gave a slow deep sigh, then raised her hands and placed them on both sides of his face. She lifted her head from the pillow and put her face close to his and spoke in the deliberate manner she had used while giving him his speech lessons.

"*Thank you.*"

She gave a little wondering smile and drew his head down closer, and spoke in a tone between a sigh and a whisper.

"*Thank you, Francisco.*"

As to what happened next, how would either of them give an account of it, or even explain it to themselves?

For Goya, there must have been a burgeoning sense of gratitude. In the ordinary course of events the Duchess would have taken little interest in him. When he was painting her first portrait at the Osunas, she had taken scant notice of him. Yet in these last weeks she had shown him consideration and compassion. Of course, Don Sebastián had been kind to him, but he knew he had outstayed his welcome in Don Sebastián's house. He could no longer impose on Don Sebastián's hospitality. And where could he go? There was no comfort in his empty house in Madrid. His poor Josefa was far away, unstrung by the deaths of their children. To join her would only have added his burden of grief to hers. And in his extremity, although the Duchess's health was as precarious as his, she had taken him in and provided him with shelter. More, she had also offered him the opportunity to work, to paint again.

Naturally, he had grown increasingly aware of her personal allure, spending as much time as he had at close quarters with her in the studio, the dining room, the courtyard and now in this bedchamber. She was one of the most beautiful women in Spain and he had always been stimulated by beautiful women. Since his illness he had wondered if all that would not be over. He had pictured himself creeping back to Madrid, to La Tirana, La Luna, La Zárate a pitiful and played out wreck.

And she, was she too experiencing an unlooked for tide of the blood? Was she too about to be caught up and carried away on a crest of a great wave that can sweep one up and change the whole direction of one's life in the course of a minute? Had she been growing susceptible to the potency of this singular man? Had she fallen under the spell of that powerful temperament? Powerful mind, powerful character, powerful body. It was that power, power of personality as much as power of talent, that had enabled him to bullock his way from a poverty-stricken village in Aragón to a position not far from the center of the court. Not that she had not known other powerful men, of course, men like young Pedro Romero and old Costillares, bullfighters as he had once been. But there were other men who had played an intimate part in her life, not men of force and power, but weak men, puny men, men with whom she should have been ashamed for the great name of Alba to have been associated.

Goya. He was here. He was leaning over her, holding her, caring for her. A firm hand. A strong body.

The dizziness in her head and the shaking of her limbs were fading away. One last spasm of coughing and she let her limbs go slack. She lay quietly, his arm still stretched across her body, his face drawn down close to hers. The smell of lotion, the smell of paint and oil and Seville cigars was comforting now. She put up a hand over the white sleeve to keep in place the arm that encircled her. She closed her eyes.

She felt herself being unbound, unlaced. She felt a strange new quaking in her limbs and a fluttering in her belly and a sensation of wetness trickling between her thighs.

So what then, after all this, of the portrait?

The sittings had continued, though on some days now they stayed loitering so long over the breakfast table that the sittings had become little more than a brief prelude to their removal to the bedchamber. In the studio he would make a show of putting a little color on the canvas while she took up her pose on the platform, with María Luz watching them with barely repressed misgivings from her chair in the corner. Then, after a few minutes, the Duchess would step down from the platform, brusquely signal to María Luz to follow her and hurry back to her bedchamber, leaving Francisco to put away his paints and dry his brushes and cover the canvas with its cloth and wait for quarter of an hour or so before making his own quick departure.

This afternoon, as she eased her damp limbs on top of the rumpled sheets, she could feel the moisture running down her arms and between her breasts and along her flanks and thighs. Spanish ladies were not supposed to perspire, let alone sweat, at least not in public, and by nature she had not been given much to sweating, except for the recent evil-smelling night sweats that Doctor Arrieta's potions were supposed to be curing. But these afternoons sweats, these love sweats, were good sweats, honest sweats, sweet sweats. They made the twinned bodies swim and slide in the long rhythms of their coupling.

Not that the sensation of sweating, or even the mildest hint of perspiration, had ever figured in her bedroom exertions before the appearance of Francisco. Certainly the pathetic ministrations of her sickly husband had never managed to raise a sweat, and the same could be said of the other men who had made love to her in the fourteen or fifteen years since her marriage. She sighed and twisted her body fretfully as she thought of them. Not that there had been as many of them as popular rumor had credited her with. Imagine it, a woman with the opportunities of the Duchess of Alba who could boast of no more than three lovers, four if you counted her non-performing husband! A sad collection when all was said and done. Still, she had to admit that they had all shared a quality which had made them attractive to her, her husband excepted. They had all had charm, lots of charm. She had always seemed to be hoodwinked by charm. Miguel de Altolaguirre had it in abundance. She had been tempted from time to time by other notable charmers—Pedro Romero was a famous charmer, and during their carriage rides in Madrid she had been tempted to offer him the prize he had only too obviously been hoping for.

But all that had vanished with the advent of Francisco. No one could accuse him of possessing too much charm. He had acquired a certain amount of polish during his years at court, but he still retained the unmistakable stamp of an Aragonese provincial. However, his background had not been entirely unrefined and uncultivated, indeed it had been quite elevated for someone brought up in a provincial backwater. But charming? No. Like Pedro Romero, he had been a *torero* of sorts but she never thought him to have had the adroitness and address that Pedro Romero possessed. In fact when he first began to make love to her, she thought he would make love to her like a clumsy peasant and had been afraid of the crushing weight of his body on hers. When she had put a hand down to guide him inside her and had felt the length and thickness of his member, like the pizzle of a bull, she had been frightened he was going to hurt her.

And yet, to the contrary, he had proved to be both skilled and tender. How could she express her sense of surprise, her gratitude? Here was a man who had enjoyed women and knew how to treat them. Of course, he had had plenty of experience. What about the women at court who had refused to stay on their side of the easel? No wonder his wife spent long periods of time in Zaragoza with her family!

And yet he had hurt her. Hurt her physically, twice, the first time quite sharply. And on both occasions there had been a definite moment of fright. She had learned from Don Sebastián about the incipient strain of violence in his nature. Now she had had a personal glimpse of it.

The first of these episodes occurred as early as the second afternoon they had spent in her bedchamber and concerned her gold locket containing the miniature of Miguel. It was not surprising that he had paid no attention to it during the convulsive unpremeditated coming together of their bodies the previous day when she had been lying on the big canopied bed stripped and naked except for her locket and bracelets and rings. In the heat of their lovemaking the locket had slithered sideways from between her breasts and lodged itself beneath her. It was only on the following afternoon, in the tranquil lull between bouts of lovemaking, that he had reached across her and idly taken hold of the velvet ribbon, running his fingers down it until they encountered the locket. Languidly he had supported himself on one elbow and fumbled with the catch, yawning and mildly curious.

Abruptly he pushed himself upright, his unfastened shirt falling away from his chest, and uttered a short harsh grunt. He was staring hard at the miniature. The Duchess, who had been yawning too and lying slack-limbed on the tousled sheets, had opened a sleepy eye and turned her head toward him on the pillow. She smiled at him, then caught her breath as she saw him gazing at the miniature. Why, she asked herself, had she not had the sense to take it off?

She sat up, shifting her body way from him but finding herself held fast by the taut string of velvet around her throat. He was staring at the miniature, his heavy brows darkened in fury. He would recognize Miguel de Altolaguirre from their days together in court.... He lifted his smoldering glance from the locket and fastened her with a long fierce look of scorn and disbelief. It was a look she had seen on the faces of many of the characters in his sketchbook.

What he did next increased her swelling sense of fright. He closed his fist around the locket, twisting the ribbon until it was even tighter around her throat. He gave it a savage yank that tore it loose, jerking her head violently forward. If the ribbon hadn't parted with a sharp snap, her neck would have been badly injured. Nevertheless it stung like a lash from a whip.

He uttered a growling sound and raised the fist with the

trailing ribbon. She cowered, thinking he was going to strike her. Then there was a flash of gold as he hurled the locket across the room, the smashing of glass as it hit the wall, reminding her of the sound of the guitar striking the wall of the studio when she had entered it for her first sitting.

The second time she had a fright was about a week later. Again, it was due to her carelessness, and again it involved Miguel. They had just made love and he was sitting on the bed with his back against the headboard as she paraded around the bedchamber, preparing to make herself decent before María Luz came to rouse her from her supposed siesta and dress her for the evening. She had gone to her dressing table to look for a comb for her tangled hair and, rummaging about in a drawer, had dumped its contents loosely on top of the dressing table. She found her comb and wandered away, leaving the pile from the drawer lying where it was. Among the contents was the bundle of letters from Miguel, tied up in their black ribbon. And Goya had got up from the bed and with a smile on his face, and with the idle curiosity of a lover, had begun poking through the little untidy pile. He lifted the bundle of letters and looked at it. The Duchess had been dancing dreamily around the bedchamber and was between him and the bed when she saw him holding the packet and scrutinizing the writing on the letters. Why had she been so careless and so stupid? Why hadn't she got rid of the things altogether? Foolish, foolish woman! She could only watch as he picked up the packet and weighed it in his hand. He ripped the top one open and read for a few seconds. Then he swung around and looked at her with the same furious expression on his face and with the same angry grunting sound deep in his throat she had seen and heard when he had discovered the locket. She stopped, fearful, standing still with her hands crossed over her naked breasts as he took two quick paces towards her. He gave her a violent shove that sent her flying backwards onto the bed. She lay there sprawling, heart pounding, her legs parted and her arms flung wide. He bore down on her, kneeing his way between her open legs and pinning her down on the bed and when she tried to struggle up thrusting her brutally down again.

Straddling her, keeping her locked beneath him, his muscled and naked thighs jammed against her soft and quivering flesh, he tensed himself and proceeded to tear each offending letter from his rival, the contemptible *señorito*, into small pieces. He tore up the letters one by one, very calmly and deliberately. And when he had torn them into tiny fragments he let the pieces drift down on her exposed body until her breasts and belly were covered with a small snowstorm of white paper. And then he laughed. A hard loud laugh. A genuine laugh. And then she felt him bulling his way into her and felt his long thick glorious thing sliding into her as she gave a cry and closed her eyes.

SHE SMILED SLEEPILY and yawned and stretched her limbs luxuriously on the rumpled sheets. So sweet, this afternoon. So delicious. But really they must not get into the habit of hurrying straight to her bedchamber at siesta time, as they had today. They ought to at least keep up some brief pretense of staying in the studio and getting on with the portrait. Wouldn't people already be asking themselves why he was taking so long to finish it?

Her portrait! In the last few days she had found herself becoming increasingly curious about it. Since they became lovers, her desire to obtain a glimpse of what lay beneath that dampened cloth had been growing. Would the portrait reveal what he truly felt about her? Would it contain some clue about the nature of the unanticipated passion by which they had been seized?

María Luz was not with her, as the girl usually indulged in a few hours' repose before returning at nine and dressing her mistress in preparation for the evening meal. The Duchess scrambled out from beneath the light coverlet and took an ivory colored wrapper from her closet. She knotted a sash about her waist and slipped out of her bedchamber. The footman on duty had long since been dismissed. Her hair loose, her feet bare so as not to alert any servants who might be within earshot, her skin and flesh still imprinted and impregnated with the flush of love, she stole down through the quiet corridors towards his studio. She knew that, when their lovemaking was done, Francisco usually returned to his own room to sleep until it was time to present himself in the dining room.

Then she slackened her pace. What if, for once, instead of going to his room he had returned to the studio? What would he think if he found her slinking into it behind his back to sneak a look at the picture? For all she knew he might be so obsessed with his eternal painting and sketching that some flash of inspiration may have driven him back to his easel to add a few extra strokes to her portrait or to one of the other canvases that had appeared there in recent weeks, stacked in groups with their faces turned to the wall. Working, working always working! Sometimes even when they made love he would suddenly ease off briefly and his face would go blank. He would drift away and make her wonder about what he was thinking, perhaps of his wife and family, making love to some other woman or just some new idea connected to his painting? Those sketchbooks! One afternoon a few days ago, between bouts of lovemaking, he had sat himself up against the headboard and made her pose for him, naked. She was no longer Cayetana the Duchess, but Cayetana the *maja*. And she had willingly joined in the game, flitting light-heartedly around the bedchamber striking a *maja*'s provocative poses, determined to prove she could be every bit as wanton and provocative as any of his dancers or actresses. And when she had chased him around the bedchamber, laughing and wheedling and trying to wrestle the sketchbook away from him, he had only laughed and pushed her down on the bed and refused to let her see it.

The corridor leading to the studio was empty. She stole quickly down it, her bare feet making no noise. She tried the handle of the studio door. Unlocked. She darted inside and softly closed the door behind her. She leaned back against it, hearing the beat of her heart in the silent room. Feeling a little shaky, she looked around and saw María Luz's chair in the corner. She made her way unsteadily towards it and sat down.

Waiting to recover her breath, she stared down the length of the room at the easel with its shrouded canvas and the tables with their pots of paint and brushes. The room seemed as masked and mantled as the picture on the easel. The tall windows were closed, only a thin trickle of light seeped around the edge of the shutters. She could dimly make out the square shapes of the portrait and an untidy row of canvases standing against the wall. A close and malodorous smell hung in the air. She imagined him there, humming tunelessly or whistling under his breath as he spent his nights working on his paintings by the light of the candles in his queer hat with the circle of candle holders.

She continued to sit, staring across at the cloaked shape on the easel. The canvas was tilted slightly forward so that the cloth would not touch the painting behind it. The blank smooth sheet, hanging straight down, possessed a disquieting air. She remembered the dislike she felt for the first portrait Francisco had painted of her, feeling her heart beating faster at the prospect of unveiling her new likeness. How did he see her now? How had his image of her altered? How had it been transformed after their afternoons in her bedchamber? Driven as she was by a desperate curiosity, she felt her heart beat even faster with the fear of what she might discover when she finally summoned up the courage to get up and go to the easel and lift up the cloth....

It was several minutes before she could nerve herself to rise from the chair. She went to a window. She fumbled with the latch of the shutter and pushed it back. The sudden shaft of late summer sunlight struck across the studio and cast a glaring pool of light on the easel. It hurt her eyes so that she had to shut them and turn away.

Again, she had to remind herself that if she wanted to inspect the portrait and get back to her room undetected she must waste no time. All the same, gingerly approaching the easel, she couldn't help procrastinating, toying with the brushes and knives and spatulas and pots of paint, their contents glowing in the beam of sunshine. She fingered them, thinking of how Francisco's fingers had touched them. She picked up a pot and read the label. *Estrato de Saturno*. Extract of lead. She shuddered and put down the pot, remembering how he licked his brushes and recalling the faint trace of paint she could often taste on his lips.

She could put it off no longer. She reached out and touched the dingy white cloth stained with spots of paint. She snatched her finger back, she had forgotten that the cloth was wet. She felt her pulse race at this small shock and wiped her fingers on her quilted robe. Then she stepped forward and took hold of the extreme edge of the cloth, carefully drawing it aside. She had to stretch her arms high, standing on tiptoe and taking care not to let the front of her robe come in contact with the moist paint on the surface.

She moved back, a little off balance now, knocking her hip against the edge of a table, smearing the bottom half of the robe as she steadied herself. The canvas was bathed in sunlight. All she could make out was a blur of fine strokes applied with a thin brush intermixed with a bold mass of color applied with his thumb or a knife. She had to move back further to bring it into focus. She pressed a hand under her breast and ducked her head down, softly squeezing her eyes shut and swaying a little on her feet. Finally she took a deep breath, wishing she had remembered to slip her bottle of smelling salts into the pocket of her robe. She stood in front of the portrait with her head lowered and her eyes closed. Only when she felt in command of herself, did she lift her head and open her eyes....

It took a full minute for her mind to clear before she could make sense of what confronted her. And then her reaction was one of gratitude and relief. This was no caricature she was looking at. This was not the woman of the first portrait, the spoiled and scatterbrained young woman who seemed to have barely emerged from adolescence. This was not the portrait of the silly girl with the red bows in her hair, but a portrait of a confident and voluptuous young woman painted with admiration, with excitement and, yes, with love....

But what was confusing her and setting her mind in a whirl was the fact that the painting was so unfinished—not even *half* finished. Could this be the painting to which they had devoted so many sessions? Was this the work of a man reputed to be able to complete a portrait in a minimum of sittings? Or was it the work of a man who had never intended to finish it quickly, a man who wanted to drag it out as long as possible?

It looked disembodied. Only three areas of the figure had been completed, three islands surrounded by the reddish ground of the canvas. They portrayed only the head, the right hand and the feet. They swum in a void except for a vague yellowish strip beneath the jeweled slippers. Highlighted by the red aureole around it, the head was a small striking portrait in itself, seeming to float from the canvas towards her. The oval features surrounded by their Medusa-like mass of flaring curls were further haloed by the black lace shawl, suggesting both the aristocratic widow and a woman of the streets. Goya had imbued the features with audacity and independence, painting them with the precision of a portrait on porcelain. And what was that at the far end of the right eyebrow, tucked in so close to the hair and shawl that a casual viewer would miss it? A large black beauty spot. The emblem of the *maja*. The *maja's* mark of love and passion She raised her hand in a spontaneous gesture to her thick and furry eyebrows and caressed her temple.

And next the arm and the hand. The painting of these was equally striking. Only the lower part of the arm was visible, cut off just above the wrist, the arm fully extended downwards over the black lace skirt. Beneath the few strands of gold thread above it, a long slender forefinger was stretched imperiously earthward. And then followed a long gap to a little oasis containing her feet in their Turkish slippers, with their high heels and tapering toes, the feet turned outward in the manner characteristic of both the *maja* and the fashionable lady....

Yes, but what of the hand itself? Her eye returned to it. The rings. Surely there was something unusual about the two rings? Not the big oval topaz on the middle finger, emblazoned in large letters with the name of the House of Alba to which he had given a pearly tint—no doubt to lend contrast to the brown of the fingers and the rosy tint of the knuckles. No, it was the other one, the smaller ring on the forefinger which commanded her attention. It was a mourning ring, a small band of gold filigree with black enamel bearing the name of her late husband. She bent down to examine it more closely. The script was difficult to read. But then, by tilting her head and narrowing her eyes, she finally managed to puzzle it out. The four letters sprang at her so sharply she straightened abruptly and felt her heart beat faster. She saw the name that had been painted on the ring instead of her husband's.

GOYA

And what was this? Again she bent forward. What were those other words traced faintly at the bottom of the canvas, below the pointed toes? Craning forward, leaning to the right in order to scan the sun-struck surface of the canvas at a sideways angle, she could just make out the two words that had been written upside down and in a semicircle. It was as if the woman in the portrait had bent down herself and written them on the moist sand of the Quadalquivir on which the artist had fancifully posed her, straightening her back in order to point to them. Two words incised on the sand with a purposeful finger encircled by the ring on which Francisco had imprinted his own name. The two words leaped out at her.

SOLO GOYA

She put out her finger and slowly traced the painted forefinger with the enameled ring and read again, more slowly, the words on the sandy ground beneath the slippers. She lifted her finger and sucked the wet paint from her nail as she stood staring at the half-finished picture.

Only Goya. Yes. It was true. *Only Goya.* Yes! *Only Goya.*

She moved away from the easel, taking care not to strike her hip against the table. She felt the back of her knees make contact with his chair. She glanced down and saw his palette lying on a chair. She picked it up and placed it with the pots and other paraphernalia on the big table. His brown smock, speckled with paint, had been flung over the back of the chair but she ignored it and sat down, glad to feel support for her shaky limbs, telling herself that another smear on the skirt of her wrapper hardly mattered. For a long time she stared at the word on the small ring and at the words written in the sand....

SOLO GOYA

Her eyes brimmed with tears. She put up a hand to cover them. Then she choked back the tears and stared again at the portrait.

A long minute passed.

Suddenly she turned.

She leaped to her feet.

Was that a footstep she had heard outside in the corridor?

Hurriedly, she ran to the easel and seized the damp cloth and draped it awkwardly over the canvas.

She darted to the door and opening it a fraction peered into the corridor.

She sighed with relief. There was no one there. She hastened back to her bedchamber and flung herself on her bed. She asked herself why there should be any hurry to finish the portrait, why should there be any hurry for her or Francisco to return to Madrid?

Then she suddenly remembered the foolish letter she had given to Carulli to send to Miguel in Galicia. She prayed Miguel hadn't received it. She recalled with dismay and alarm the expression of rage on Francisco's face as he wrenched Miguel's picture from her throat and tore up Miguel's love letters.

Miguel must not come to Sanlúcar! Oh God, what if he was already on his way? At all costs Miguel and Francisco must be prevented from meeting face to face. She was seized with a premonition of disaster. She must write immediately to Miguel and put him off. She would tell him she was seriously indisposed or that she had been summoned by the Queen and must return immediately to Madrid.

She must write tonight. She must write this afternoon.

She must write—*now!*

She rose from the bed and ran to her dressing table and hunted frantically for some paper and a pen and some ink.

Only when she had finished scribbling and had rung the bell for María Luz and had sent her maid scurrying off to fetch Carulli, did she permit herself to relax and sink back with a sigh of relief.

Their first meeting of the day, in the courtyard, gave them particular pleasure. Apart from the weather, which on some mornings was overcast and slightly chilly, there was no alteration in their breakfast routine. They took their chocolate and pastries and sweet rolls in the same leisurely manner, the Duchess with her little dog Conchita in her lap, the little black child Estrellita frolicking around them and María Luz looking on from a discreet distance, having long since grown aware that her close attendance as guardian and *dueña* was unnecessary. Her mistress had made it abundantly clear that she and her visitor, whom the servants now regarded as a permanent guest, wished to spend their time alone together. María Luz was now stationed on a chair inside the nearby room in the antechamber beyond the double doors, out of sight but within earshot if the Duchess needed to summon her to bring an additional shawl or a fresh supply of chocolate. As for her butler, she had indicated in plain terms that he was not to perform any major services until his customary appearance to supervise the evening meal. Like Francisco's truculent hound, the finicky Neapolitan had been banished to the interior of the palace.

For the most part, the Duchess and Francisco would simply sit toying with their food in decorous silence, like a married couple. Now and again Goya would clear his throat with a jarring noise that startled her and sometimes, when they dined together in the evenings, she felt he handled her delicate tableware and her silver from the fabled mines of Potosí a shade too roughly. Nor could she help wincing when, touching his glass against hers in a toast, he did it with such exuberance that it threatened to shatter the red Venetian goblets that had been in her family for two centuries, since the victorious Iron Duke of Alba had brought them back to Spain after the battle of Pavia.

Nevertheless there was no doubt that love, deafness or no deafness, had wrought a softening influence on him. For one thing he had stopped bringing those wearisome sketchbooks to the table with him. Before it had been scribble, scribble, scribble the whole time. Now, seated close to her, he was as alert and attentive as his handicap would allow him to be, his velvet jacket freshly pressed and his white cuffs and shirtfront crisp and snowy. Looking at him over her cup of chocolate, she felt she was entitled to consider the absence of the sketchbooks as a minor token of a larger victory.

They had continued with their lip-reading sessions and there were signs he was making progress, but some mornings she had a sinking feeling that, however hard she made him try and however many books Doctor Arrieta might send to Sanlúcar, they would never really achieve more than partial success. She had to face the fact that it was likely that her new lover would never hear her voice or be able to exchange more than a few scattered phrases. For the most part, instead of the painful struggle to bandy a few commonplace sentences, they simply sat together in companionable silence. While she drank her chocolate and licked the last crumbs of the sweet roll from her lips, she reflected that it was that very deafness and their attempts to overcome it that had brought them together. As she watched him, smiling, she considered how it would be possible for them to stay together. She knew it would be difficult but, surely, for an influential and resourceful woman, for a woman in love, it could not be wholly inconceivable?

There had been, for some days past, a brief cessation of their lovemaking. She could hardly believe that it was nearly a whole month since that afternoon when he had carried her to her bedchamber, but a hiatus in their lovemaking had come about due to her monthly menses which, as María Luz who had to dispose of the bloody rags could testify, had been increasingly prolonged and painful. It also fell to her maid to dispose of the wadded up squares of cotton soaked in almond and other oils which she found every afternoon in her mistress's chamber pot, scraps of cotton that were not mentioned by the Duchess but whose use was obvious. Before the onset of her menses María Luz had noticed that the Duchess had been particularly agitated, for their arrival had been almost ten days late. But the little sticky scraps, recommended to the Duchess when she was in her teens by a high-born and knowledgeable woman friend, had done their work, and there had been no sign of a thickening of the Duchess's belly. Her relief, in spite of the griping pains in her abdomen, had been palpable. So had María Luz's, since the latter had no illusions about the consequences that would arise from such a ruinous pregnancy. She was glad when her mistress suffered from her menses as then there was no chance of such a calamitous mishap. It was the dread of this that had more than once prompted María Luz to disobey the Duchess's strict injunction to her and the footmen who were normally stationed at the bedroom door, to stay away during the hours when her mistress and Goya were closeted together. On three or four occasions the Arab girl had not been able to bear her feelings of anxiety any longer, and had stolen as quietly as she could down the deserted hallway and put her ear against the panels of the door. She remembered how, on one occasion, she had been shocked at hearing the Duchess cry out, a cry that started softly then mounted to such a pitch that María Luz was sure it would reach the ears of everyone in the palace. Not that such cries of pleasure would have startled or unsettled María Luz, who in bygone years in North Africa had heard them frequently and had herself uttered them during the transports when she was begetting Estrellita. But what shook her was hearing these sounds uttered by a woman of the station of the Duchess of Alba, discomfiting sounds accompanied by the harsh panting of the deaf man. His strident grunts and gasps must surely resonate, she told herself, all over the palace.

 Ear pressed to the door, she found herself a reluctant witness to the playful preliminaries with which the pair in the bedchamber were evidently accustomed to preface their lovemaking. These were a variation, or rather a continuation, of their usual morning lip-reading exercises. Mouth dry and heart palpitating, María Luz would catch the sound of Goya's voice, low and throaty at first, as he announced, "Toe!", followed by an interval before the Duchess, her voice low and laughing, would respond with "Ankle!" after which it was Goya's turn, after a tantalizing pause in which María Luz imagined them fondling and kissing the part of the naked flesh in question, to continue with "Calf!" to which the Duchess answered "Knee!" Then came "Thigh!" attended by another bubble of laughter and an even longer pause, during which María Luz could all too vividly imagine what portion of the Duchess's white body Goya's mouth was seeking. And listening another time, unwillingly but unable to tear herself away, she would hear them divert themselves by starting from top to toe instead of toe to top. Then it was a whispered litany of *"Forehead!"*, *"Eyebrow!"*, *"Eyes!"*, *"Chin!"*, *"Mouth!"*, then lingering, *"Throat!"*, *"Breasts!"*, lingering long here, *"Belly!"*—the alternating voices swelling steadily now, the Duchess's fluttery gigglings and half-hearted and futile attempts to hush his guttural laughter giving way to gasps and broken murmurs that María Luz's straining ears failed to catch. There would follow a minute or two of complete silence, the Arab girl picturing what came after the throbbing and triumphant declaration of *"Belly!"* Then the sound, what else, of another portion of her taut, recumbent flesh being saluted and savored.

Then another long silence which was succeeded by more muted and confused sounds. María Luz closed her eyes, knowing she would now hear the motion of the limbs, slow and stealthy at first, interspersed with intervals for prolonged kissing and breathy mutterings, before mounting, accompanied by sharp cries on the Duchess's part and hoarser ones on his, until they attained that unrestrained, exultant, long-drawn-out crescendo that the Arab girl, pulling herself away from the door and clapping her hands over her ears, was certain could be heard by everyone. Then half-sobbing, María Luz stumbled, hands still over her ears, down the long corridor. Those unbridled afternoons! Was it any wonder that she was in a constant state of dread over the prospect of her mistress's illicit pregnancy? Was it any wonder that she regarded the days of the Duchess's menses as a welcome suspension of the probable consequences that could flow from such a dire eventuality? And although she had developed, as had the other servants, a decided partiality for Señor Goya, she could not help wondering whether such an unpredictable and immoderate man might be able to rein in his appetites at such a time. But she was wrong. Once, on an afternoon when the Duchess had started her menses, María Luz, her ear fastened to the door, had fancied she heard the usual humid sounds of their lovemaking. Indignant and assuming that Goya was taking advantage of her mistress, she wanted to throw her orders to the wind and rap loudly on the door. As her hand was raised to knock, her other hand had taken hold of the handle. To her surprise, the door was unlocked. It suddenly swung open, although she had the presence of mind not to let it swing widely open and through a very narrow gap, her hand still on the handle, she had a direct view of the Duchess's high-canopied bed with its tapestried headboard of tumbling Cupids. She expected to see a scatter of bloody rags on the side of the bed, her mistress pinned beneath Goya's heaving bulk, clamped by knees and elbows as he furiously drove into her. Instead the Duchess was sitting in bed partially in her *maja* costume and Goya was seated fully dressed on the side of the bed, seeking to ease her fevers and cramps by bathing her breasts and temples with fragrant *agua de colonia*. It had been touching to observe that thickset man leaning so solicitously above the slender figure stretched out in the gilded immensity of the bed administering to her with such infinite care. María Luz slowly tiptoed away.

AFTER THIS DISPLAY of tenderness, the terrible scene that took place two mornings later came as a terrible shock.

Even as it was happening, Goya and the Duchess must have recognized it as the turning point of their idyllic days at Sanlúcar. But how could they have foreseen that an unpredictable accident on this early autumn morning would wrench them so savagely apart? Yet surely the Duchess should have divined, from the evidence of the sketchbooks, that it would be likely that some such scene would eventually erupt? The irony was that the incident could have been easily avoided if only María Luz, or another of the servants, had thought fit to mention to their mistress something they all knew but thought too unimportant to tell her....

She reflected afterwards that it was absurd that a relationship, built up so painstakingly over the course of the summer, could be destroyed in the matter of a dozen minutes. They had achieved so much since coming to Sanlúcar. She had felt herself ripening into a more mature and serious woman, less given to waywardness and caprice. And her health had shown definite signs of mending. No more night sweats, no more headaches, and a remission of the lacerating pressure in her breast. And as for Francisco, seated there in the courtyard opposite her, his ruffled white shirt open at the neck in defiance of the early morning chill, his black hair with its streaks of gray tousled by the breeze that rattled the vine leaves in the arbor overhead, surely Francisco was also mentally and physically improved? The burden of disease and of deafness, those domestic calamities, surely they had been lightened to some degree? Following her attempts to teach him to lip-read he seemed to be growing more reconciled to his affliction, more adept at coping with it. But after those next few fatal minutes, nothing of this would count.

What added to the Duchess's bitterness was the fact that the catastrophe was to occur in the same pretty blue and white tiled courtyard where they had leaned across the table and ventured their first kiss. This morning María Luz had tried to protest when the Duchess had instructed her to prepare their breakfast outside since the weather was definitely on the turn, rain was threatening, and the winds of oncoming winter were more blustery. But the Duchess of Alba was not lightly to be talked out of her whims. The most María Luz could do was to see that the Duchess was well wrapped up. Over her white morning gown, woolen and with long sleeves, she wore a white silk fichu and a white wool wrap, together with a little black lace cap.

It was only later that María Luz fully recalled the deep sense of unease she had had that morning as she went about the business of sweeping down the courtyard, arranging the tables and chairs and preparing for the meal. As she was bringing out the basket of pastries and the *chocolatière,* she remembered how a single red vine leaf, withered but still perfect in shape, had come spiraling down from the arbor overhead and had settled itself like a scarlet stain in the middle of the white tablecloth. She had an odd feeling of foreboding as she bent across the tablecloth to remove it. Then when everything had been disposed to her satisfaction, she had left the courtyard shortly before the arrival of Goya and the Duchess and taken up her station on a chair in the nearby room.

Later, when she had hastened to respond to her mistress's call, she discovered the painter and the Duchess bent across the table staring at each other with the secret smiles of lovers. They were unusually restrained, they did nothing more suggestive than take turns scribbling notes to each other in Goya's sketchbooks, though then too they would exchange the conspiratorial looks of lovers. From time to time, María Luz would catch the throaty rumble of Goya's voice and the high tones of the Duchess as they spoke tentatively to each other, mostly in single words but sometimes now in short sentences, and when she heard the tinkle of the silver bell she jumped from her seat to replenish the chocolate.

Today, snatching the *chocolatière* from the serving table and hurrying towards the double doors, she almost tripped over her child, who had sneaked in from the servants' quarters to be with her mother and was playing quietly on the floor by her chair. Pascual, the young coachman, who had been doggedly courting the young Arab girl, had made Estrellita a set of beautifully carved and painted wooden horses and she was propelling them vigorously across the tiles. Estrellita was sometimes permitted to accompany her mother in the mornings but was not allowed to play in the courtyard and climb on Señor Goya's knee or frolic with the Duchess's little white dog. As for the latter, so strong was the Duchess and Goya's desire to be completely alone, it too had been banished from the courtyard and was dozing in a basket close to María Luz's chair.

As María Luz entered the courtyard with the fresh chocolate, the Duchess was setting down the bell with one hand, her other hand stretched out across the tablecloth in Goya's strong grasp. Where María Luz was concerned, the Duchess had obviously decided that there was no longer any point in attempting any concealment. She and Goya did not take their eyes from each other and María Luz's eyes were expressionless. As she was whisking the foam with the *molinillo*, she took care not to look at them directly, although she couldn't help glancing at them out of the corner of her eye.

As she was tilting the *chocolatière* in order to refill their cups and the thick dark liquid was beginning to issue from the spout, there was a loud startling sound from within the confines of the palace. The heavy silver pot slipped in her hand and a jet of chocolate went streaming across the tablecloth. There was a crash followed by a loud shriek and then a whole series of crashes accompanied by even louder wails and shrieks.

María Luz recognized the wails and screeches as being those of her daughter. She dropped the pot on the table, saturating the material with a scalding gush of liquid. As she turned towards the double doors, Estrellita came rushing out into the courtyard and hurled herself into her mother's arms.

María Luz, hoisting her aloft in her arms, thought her child must have knocked over the serving table in the anteroom. But the series of shrieks went on, getting louder and louder as if a madman was lurching around breaking all the glasses and dishes and furniture.

The Duchess pushed back her chair and jumped to her feet just as her little white dog came scampering frantically into the courtyard followed by the huge mastiff Baltasar. Goya, sitting with his back to the double doors, went on sitting where he was, oblivious to the commotion and regarding with a kind of professional interest the shape that the chocolate was making as it spread out over the tablecloth.

It was only when the white dog came dashing around the table for the second time that he grasped what was going on. He came to himself with a start and lunged sideways in his chair to make a grab at the mastiff's leather collar.

He missed, and the two dogs went racing around the courtyard, the small dog making a succession of desperate darts as it tried to seek shelter behind its mistress. The big dog's huge jaws were dripping drool and its saliva flew in a fine spray around the courtyard. Somehow it had got loose from the stables and had gone searching for its master and had then come across the Duchess's lapdog sleeping in its basket.

The Duchess and María Luz kept their heads. The Duchess called out something above the hubbub and María Luz thrust her child into the Duchess's arms and ran through the double doors to summon help. There was no need. A crowd of servants was already flocking into the courtyard, crowding back in the doorway, bewildered by the spectacle and dumbfounded by the noise which was now reaching a pitch of delirium.

The Duchess pressed the child's head to her shoulder, sheltering it and soothing it, swaying from side to side to avoid the dogs as they pelted past her in ever-tightening circles.

Goya was lunging from side to side and roaring "BALTASAR! BALTASAR! BALTASAR!" at the top of his lungs, only adding to the pandemonium. The small dog was insane with terror, the great dog beyond all restraint, intent on seizing the small creature and tearing it to pieces. In an attempt to block its path, Goya thrust out a leg and the mastiff's massive chest went slamming squarely into it and Goya was knocked sideways out of his chair. He snatched at the tablecloth as he fell and brought the whole table down, sending the cups and plates and the *chocolatière* crashing to the floor where they bounced and shattered on the white Tarifa tiles.

The mastiff, its studded collar a streak of scarlet, leaped over Goya's body as he lay sprawling and got the hindquarters of the lapdog between its teeth. Little Conchita squealed like a rabbit in a snare. It tried to tear itself away as its flanks were ripped open and its blood was spattered onto its white fur. Its legs buckled under it as the mastiff got a solid grip and hoisted it high in the air and shook it triumphantly this way and that. The small dog was a white and ruby blur in the air and the courtyard was filled with a crimson film that splattered Goya and the Duchess's clothes and faces, the child in her arms and the servants milling helplessly in the doorway, running in small crimson trails down the blue and white *azulejos* of the walls. There was blood on Goya's white shirt and the Duchess's white dress, fichu and woolen shawl. The whole courtyard was tainted with the smell of blood, the reek of the animals, the stink of fear.

Goya managed to struggle to his knees and got a grip on the mastiff as it came careering around again, flourishing in its jaws the now floppy body of the little dog. He grasped Baltasar with one hand and wrestled it to the ground, trying with the other hand to extricate the small corpse from between the glistening teeth and the bloody gums. The beast growled at him furiously and clamped its jaws down tighter and Goya had to hit it with his clenched fist.

He then grabbed the *chocolatière* and struck it with it. As the dog was robbed of its prize, it swung around and sank its teeth into the fingers that were twisted around its collar.

Goya gave a shout and wrenched his hand free and some of the bolder servants finally screwed up their courage and ran forward to subdue the dog that Goya was now pinning down with a forearm across its massive throat. Somehow they got hold of the beast's legs and its bloodied brown pelt and managed to drag it out and through the double doors, snarling and flailing the air with its huge paws, leaving a wet crimson trail behind it

María Luz rushed forward to pry her small daughter from the Duchess's arms and ran out weeping after the other servants.

Goya and the Duchess could not move. The courtyard was silent. Goya stayed where he was, kneeling on the smeared white tiles. He sank slowly back onto his haunches.

After a moment he brought up his injured hand and brushed it across his forehead, leaving a ribbon of blood and chocolate. He lowered it shakily, staring at the skin that was torn by the teeth and the flesh that was oozing blood.

He reached across and pulled the end of the crumpled tablecloth towards him. Clumsily, with a trembling hand, he got his broad-bladed knife out of his pocket, fumbled it open and began to try and saw off a strip of the cloth.

The Duchess moved slowly around the fallen table, stepping over the welter of broken glass and china and knelt down opposite him. The body of the dead dog lay on the tiles between them. The courtyard was like a miniature bullring after a *corrida* had taken place. Her skirt and bodice were flecked with red. She stared at Francisco's sketchbook, strewn now among the wreckage on the ground. She shivered. Perhaps among its pages were drawings of real life *corridas*. Had she not been warned in Cádiz that he might bring ill-fortune to Sanlúcar? That he was not a man who could easily slough off the aura of disaster which surrounded him? She found herself to be in love with a man who moved within some calamitous orbit.

He had managed to cut off a corner of the tablecloth and was trying to wrap it around his wounded hand. She reached out and took the knife from him and placed it on the ground. then took the strip of cloth and began to bandage the wound. She noted with relief that the dog had bitten his left hand, not his right.

She felt in the pocket of her blood-daubed skirt for a handkerchief and wiped his forehead and his face. He remained quite still, wearing a look of stupefaction as if he were stunned by the way one of his brain's dark visions had been translated into violent reality.

A vine leaf came curling down from overhead. It landed softly on the sticky brown residue trickling from the broken *chocolatière*.

She heard a quiet cough behind her, unnaturally loud in the hush.

She turned and glanced up. Carulli was standing behind her. He was looking down at them as they knelt closely together, a blank expression on his brown face. His appearance as usual was immaculate. He had taken care to be the last to arrive at the sanguinary scene. He coughed again into a white-gloved hand and lowered his white-wigged head to survey the litter of debris around his gleaming black pumps.

He cleared his throat, bowed low and spoke with studied politeness.

"I have given instructions for the animal to be destroyed, Duchess. I take it that will meet with your approval?"

He spoke quietly but nevertheless the Neapolitan accent grated on the Duchess's ear.

She looked at poor deaf Goya, staring straight ahead, unaware of Carulli's presence. There was no response.

Carulli waited.

And then the Duchess made the first of her two great and fatal mistakes.

She turned and nodded. She whispered.

'Yes, Salvatore. Will you please attend to it?"

The Italian smirked.

"Right away, Duchess."

Esteban and Pascual, the two men on the box, knew it was no secret that Goya possessed a bad reputation as a coachman. For several years his frequent spills and collisions had been the talk of Madrid. The whole city had been familiar with the accidents that had kept him in continual trouble with the authorities. Only his connection with the royal household and the lavish way in which he paid for any damages saved him from being banned from driving in the streets. When they saw the rakish yellow *berlina* bearing down on them, citizens flattened themselves against walls and had even been known to jump off bridges. In short, he was a menace when in a carriage, and Esteban and Pascual had been troubled ever since his arrival at Sanlúcar that he might take it into his head to take a spin in one or another of the Duchess's coaches. They had entered into a pact that if he did they would try to head him off, pretending that all the coaches were laid up for repairs or absent on errands. To their relief, however, except for some leisurely afternoon excursions around the countryside with the Duchess, he had not shown the slightest interest in the carriages. He hadn't even asked them to saddle up a horse for him for one of his midnight rambles. Esteban, the old bow-legged and weather-beaten senior coachman, had often told his young assistant, the fresh-faced peasant lad, Pascual, that Goya had probably not been interested because his deafness had probably affected his sense of balance—a man could hardly fool around with horses and coaches if he was unable to hear a single sound. But later, during the course of what turned out to be a rain-drenched afternoon, the two coachmen found out at first hand just how reckless Goya could be when on the box with the reins in his hands.

But in fact the excitement began even before the coach left the palace yard. The coachmen were out in the stable-yard making preparations to shoot the dog. They helped the other servants get the big beast firmly strapped up with spare leathers from the stables and to muzzle its jaws firmly shut with twine. (Goya had not been the only one that day to have a hand injured by those keen teeth). They then dragged and shoved and kicked the beast into the middle of the yard, and Esteban had drawn a large horse pistol from its holster and primed and loaded it in readiness. The male servants had now been joined by a number of females, who formed a rough circle around the creature as it writhed on the ground, striving desperately to break its bonds. Pascual, a strong boy, had heaved the animal over to its side to ready it for a bullet behind the ear, and Esteban was squatting down beside him and cocking his pistol. He curled his fingers around the trigger and turned his head, looking through the legs of the crowd to where Carulli was standing beside a stable door in the corner of the yard. The Italian wore his green livery and three-cornered hat and powdered wig and carried a silver-topped cane, pressing a white silk handkerchief to his mouth and wrinkling up his nose in disgust at the smells of horse-piss and manure. He had stationed himself at a distance so that the overhanging eaves of the stables would protect his exquisite uniform from the impending threat of rain. He had been keeping an uneasy eye on the heavens as the sky had been steadily darkening. He was watching Esteban and Pascual impatiently, wanting to get the business over with before the first drops fell. It was he who was to give the signal for the shot to be fired so he could report to the Duchess that he had personally attended to her order to destroy the dog.

He was about to raise his cane to give Esteban the signal when there was a sudden violent interruption. He was lifting his cane, and the crowd of servants abruptly stopped chattering and craned forward, when there was a deep, full throated angry roar. They all swung around to see the powerful figure of Goya come bursting into the yard from a rear door of the palace, wild-eyed, his black hair tousled and streaming, his shirt gaping at the throat and still befouled with the blood of the little white dog, a blood-soaked bandage trailing from his wounded hand. He paused to take in the scene before charging at Carulli, wrestling the cane from his hand and dashing it to the cobblestones, then seizing the butler by his velvet collar and shaking him and throwing him against the stable door. He stormed over to the crowd of servants, still roaring with that same wrathful cry. He went barging through them with such force he knocked some of them down and then he hurled himself at old Esteban, knocking him down too. He snatched the pistol from his hand and sent it cartwheeling across the courtyard. It hit the cobbles and exploded in a shower of sparks and a bullet thudded into the stable door, a hand's breadth from the butler's head.

Pascual, bowled over in his turn by Esteban, picked himself up and saw Goya stooping over his dog. The dog, a skein of slobber dripping from its tethered jaws, had seen the pistol and had sensed what was going to happen and had stopped struggling and quivering. Pascual saw Goya thrust both arms beneath the brute and set off across the courtyard in the direction of a coach standing on the other side. This was the Duchess's own coach, whose wheels the two coachmen had been greasing before the butler had appeared to oversee the destruction of the dog. As Goya wove his way towards it, Pascual heard him repeatedly bawling in a thick strident voice something that sounded like *"Montera!"* or *"Frontera!"* or possibly a person's name—*"Herrera!."* Neither Esteban nor Pascual could make head or tail of it. With the other servants bunching up behind them, they followed Goya to the coach, the door of which was standing open. They saw the muscles in his back growing taut beneath the bloodied shirt as he lifted the body of the dog and pitched it through the door on to the blue silken cushions of the Duchess's coach. He clambered up the iron steps after it, the onlookers falling back with murmurs of consternation as they saw him bend down inside the carriage, take out his clasp knife and cut away the leather straps from the dog's body and the twine from around its jaws.

Pascual's next impressions were hazy. After leaping down from the coach and slamming the door shut on the dog, Goya kept him and Esteban and the troop of servants busy as they ran about the palace and courtyard obeying his bellowed instructions to load up the coach with provisions and get ready for a speedy departure. Carulli had pulled himself together, but at the sight of Goya's threatening fist and the menacing tone of his voice, he quickly turned and scuttled away with what little dignity he could muster, pausing briefly to look back at Goya over his shoulder with an expression of undisguised hatred on his lean face.

It was only when the two coachmen were making a last trip across the courtyard that Pascual found out why they were bustling this way and that. Esteban was carrying some feed bags over his shoulder and Pascual was carrying some oilskins. The older man hung the bags on the hooks at the back of the coach and he and Pascual were shrugging themselves into their oilskins, when Esteban told him what Goya had been trying to say in his deaf man's voice. The sky was already growing black and the clouds were now swollen and purple and the first big drops of rain were starting to fall.

Goya had not said "Montera!" or "Frontera!" or even "Herrera!" but *"Utrera!"*

Utrera. The town to the north-west of Sanlúcar at the junction of the road from Cádiz to Seville. Esteban explained to Pascual that they would be heading for Utrera so Goya could intercept the mail coach and give them instructions to transfer the dog to the express coach to Madrid. Goya was determined to get the wretched creature out of harm's way and have it taken to the shelter of his house in the capital. Then presumably the three of them would spend the night in Utrera and return to Sanlúcar the next day.

"We must hurry, Pascual," said Esteban buttoning his oilskin. "It's a fair stretch to Utrera. We'll have to get a move on if we're to get there in time to meet the mail coach."

At that moment Goya marched up to them, waving away the oilskin Esteban offered him and poking Pascual in the back with the muzzle of the hunting gun he was carrying. In his garbled voice he barked out something like, *"Let's get on with it, what are we hanging about for. Let's GO!"*

He spun around and wrenched open the door of the coach, throwing the gun onto the floor and jumping in after it, banging the door shut and leaving Esteban and Pascual to scamper to their places. As Pascual swung himself up onto the box, he glimpsed Goya glaring up at him through the window, the head of the shivering dog on his knee, making urgent motions for them to be gone.

With a crack of the whip Esteban got the four horses in hand and there was a great drumming of hoofs on the cobbles as the coach clattered out of the courtyard.

The rain was already beginning to turn the track into mud. It was a side road and would join up with a wider one at Las Cabezas de San Juan, half-way to Utrera. It was little more than a trackway skirting the marshy left bank of the broad basin of the Guadalquivir. Nonetheless, they made good time on this first leg of the journey even though Esteban, a skilled driver, could not cut too fast a pace through the swirling rain. He had to keep alert every minute as this part of the trackway consisted mainly of a series of long sweeping curves. He was glad when, after a couple of hours, they caught sight of the small village of Trebujena, a little straggle of houses without even a church. He had not planned to make a stop at Trebujena as he reckoned he could get as far as Lebrija or even Las Cabezas before he had to halt to rest and feed the horses.

However, when they were approaching an inn that stood at the far end of the village, he heard a furious drumming on the roof of the coach below him, and when he bent down and looked he saw his passenger leaning out of the window making urgent signals for him to stop. Straining hard, he brought his team to a standstill outside the door of the inn.

He assumed Goya was feeling cooped up with the dog and wanted to stretch his legs or relieve himself. In any case, they had left Sanlúcar in such a rush that Esteban had not had time to tend to the horses properly and thought this a good time to treat them to at least some water. He didn't think they needed to pull the coach into the yard behind the inn but left it standing on the road by the inn door. Then he and Pascual climbed down and went into the inn to ask for water and borrow some buckets.

It was wonderfully warm and dry in the inn. While they were thawing themselves out in front of the fire and the innkeeper was rummaging in his storeroom, his wife came in carrying a steaming bowl of what smelled like hot rum punch. They were both eagerly holding out their tankards when Pascual happened to glance out of the window. He uttered a cry and the pair of them abandoned their tankards and almost collided with each other in their haste to rush out of the door.

Goya, an unlit cigar sticking out of the corner of his mouth, was putting his foot in the spokes of the forward wheel and was hoisting himself on to the box. They gasped as they watched him settle himself and take hold of the reins in one hand and pick the whip from its holder with the other. He looked down at them and called out in a gruff and commanding tone.

"You get up here with me, Esteban. Pascual, you get on the step behind."

Neither of them wanted him to drive. When Esteban was about to protest, Goya thumped the seat beside him with the butt of his whip and the old coachman had no option but to clamber hastily on the box and take his place. Pascual cursed under his breath and ran around to the step at the back where the footmen usually rode. He paused and looked through the rainy glass at the dim shape of the dog inside the carriage. Its head was drooping over the blue cushions, its eyes shut and tongue lolling. Why all this fuss and bother over a dog? Why couldn't they have just shot it? He was thus grumbling to himself and reaching for the iron bar to pull himself onto the step when the carriage took off with a flying start. His hand slithered on the wet bar and he just managed to get a grip on it and heave himself up to stand panting on the now swaying step.

Sixteen hoofs dug into the track and they flew off at such a pace that Esteban slid sideways on the rain-slick leather of the seat and almost toppled off the box. Barely had the horses leaned fully into their harnesses before Goya started flicking them with his whip to encourage them to gallop. The curtain of the rain made it impossible to see more than a very short distance ahead and the haze was growing denser as they approached the river. A thick miasma was rising from the marshes between the track and the Guadalquivir. They were now entering the evil-smelling region of the fever swamps, which travelers treated with extreme caution, if they weren't able to avoid it altogether.

Esteban and Pascual were relieved to see the track was now running straight. But it was still very narrow and the slightest twitch of the reins to right of left could send the coach veering off the track to be bogged down in one of the treacherous patches of quicksand with which the swamps were sprinkled. As the coach picked up speed, showering them all with mud and stones thrown up by the wheels, the coach began to pitch like a ship in a storm. Pascual hung on grimly to the iron guardrail. If Goya kept on like this, he thought, it would only be a matter of minutes before the coach hit a rock or a hole in the road and overturned, pinning them all under it.

Esteban stole a glance at Goya and saw his thick and broad-shouldered figure sitting like a stone. His expression was blank and fixed like a statue's. He was impervious to the violent motions of the coach. Esteban was not an imaginative man but it seemed to him as though Goya were in the grip of some inner demon, some inner fury, as if he was being urged on his mad flight by some irresistible force. The man beside him appeared to have gone beyond all sense and reason, overcome in his anger at the treatment of his dog, anger at the Duchess, and for all Esteban knew, an anger at the whole world and at life itself. And the next moment, as they topped a slight rise and started to descend on the other side, it looked as if he meant to put an end to his anger by killing himself and his two companions with him.

The rise was steep and the descent severe enough to give an added momentum to the onward flight of the coach. And there, bulking very large and visible through a hole in the swirling mists, Esteban could see the square outline of an approaching coach coming straight towards them down the middle of the track. He shot upright on the box. This was one of the most deserted roads in Spain yet, suddenly looming out of the fog and barreling down upon them, was a high wide coach that seemed to his startled eyes as large as a house. What could such a huge coach be doing at this hour and at this season on this lonely road? Moreover, the track at this point was raised onto a sort of narrow causeway, and Esteban immediately saw that there was no room for the two coaches to pass each other. His first thought was that both coaches would have to slow down and draw over to their respective sides of the track and stop. That way one or other of them could cautiously edge its way around the other vehicle and onto the clear track ahead. This would have to be executed carefully, the grooms and coachmen holding the horses' heads to keep them quiet. It was quite possible, moreover, that they would be unable to make it and would simply have to remain staring at each other through the pelting rain until they could get down and consult each other and see what to do.

Esteban now saw that the coach was not traveling quite as fast as he thought but was laboring as it came up the slope towards them. It drifted slightly from one side of the track to the other, as if the horses were tired or as if one of them had gone lame. As it came nearer still Esteban realized that it was no shabby or rickety mail coach, but the rich equipage of some very important person. Beneath the coating of mud he discerned a gleam of black paint picked out with gold, together with heavy gold braided tassels on the saddlecloths and on the flounced material around the box.

Goya would have to stop. Esteban thrust his feet against the guardrail and leaned back and prepared to take the shock. The driver of the other coach was obviously a practical hand since he had already slowed and was steering his team as close to the brink of the causeway as he dared.

But Goya did not stop. Esteban's heart leaped into his mouth as they kept hurtling down the slope. The towering black shape in front of them swelled larger and larger by the second as the mist shredded away. The horses of both teams started to whinny in panic. Esteban could hear himself shouting and could hear Pascual shouting from the back. Goya's fingers with the bloodied trailing bandage were knotted in the reins. He was forcing the four horses to veer on his side of the track but without slowing down and still sitting impassively as if he had been hewn from marble.

Esteban was too terrified even to close his eyes. He waited numbly for the crash. Pascual was frozen on his step, his wrists aching from his convulsive grip on the iron stanchion. Afterwards he could only remember a dim impression of the coach lurching over the bank of the causeway as the offside wheels lost their grip on the rim of the track, spinning in the empty air before biting once more on the muddy surface. The coach shuddered as it righted itself and the wheels of the two coaches collided, scraped together and then bounced off one another. As he clung on for dear life, Pascual got a blurry glimpse of a coat of arms painted on the door of the big coach and saw as he whirled past the white faces of the coachmen and the passengers gaping at him from the plush interior. Then his own coach righted itself with a sickening lurch and went thundering away down the track. Goya did not even turn his head.

Esteban's legs were rammed against the rail in front of him. He couldn't move. He could scarcely breathe. He took the roaring in the ears to be the sound of the crash they had by some miracle managed to avoid. He knew what he had to do. He lunged sideways and made a grab for the reins. Goya's unwavering glance fastened on the empty track ahead and his forearm flew sideways, hitting Esteban in the chest like a blow from an iron bar. The coachman was almost knocked off the box but struggled to make a second snatch at the reins. Again Goya hit him and made him double up with the force of the blow. But Esteban knew he had to try again and when he had caught his breath, he flung himself at Goya and managed to seize the reins. They struggled, Goya never taking his eyes from the rain-dimmed track. Again the coach tilted and Pascual feared the worst. But then, just as the coach was righting itself once more, the duel between the two men was suddenly interrupted by the sound of smashing glass.

Pascual thought the window of the coach window had been shattered by the shuddering thump of the vehicle on the road. But when he craned sideways and shot a glance down the side of the coach he saw a long brown streak sail through the air below him. Later neither Esteban or Pascual could account for what caused the dog to jump. The yelling of the coachman and the rackety motion of the coach had evidently shaken it out of its torpor. Perhaps it panicked and wanted its master, or it had reared up and spotted a hare or rabbit browsing by the edge of the marsh. Whatever the reason, it landed hard and picked itself up and went chasing around in wild circles. Then it started to bound after the coach, catching up with it and overtaking it, almost getting tangled up between the hoofs of the horses.

It was then that Goya saw it. He heaved back on the reins and tossed away the whip and managed to bring the steaming horses to a halt.

He stood up on the box and shouted out the dog's name.
"Baltasar! Baltasar!"

The dog had stopped racing after the coach and was once more careening around in demented circles. Goya leaped down from the box. He reached for the guardrail with his wounded hand and missed it and hit his shoulder on the wheel. He went sprawling into the road. Pascual saw him struggle to his feet and hobble up the track toward where the dog was performing its crazy gyrations. Again he fell and forced himself to his feet and Pascual realized he had injured his ankle while jumping down from the box. But he went clumping forward with great limping strides.

"Baltasar! Baltasar!"

Esteban now jumped down from the box and when Pascual too stepped down unsteadily from the back of the coach Esteban ran around and punched him in the chest.

"Get back on the box! Steady the horses! Make sure they don't bolt!"

Pascual scrambled up onto the box and grabbed the reins and saw Esteban running down the road towards the mud-daubed figure of Goya as it continued stumbling forward.

"Baltasar!"

The dog had left the road and was now on the marsh. Pascual saw Goya drop to his knees at the edge of the track and stretch out his arms to the dog. The rain was streaming down his cheeks and making unruly spikes of his hair.

For a moment his calls seemed to be having an effect. Pascual could just make out through the drifting drizzle that the dog had stopped in its tracks and was standing stock still with its ears pricked. As Goya kept shouting its name it began to trot towards its mud-smeared master, its own shaggy coat equally plastered with mud. Goya uttered guttural cries of encouragement. The dog started to trot towards him, pausing only to shake a clot of mud from its paws. It was almost within striking distance of its master's outflung arms.

Then, between Goya's shouts and the restive snorting and stamping of the horses, Pascual suddenly heard a sucking sound emanating from the spongy ground beneath the animal's paws. It was the sound all travelers in this region had come to fear.

Neither Goya nor the dog seem to recognize what was about to happen. The dog stopped and stared glassily at its master. It stood there trembling. Its back legs began to sink. Goya shuffled on his knees toward the edge of the track. Esteban darted after him and seized him by his shirt collar. Goya tried to bull his way forward but Esteban got an arm around him and wrestled him back.

Goya's thick frame was shaking in an agony of uncertainty. He swayed from side to side as he knelt on the track shouting hoarsely to the dog as it lifted its paws out of the gluey sand and tried to plough his way towards him.

The dog continued to stare wide-eyed at its master. It made no attempt to bark as the marsh itself developed its own diabolical voice. It emitted a series of thick smacking sounds as it slowly drew the animal under. It slowly swallowed the dog like some giant snake. It took its time. It paused at intervals to enjoy devouring and digesting it. It heaved and slurped and belched. First the dog's legs, then its chest and hindquarters, sank steadily from sight.

A last eructation from the wet sand. The plop of a few final bubbles. Then all was silence and stillness.

"Baltasar!"

Goya let himself fall forward and lay prone on the muddy track. Esteban stood motionless and stunned. Pascual knotted the reins around the guardrail and got down from the box and moved up the road towards them. He gawked at the flat dimpled surface of the marsh fringed with reeds where the dog had just vanished.

Esteban shivered. After a moment he motioned to Pascual and between them they got Goya to his feet. They walked him back to the coach, half supporting him and half carrying him. His left leg now gave way beneath him and his foot stuck out at an unnatural angle. It was now raining so steadily that Pascual was unable to tell how much of the moisture on Goya's face was raindrops, or how much was tears.

It was cold. It was getting dark. The stricken Goya was a dead weight. His clothes were heavy and slimy with mud. They managed to hoist him into the coach and lay him on the cushions. He lay still with his head turned away and his eyes shut.

Esteban told his fellow servants later that he couldn't help feeling that he was driving a hearse back to Sanlúcar, not a coach emblazoned with the proud arms of the Duchess of Alba.

THAT HORRIBLE BEAST, that miserable brute of a dog. How could she have been expected to *know*? Why had nobody *told* her...?

What time was it? Two o'clock? Three? She twisted and turned in the tangled and sweat-soaked sheets. Couldn't lie still. Hadn't slept since they had put her to bed.

Dark. So dark. A sickening smell of burnt-out candles. Where were the servants? Where was María Luz? Why hadn't she brought fresh candles? Where *was* she? Dark, dark. Where was that bell? Groping for it. Reaching for it. Why would no one come?

Listen to that rain. Where was *he*? Oughtn't he to be back by now? They told her he was only going as far as Utrera. Where *was* Utrera anyway? Oh, why hadn't she taken better notice of the names of the towns she had passed through on the way from Madrid?

How long since he had left the palace? Ten hours? Twelve?

And again that frightful thought. What if he had had an accident? What if Esteban and Pascual had let him drive? What if he were lying helpless in a ditch?

And then a worse thought. What if he had reached Utrera and hadn't stopped there and had gone straight on to Seville? Or to Madrid?

And all because of that damnable animal. Could it all come to an end over something so trivial? After all they had been to each other? Surely she had been right to tell Carulli to get rid of the dangerous creature? How could she have known it had belonged to his children? That it was a last link to his two dead sons? Why had nobody mentioned it all these weeks? Why hadn't she remembered the sketches of a dog and a pair of boys in the first sketchbook she had thumbed through in the studio? Why hadn't she put two and two together? It could have all been so simple!

So dark. So cold. She threw out a hand. Nothing. *Francisco!* She clutched the damp sheet and felt a fevered wetness on her forehead. Mother of God! Why would he drive in this nightmarish weather to Utrera? Or Madrid? *Dios mío!* Not that. Please not that.

Should she pray? She turned her head to where the crucifix and the image of the Virgin hung beside the dressing table mirror. It was too dark to see. She felt a sting of fear. Surely she had done more than her share of praying since the death of her husband? Stiff ceremonies and endless ritual masses, all the obligatory mourning in those unbecoming black dresses. The pretense of weeping for a man she had never loved.

She felt the bile rise in her throat. A cough. A harsh and horrid sound. The bed started to heave and tilt and to rock and sway....

A runaway horse. She was groping for the reins and gripping its mane. Her legs were spread wide over its sloping back. Her skirts were billowing in the cold black wind. She felt the great bunched muscles working beneath her thighs. Why was the saddle so wet and slippery beneath her?. What was this iron band fastened around her waist squeezing and crushing her tighter and tighter...?

Steeper and steeper still and only the iron band holding her in place. Her hands were digging desperately, trying to find something to clutch on to. They touched something springy, something dry. Something not at all like a horse's mane.

And what was that sound? That curious sound? It sounded like the beating of an enormous pair of wings. A pair of wings spreading out on either side of her. A pair of feathered wings driving through the dark with the rhythmic pulsation of vast sails. A colossal span of wings cleaving the night sky beneath the glimmer of starlight.

Upwards and upwards! The wings of a bird and the body of a horse. A bloodless horse with a furry down of ashy white. A horse with a bony beak, its white eyes sunk into fleshless sockets. Crocodile jaws with pointed teeth.

Her arms were flying upwards. She was falling backwards, losing her grip on the feathery pelt. The iron clamp was tightening beneath her breasts. A pair of hands was locked about her.

Francisco was mounted beside her on a winged beast, its cries like sharp knives. She could hear the deaf man shouting. She could feel her own mouth stretched wide in a scream. They were riding, riding through the night together. Riding to the rim of the sky and the edge of the earth into the heart of the nightmare.

She could smell his sweat. She could smell the leathery reek of the horse. She could smell the ammoniac odor of the feathery wings cleaving the darkness.

The fingers hooked through her sash to hold her steady were loosening. She was slipping. She was sliding. She was falling.

Falling. Falling. Falling.
Coughing. Choking.

Someone was shaking her.

"Duchess, Duchess—wake up!"

Her eyes sprang open and she lifted her head. Candlelight! Above her was the wavering black oval of María Luz's face with its tight cap of ebony curls.

Her maid was shaking her and pulling at her nightgown. The Duchess was still in the grip of the nightmare and stared at the girl stupidly. María Luz went on speaking to her urgently as the Duchess tried to find the strength to sit up. She tried to focus on the dark lips between which the small even teeth were flashing brightly in the light of the candles. There was a blockage in her ears caused by the heights she had reached in the dream and then María Luz's voice came bursting through. At the same time she heard a clap of thunder. A flicker of lightning lit up María Luz's face so that the Duchess was able to catch a few of the words the girl was telling her.

"Came back an hour ago... standing outside his room in the rain... won't take any notice of Esteban and Pascual... trying to get him inside... the dog is dead, Señora, drowned in the marshes...."

The words were a mere buzz in her ear. The girl continued to pull at her but she was still unable to rouse herself. She lay as if dazed from the speed of the fall and the bruising contact with the earth. She had a dim memory of falling through the branches of trees in which owls and bats and hooded figures sprang out as she somersaulted past them. She lay prone on the bed, her arms flung wide, the sound of the girl's voice swelling and fading as a picture of Francisco, standing in the storm soaked and silent, gradually began to form in her brain.

He had come back! He had returned to Sanlúcar!

She reached up and took hold of María Luz and managed to pull herself up and sit on the edge of the bed. The movement made her head swim and prompted a wave of nausea. It was several minutes before she felt strong enough to stand up and let María Luz drape some clothes around her. She shivered as she felt the night sweat drying on her body. María Luz put a robe over her nightdress, tied the ribbons and inserted her feet into her silk slippers. She felt the girl giving her hair a hasty comb, smoothing out the worst of its tangles. Still numb from the aftermath of the dream she was vaguely aware that the bedchamber door was open and that a group of servants were waiting outside in the corridor holding candlesticks and whispering together. She was conscious only that it must be the middle of the night, that it was cold, that the rain and thunder seemed to be growing in intensity.

She must go to him! She must go to Francisco!

She let María Luz lead her from the bedchamber, leaning heavily on the girl's arm. Her head ached and she could barely put one foot in front of the other. As she reached the door, the throng of servants fell back to let her pass.

Once outside the door she tried to take command of herself, pausing a moment to straighten herself and make a determined effort to shake off the last shreds of the dream that still clung to her like the filaments of a web. She pulled her shoulders back and tilted her chin and walked down the corridors followed by the band of servants, with María Luz a watchful step or two behind her. A whole labyrinth of passageways lay between her quarters and Francisco's. The flagged floors struck up a chill beneath the thin soles of her embroidered slippers.

She had not realized what a distance separated their quarters. She quickened her pace, wrapping her arms around her body to hold in the warmth of the silken nightdress and the satin robe. María Luz, carrying one of the candelabra from the bedchamber, had drawn level with her and was whispering urgently in her ear as they hurried forward.

"We wanted to let you sleep and not disturb you until the morning, Señora. But we weren't sure what to do. He is standing in the rain and we can't get him inside." She spoke breathlessly, struggling under the weight of the heavy silver candelabra. "*And the door to his room is locked. It is always locked. He never lets anyone in—not even little Estrellita.*"

The Duchess halted for a moment, the bunched servants behind her almost running into each other. She stared at the fine features of the Arab girl gleaming in the candlelight. So he kept his door locked at all times? What strange kind of secret existence had her lover been leading these past few weeks? Why had it never occurred to her to find out for herself? Was it because she had sensed there was always to be something alarming about this paradox of a man, always something unsettling and unexpected to discover? Would she never come to the end of him?

She shook her head and walked forward, working her toes more firmly into her flimsy slippers. And now she and her retinue, muttering behind her rather like a stage chorus, made their way from the confines of the maze of corridors into the warren of passageways that led them through and into the chapel. In the small windowless, box-like space the air seemed heavy and laden with stale incense. Her footsteps and those of her nocturnal procession echoed from the vaulted ceiling, the sagging figure on the tarnished bronze crucifix hanging crookedly on the wall behind the bare altar seeming to stare down at them accusingly as they shuffled by. She averted her eyes from the crucifix and from the flaking images of the Virgin and the saints in their respective niches as she hastened down the aisle and through the door at the far end.

It was then, in the final passage that lay between the chapel and Goya's quarters, that something caught her eye and caused her to halt abruptly. In the distance she could now see the dark oblong of his door, and between it and the rear of the chapel stretched a length of whitewashed wall. Glancing at the wall, she saw its white surface was now covered along its entire length with a kind of fresco, with images of humans mixed with animals and fantastic figures, of wildly different shapes and sizes, in no conceivable pattern or order. Some of the humans and assorted creatures were the right way up, some were sideways, some standing on their heads and some upside down. She took the candelabra from María

Luz, recoiling slightly as some hot wax splashed onto her hand, and stepped closer to the wall.

María Luz came up behind her and whispered.

"Señor Goya did these. He calls them his *garabatos*, his scribblings. We are all afraid of them—we think they look like the work of the Devil!"

Running the candelabra back and forth over the wall, the Duchess had to agree there was something devilish about it. This would surely ensure his privacy. No servants would want to come close to his quarters if they had to look at this!

Holding the light even closer, she saw the figures, executed with short, meandering, jiggling strokes, were even odder than at first glance. This was a neglected part of the palace and the whitewash on the wall was crumbling, with patches and pockmarks where the plaster had peeled away. It was this leprous background that Goya had used to fashion his mural. She could see that he had made his figures out of the lumps and blisters, using them to fashion the heads and bodies of his monstrous animals and humanoid creatures. He had joined up the holes and bulges to provide their outlines, and it was only after she had been looking at them for several minutes that she realized what she was seeing was not disordered at all but was a means of rendering something random and meaningless into something resembling order. The conjuring of something real and palpable out of nothing. Who but her Francisco could have concocted anything so close to that borderline between madness and meaning?

For a moment she was oblivious to the band of servants jostling behind her, all of them peering at the mural with hushed exclamations of awe and dread or with weak attempts at facetiousness. Her heart turned over as she pictured him night after night at this cankered wall, scrawling his eerie designs on its grimy surface, bringing to life the seething mass of phantoms that swam in the depths of his brain.

But now she could no longer ignore the crowd of servants at her heels. Francisco was somewhere out in the rain beyond the door at the end of the corridor. Candelabra in hand she advanced towards Goya's room. Of course, the door was locked. She wondered if some of the stouter servants could put their shoulders to it and break the lock. And then, from out of the shadows, carrying a huge ring of master keys in a white-gloved hand, stepped Salvatore Carulli.

Where had he come from? Why was he fully dressed in his elaborate livery, tightly buttoned up and with his gold-laced cocked hat under his arm, at this hour of the night? He stood there, bending with his usual obsequious air, not speaking a word and holding out the outsized ring of keys. He deftly detached one and presented it to her with a little flourish. Taking it, she stared at him as hard as the wavering light of the flickering candles allowed. He bowed low, straightening up with that slightly ironic expression on his face that was never quite pronounced enough for her to feel able to rebuke. As he bowed and backed away it seemed to her that there was something unpleasant about that secretive half-smile, something that hinted he was keeping something to himself…. And all at once, as he retreated with another bow, she determined then and there that she would definitely dismiss him when she returned to Madrid. She had long suspected that he might be a sneak and a spy, foisted on her by those at court that wished her ill. She would give him his dismissal and send him packing. She should have done it sooner. Let him carry his parcel of rumors and insinuations to the Queen and the toadies around her, who would be only too ready to believe them. Let them do what they wished with them!

With the candelabra in one hand and the key in the other, she motioned to Carulli and the other servants to leave. They were clustered in a half-circle, caught up in the drama of the scene. She stamped a slippered foot.

"Go. Go now. All of you. Go!"

She stood by the door waiting until Carulli had ushered the servants away with his usual show of officiousness. María Luz did not want to leave, calling out to the Duchess until Carulli grasped her, none too gently, by the elbow and took her away with the rest. She hovered and resisted, casting back anxious and appealing glances.

The Duchess waited until all the other lights were extinguished and only the light of her candelabra remained. The shadows crowded around her. She shivered. Without the warm companionship of the crowd she felt suddenly cold. Surely Goya would be in his room by now? She summoned her courage and rapped on the door. From above she heard the muffled growl of the thunder.

But there was no answer. But of course. There would be no answer, why was she always forgetting his deafness? She put the key in the lock and turned it and went inside.

Her heart was beating and she expected to find the room in darkness. She was relieved to discover it was lit by a dozen stumps of candles which were stuck haphazardly in candlesticks on the pieces of furniture in the room. She detected a smell of singeing and burning and she went around the room pinching out with a thumb and forefinger the flames of the dangerously placed candles. She put her candelabra on the chest. As she did so she stumbled on something on the floor and almost fell. She could see in the flickering light that she had tripped over Francisco's guitar, the guitar with the broken strings.

There was no sign of him. The room was empty and the wide windows with their low lintel and double shutters stood open to the night. The rain was pouring in. So he was still outside. The light of the silver candelabra fluttered wildly in the wind.

She looked about her. She felt a pang. She had had no idea that he had been living like this and that his room was so poorly furnished. She should have seen that he was more comfortable. Again she was angry with Carulli.

The room was a mess and not simply because of all the clutter on the floor. In the guttering light she could see clothes trailing from the backs of chairs. The bed was pulled out at an angle from a recess in the wall, its sheets and blankets bunched up at the foot in a tangled mound. It was obvious no servants had been allowed in to clean the room.

But it puzzled her. When Francisco came to her in the afternoons in her bedchamber there had been no hint of anything slovenly about him. He had been closely shaven, his linen clean, his clothing brushed. Yet privately this was the way he had chosen to live. Had she known anything about him? She had given herself to a man who had hidden himself away in a dark den like a beast in its lair. On top of the smell of the rain driving in through the open window, there was something animal hanging in the air, mingling with the ineradicable effluvium of linseed and turpentine and stale cigars which always clung to him. A flash of lightning lit up the room like the bursting of a rocket, throwing the darkness of her surroundings into stark relief. She looked around at the soiled bed sheets and the unemptied washing bowl in the corner, at the dirty towels and the overflowing chamber pot at the foot of the bed. The whole room stank of despondency, verging on despair. Despair she had done her best to dispel. As she looked around she had to ask herself if she had made the progress she had thought she had.

She put a hand to her breast and felt her heart fill with pain. She stood irresolute for a moment and then felt herself prompted to do something she hadn't done since she was a child. She began to tidy the room. As if the thunder and lightning had suddenly stirred her into action, the Duchess of Alba began to shake out sheets and blankets and fold them on the bed. She picked up the crumpled clothes from the floor and put them in neat piles on the chairs. Carrying a load of shirts she went to the chest of drawers on which stood the candelabra and started to pull out the drawers to put the shirts inside them.

Like the rest of the room, the chest itself was a mess. On its surface lay his razors and toilet articles, a drift of cigars, a fly-specked mirror and some brushes and pots of paint, together with something she couldn't identify. She picked it up and twisted it in the light. It was a long heavy strip of leather, greasy to the touch, ornamented with brass studs. It was the spare collar of the dog. With a sharp pang she let it fall on the chest top with a dull clatter.

There were two stacks of pictures, six or eight to the stack, propped against both sides of the chest. Some of them must have been the pictures swathed in sacking she had seen him stow on top of the roof of the coach before they left Don Sebastián's. Others may have been some of the pictures he had been working on in the studio and which he had taken back to his bedchamber to finish. Only the backs were visible. She lifted them up one by one and turned them over and held them up to look at them.

There was sufficient light for her to make out that the paintings in the first stack were devoted to cheerful subjects, subjects typical of Goya in the years before his illness. These she was familiar with. She had seen them on the walls of the royal palace in Madrid and on the walls of her aristocratic friends, the sort of innocent scenes she had seen him sketching on the lawns outside her bedchamber or at the harvest feast on the banks of the Guadalimar. The paintings were the works of a young man, a young painter hopeful in spirit. They were infused with a sense of joy. Some were on canvas, some on wooden panels, still others on sheets of tin whose sharp edges she quickly realized she needed to handle carefully.

These mostly depicted young country folk, dancing and making music, playing at blind man's buff, tossing a puppet in a blanket, or trying to climb a greasy pole or walk along a low rope slung between the trunks of two trees. Many were of children running or racing each other or engrossed in such games as playing leapfrog, dressing up as soldiers and parading around with tiny drums and wooden rifles, or pretending to be giants by standing on each others' shoulders. This was obviously a painter who loved and understood children, a love made doubly poignant by a small panel depicting the small boys embracing a gigantic brown dog. An obvious image of Baltasar and his two sons. All three of whom were lost to him now. She felt a tug at her heart.

It was when she had finished the first stack of pictures and was beginning to examine the second that her senses began to flutter and tremble. The candlelight itself began to flicker on their surfaces, as if reluctant to reveal the nature of their subjects. No greater contrast with the first group could be imagined. There was no trace of sunshine here. They were filled with a frank terror. The two groups of paintings could have been painted by a different man. Gone was youth and harmless pleasures. These pictures were of an unspeakable darkness. It seemed right that they were hidden away in this dark chamber where their creator had passed the darkness of his nights and spewed out the darkness in his soul.

Her first reaction was disgust. Handling them in itself was abhorrent. They could only reinforce the world's prejudice that Spaniards had a tendency for callousness and cruelty. As a child she had heard of the ruthless severity with which her ancestor the Duke of Alba, the Viceroy of Flanders and the Netherlands, had put down any hint of rebellion. How could those pictures of happy peasants and children exist side by side with the pictures she was now turning this way and that in her quivering hands? Could it be that his deafness had driven him further down the slopes towards such madness?

First there were pictures of priests and Inquisitors gloating over the whipping, strangling, torturing and burning of their wretched victims. Then there were pictures of witches, witches flying, witches awake or asleep in the branches of trees, witches brewing filthy potions in their iron cauldrons, witches worshipping a horned Satan by the light of a horned moon. She shuddered as she held up a succession of pictures depicting madmen and madwomen—a huddled heap of gibbering maniacs imprisoned behind the thick walls and barred windows of their places of confinement, bound with ropes, shackled with chains, singing, yelling, writhing on flagstones, stark naked or with rags across their loins.

And then came worse paintings devoted to scenes of disaster and panic. Crowds spilling out of buildings on fire, trampling each other as they tried to escape from the flames. Survivors of a shipwreck, fighting their way through giant waves to be cast up on a rocky shore where a woman with bare breasts stretched up her arms in a fruitless appeal to heaven.

Death, death and death, death piled on death. Here was a study of a family being massacred at night by a platoon of soldiers. A mother was running with her screaming baby in her arms as bullets struck her in the back. And two sketches in oil were even more atrocious. The first showed a pair of white men, Jesuit priests or missionaries, being butchered, castrated, disemboweled and beheaded by a band of Indians. The other, a companion to it, showed the intestines of the two men being extracted while they were still alive and being cooked and eaten by their captors.

Long shudders went through her. She felt the bile rising in the back of her throat and started to cough and dropped the painting so that the whole pile of pictures collapsed and fanned out over the floor. She felt faint and held onto the chest of drawers to stop herself from falling. She lowered her head and closed her eyes for a moment. The flashes of lightning which had heightened the frightening impact of the paintings burned through her eyelids and seemed to bathe her eyes in blood.

She lowered her head, gripping the chest more tightly. So this was how Goya saw the world. Or was he, a fearful thought, some kind of prophet? Was this how he saw the world ending? Ending in death and darkness, in violence and despair? Was this what he foresaw for Spain? Yet even as she struggled to fight back the vomit and gulp back the temptation to cough, she couldn't repress a lingering sense of pity. Why had fate put such a curse on him, coupling his extraordinary gifts with such a darkening imagination? Contrasting in her mind the first series of paintings with the later ones she realized that what was pitious about his life was the fact he had somehow managed to live it the wrong way around. We all hope to sail through the earlier and more trying part of our lives and end up in the calm and more serene waters of old age. Surely after storms should come serenity, after strife come tranquility? At least after the ferment of childhood and adolescence and the initial confusion of middle age, some sort of balance and contentment should follow. How could these gruesome pictures ever show any hope for a carefree ending?

Perhaps they were indeed prophetic. What if they were actual expressions of his sorrow and anger at what he sensed must lie ahead? Could it be that one of the elements of his gifts as an artist was that he could peer into the future and descry something of what was to come? To Spain? To humanity? She turned away and went to the window to seek a breath of fresh air. It was good to stand there and feel on her hands and face the fine spray that was all that remained of the passing storm. She could detect the salt of the distant sea on the soft wind mingled with the ranker smell of the marshes.

Those pictures! She crossed her arms over her breast, as if to protect herself from them. Did such terrible ideas start with his illness, or had the trouble begun much further back than that? In his infancy perhaps? In those early and impressionable years in a stony little village in Aragon, where the country folk reveled in all manner of primitive beliefs and fantastic superstitions and stuffed the heads of their offspring with a whole host of sinister and ghoulish stories?

She pressed her arms more tightly across her breast, moving to close the windows to keep the remaining rain out so that the candles would burn more steadily. There was a valedictory flare of the lightning as the storm drifted away towards the ocean. With a hand on the shutter, leaning over the low sill and preparing to close them, she suddenly saw a broad-shouldered figure, naked to the waist, limping slowly up the slope that led to the palace from the meadow below. As the pale chain of lightning lit up the night sky with a milky glow she saw the figure halt and turn to face the receding storm. It raised its arms high, as if it had been combating the elements and had brought about their retreat and was saluting them defiantly as they departed. In one raised fist she could make out the shape of a hunting gun which the figure was brandishing at the skies as if the heavens themselves were threatening. From the figure's left hand she could see fluttering down a torn rag. And, at the same time, she saw a weak and watery glow traveling in a line along the length of the meadow just behind and below it. For several moments she was unable to make out what the glow was, then remembered the trackway across the streamlet on the far side of the meadow and realized it must be the pale lamps of a slowly moving coach. She took it to be the mail-couch following its regular route from the north towards Sanlúcar and making painful progress due to the bad weather. The silence in which the horses and carriage traveled gave an impression of a ghostly apparition, sending a shiver through her. But then the figure turned and began to limp up the slope toward her and she forgot about the coach as the landscape was claimed once more by blackness and the night.

SHE LET GO of the catch and drew back from the window.

Had he seen her there in his room, outlined against the shifting glint of the candles? Her immediate impulse was to leave quickly. She was aware of being afraid, not that he might have seen her rummaging among his belongings, but because of something deeper, a palpable physical fear of him of which she was both resentful and ashamed. Yet she could not suppress it. Who exactly climbed towards her? The tender and considerate lover? Or the purveyor of evil dreams? Was it the dilineator of her portrait, of wholesome country wenches, of beguiling actresses and beautiful noblewomen? Or was it the creator of misshapen harridans and witches who took such a twisted pleasure in depicting women as objects of rape and massacre? *Only Goya*. Were these the words of love she had taken them to be? Or were they demon words? A threat? A warning of domination and possession?

She fell back further into the shadows as he loomed up directly outside the window. As he entered the candlelight's sphere he seemed as broad and tall as a giant and his black hair was plastered across his forehead. He was brought up short by the low sill and blundered into it, swaying and almost losing his balance, putting out a hand to feel for the frame and keep himself from falling. He dropped the gun in his other hand and it fell across the sill and hit the floor with a harsh clatter that made her jump and brought her heart into her throat. He stood there rocking, not seeing her, oblivious to everything. There was a blind look on his face as if he had passed beyond comprehension, like one of the bulls in his sketchbooks waiting with head lowered for the thrust of the sword. He stood there passively for a long moment before summoning up the strength to surmount the sill and enter the room. He clambered over and slumped back against the window frame.

She knew it was useless to attempt to speak to him. She quickly stepped forward and put her hands on his shoulders. Her fear of him was gone. She was shocked to feel his nakedness and the wetness and deathly coldness of his flesh. She thought of his dog as her fingers felt his body shivering like a wounded animal.

He did not respond to her touch. She had to grasp his clammy flesh more firmly before he realized she was there. After a moment he finally came to himself and let her help him to his feet. By the glimmer of the candlelight she could now see that he was only wearing one shoe. It took a series of efforts before she could pull him up and propel him in the direction of the bed, where he could lie down. She nudged the fallen gun aside with her slipper and succeeded in making him take a few steps away from the window. He moved with shuffling steps like a sightless hulk, seemingly unaware of what she wanted him to do. He stood slump-shouldered, dripping water, still only half-conscious of someone in the room.

She was afraid that he might pitch forward and fall and that she wouldn't have the strength to pick him up. She steadied him, wondering whether she would have to summon help. After a moment, however, he seemed to be steadier, and she released her grip on him and slid slowly down until she was kneeling in front of him.

Easing off his remaining shoe was easy. The laces were untied and were loose. Something stirred in him as he felt her trying to raise his foot and he lifted it high enough to let her remove it. The ankle was cold and badly swollen and slippery as a lump of clay. His shoe was covered with mud. She could feel it on her fingers and paused to wipe her hands on the skirt of her robe before throwing it into a corner behind her. Next she unbuttoned his belt and the buttons of his fly and started to draw off his soaked breeches while he trembled beneath her fingers.

She worked the breeches down over his thighs and calves,

rapping him gently on each knee to induce him to raise his bare feet, and drew them off and cast them aside.

Now he was naked. It was impossible to tell whether he was aware of it. He had withdrawn deep inside himself, into the tenebrous regions he inhabited. She rose from her knees slowly, running her hands over his calves, thighs, hips, belly and chest. His slack and rain-cold arms were rough with gooseflesh. Not a muscle moved. He stayed completely still with his neck bent and his head lowered. If he felt her arms stealing around him he gave no sign. She raised herself on her toes, clasping her arms around him as tightly as she could, knotting her hands behind his head, She pressed her lips to his forehead, the wet and matted mass of his black hair crushed against her mouth.

She lowered an arm and unfastened her robe and untied the ribbons. Her robe was slick with the rain and the wetness of his chest and belly. She unleashed her breasts, the nipples hard in the chill of the night, and kneaded them against him. He had stopped shuddering now as they stood there breast to breast and she could feel the slow even heave of his body. In the cold room a warmth started to spread down the length of her body and flow into his.

He submitted to her embrace as motionless as a statue, locked in a dark dream like one of the prisoners or madmen in his paintings. But she knew there was one person to whom, locked in his tormented world, he would always be accessible. In his deafness and sickness he might lose himself, but he would never lose her. She would be the one to give purpose and succor to Francisco Goya. Yes, *Solo Goya*. In this cramped room, with the cold rainy autumn mist gusting through the window, in an uncertain hour before the dawn, her arms folded around the stricken man, she felt a sense of the purest elation. She pressed her cheek against his chest and told herself that the beat of his heart was steadier now she was there to calm and comfort him.

Her eyes filled with tears. She strained against him, using all the strength left in her.

All would be well.... No more bad dreams....

She felt him stir, like a creature long held in thrall emerging from a block of ice. She kissed his chest as if to warm him and hasten the thaw. He brought up his arms to hers and closed them around her.

A long slow quiver ran through their bodies as he lowered his head and kissed the crown of her head. He buried his mouth in the thick luxurious hair he had so often caressed in the long afternoons in her bedchamber.

There came a sudden low rapping at the door.

She gave an involuntary jerk and a little cry as the knocking was renewed more loudly.

Goya held her harder.

Knocking at the door at this time of night implied something disquieting. She was seized with a sense of foreboding. But when the knocking came for a third time she knew it would have to be answered.

She struggled out of his grasp, speaking breathlessly, once again forgetting in the tension of the moment that he was deaf.

"Francisco—"

She struggled harder.

"Francisco!"

He gripped her more tightly still.

More knocking and a rattling of the handle. A man's muffled voice.

"Duchess! Duchess!"

She tried to push Goya's arms away and started to drum her small fists against his chest. She tried to do it lightly. She knew he had been overcome with uncertainty and confusion.

The knocking continued.

"Duchess! Duchess!"

He would not relinquish her. But she suddenly felt him weaken.

His nightlong wandering had taken the last of his strength. His flesh was slippery as she slid free.

She went swiftly to the door, then put out a hand and spoke to him as though speaking aloud could reassure them both

"I will be back. Stay! Stay where you are."

She remembered she had unfastened her robe to let him feel the solace of her breasts. She fumbled feverishly at her robe. She pulled the door open and it swung inwards almost knocking her down. She recovered herself and slipped into the corridor, holding the top of the robe closed in one hand and shutting the door swiftly with the other so that the naked man in the room behind her would not be seen.

She leaned against the door, her breasts heaving, adjusting her eyes to the bright glare of the candelabra held aloft by the servants in the corridor.

It took her a moment to bring into focus the immaculate figure of Carulli. So it was he who had been knocking and calling for her—she should have recognized the Italian accent! It was not yet dawn but he was immaculately dressed, turned out in his braided livery, his tricorn hat stuffed under his arm.

He fell back, bowing low.

"Pardon me, Duchess."

She tilted up her chin, pleased to hear that when she spoke her voice was under control and her tone commanding, although she felt her heart beating fast and a sense of tightness in her chest.

"Yes, Carulli, what is it?"

He stepped forward, bowing again. There was something catlike in his manner. He seemed satisfied with himself and with the message he had come to impart. He regarded his mistress's disordered hair and her creased and rumpled robe with a sly half-smile.

She spoke coldly.

"Well, Carulli?"

He was taking his time. His manner suggested that

embarrassment was making him hesitate but she knew he was simply taking pleasure in making her wait.

She drew herself up, refusing to show signs of impatience, and was relieved to see María Luz running down the corridor towards her. The Arab girl hurried forward, ducking between the tall footmen standing behind Carulli. She gave a little bob and stood by the Duchess's side, darting a hostile glance at Carulli. The beautiful eyes in the black face were filled with concern.

The Duchess kept her gaze on Carulli and addressed him even more coldly.

"Do I have to ask you again, Carulli? What is the meaning of this. Speak up!"

The Italian lowered his head and covered his mouth with his hand as though reluctant to be the bearer of such news.

The Duchess felt another flash of apprehension. What could be serious enough to cause such a hubbub at this time of the morning? Had there been an unexpected death at Court? Had the kingdom been invaded? Surely they would not consider a death or disaster in the family of Francisco Goya a sufficient reason to disturb her? Unless it was the death of his wife.... Or, please God, not the death of his last remaining child…!

Her mind was in a whirl. For a moment she entertained a brief and disloyal surge of hope he might be bringing her news of the death of the Queen. But when Carulli broke his silence his news shocked her more than any tidings of mishap or mortality.

It caused her such distress she felt her knees give way and she had to support herself against the wall behind her.

María Luz placed an anxious hand on her arm.

Carulli seemed to talk from a long way away.

"*Duchess, may I beg to inform you. The Count of Altolaguirre has just arrived.*"

Miguel.

But how could that be. Hadn't he received her second letter? Had it not reached him in Galicia in time? If it had, had he ignored it, disobeyed it, decided to come to Sanlúcar anyway?

She had written to him in good time. Had her letter got lost on the way?

A sudden suspicion occurred to her. She shot a keen glance at her butler. It was difficult to read his expression in the uncertain candlelight but it seemed bland and obsequious as usual.

Had he posted the letter?

Carulli, as if anticipating the suspicion in her glance, bowed and spoke smoothly.

"The Count would have arrived at the palace at a more convenient hour, Duchess, if they had not nearly had an accident. The Count said they were nearly run off the road by a madman driving a coach at full tilt who refused to slow down for them. The Count had to stop in the village of Trebujena, several miles from here, to get a new wheel for his coach."

The Duchess's mind clouded and she seemed to hear Carulli's voice through a sort of haze.

"So the Count apologizes for his late arrival, Duchess. He wanted me to inform you that he will wait for a suitable hour later today to introduce himself and his guest so they may pay their respects...."

Still she failed to take in his words and gave her head a little shake in order to clear it. She spoke in a clear and bemused tone that seemed to her to come from a long way away.

"A *guest*, Carulli? What guest?"

He spoke smoothly.

"The *torero* Pedro Romero, Duchess. I gather the Count attended a performance by Señor Romero at the bullring in Seville. He then learned that Señor Romero was on his way to keep an appointment in Cádiz. He understood Señor Romero to be an acquaintance of the Duchess...." A faint ironic emphasis on the word *acquaintance*. "Therefore the Count felt he might venture to ask if Señor Romero could break his journey for a night or two and share your hospitality here in Sanlúcar?"

She had difficulty taking it in.

"*Pepe?* Pepe Romero is here?"

Worse and worse.

She recalled Francisco's fury when he had discovered the locket and the letters from Miguel. Would he also have heard the rumors circulating in Madrid about her friendship with Pepe Romero?

"I hope I did the correct thing, Duchess, in anticipating your wishes and acceding to the Count's request?"

He was at his most unctuous.

She gave a wave of her hand, listening to her voice coming from an even greater distance. There was a choking sensation in her throat. She could scarcely get the words out.

"Yes. Yes, of course. Tell the Count and Señor Romero I shall be glad to greet them this evening."

She gave another feeble wave of her hand.

"Please leave me now."

The little party withdrew. Only the faithful María Luz remained.

Francisco. She must go to Francisco. He was standing there, naked and bereft in the room behind her.

She suddenly heard a soft crash coming from the confines of his room, as if a heavy figure had collapsed on the floor.

She turned the handle. Her strength drained from her body. María Luz caught her as she crumpled.

A thick and evil-smelling obstruction low in her lungs broke and bubbled upwards. She gagged and heaved. Fluid began to stream from her mouth and she snatched up the skirt of her robe and vomited the sweet liquid into it. The stain glistened blackly in the light of María Luz's candle. The Duchess stared blankly at the dark patch on the white robe. She prayed this was not the baneful condition of which she had been warned by Doctor Arrieta.

"My Duchess. To your very good health, my Duchess!"

The evening meal had barely begun and already the Count of Altolaguirre was lifting his glass to toast her for the third time.

She raised her glass, inclining her head and smiling weakly.

"And to yours, Miguel."

The Count tossed back his wine and banged down his glass on the polished expanse of the table. Carulli, who seemed to have constituted himself the Count's personal assistant, stepped forward with a decanter to fill his glass. The Count signaled that Carulli had only filled his glass half-way, so Carulli poured more wine until it was full to the brim. The butler was leaning over the Count's shoulder, and as their heads came together the Count laughed and whispered something and the Italian put up a hand and laughed quietly before he stepped away.

The Duchess frowned, not pleased with the way the Count seemed to be appropriating her chamberlain and the way Carulli was attaching himself to the Count. She recalled how thick the Count and Carulli had been at court, she had seen them whispering together in corners there. Was it possible that the two of them had been in secret communication and that Carulli had kept him informed about her relationship with Goya and had hinted to the Count that it might be time for him to intervene?

Looking at him lounging in his chair as he sat beside her at the head of the table, with Carulli hovering behind him, she could not help taking offence at the familiar way in which he kept addressing her as "his" Duchess. Had he already cast himself in the role of the next Duke of Alba? Or did he consider that they were not now constrained by the formality of the court and that there was no need for him to keep a tight rein on his behaviour? Or was it just that the Count of Altolaguirre was already a little tipsy?

Her train of thought was interrupted by the voice of the second of the three men at her table tonight. There was no doubt that this still startingly handsome albeit middle-aged man was definitely the worse for drink.

"Duchess, yes...! Beautiful Duchess...! We drink to your health!"

She turned sideways to face Pedro Romero, the guest Miguel had taken upon himself to invite. Her smile was warmer now. Pedro was a long-time friend and, even though Francisco was present, she couldn't help displaying her affection for him. Nevertheless, she was surprised to find him inebriated for, although he could be an easy-going and light-hearted companion, she knew that, as a *torero*, his natural inclination was to be abstemious. But the long bullfighting season had finally ended and certainly a man who had routinely killed two hundred bulls over the course of the summer could treat himself to some well-earned months of relaxation. The look she gave him as he gulped down his fourth or fifth glass of wine was sympathetic and indulgent.

Her smile disappeared when her gaze traveled to the third man at the table. From the moment when he had been reluctant to take his chair his demeanor had made her nervous.

In contrast with the pushy manner of Miguel and the distempered one of Pedro, Francisco's manner seemed strange and ominously calm. Miguel, notwithstanding his forward air, merely displayed the kind of aristocratic hauteur with which he habitually conducted himself at court, while Pedro's deportment, despite the quantities of Valdepeñas he was tossing back, still possessed the sharpness and elegance of his movements with the cape and sword.

The four of them were seated at the top end of the long table, the Duchess with the Count at her right hand, Pedro at the corner immediately to her left, and Francisco at the other corner opposite Pedro. She noted that Francisco was sipping his wine sparingly and eating hardly anything, even though her cooks had excelled themselves in their efforts to tickle the appetites of the glamorous young Count and the *torero* who was commonly regarded as the greatest in Spain. But Goya sat very quietly, sober in mien and dress, waving away the piquant *gazpacho*, the fresh eel and mullet, the juicy duck and capon, nibbling on a small dish of anchovies or selecting an occasional praline or almond from a silver dish in the center of the table. In his short black jacket and black knee breeches he looked staid and straight-laced compared with the dashing outfits of the Count and the bullfighter. The Count was dressed in the latest of high fashion, in a long loose jacket of dark emerald silk piped with gold braid and the new French trousers with flared bottoms. Above his French gauffered shirtfront his free-flowing white cravat was knotted with artificial carelessness and fastened with a large ruby. As for Pedro, he was sporting a flamboyant civilian version of his bullfighting costume, a short light blue silk jacket cut off above the hips and with a broad purple sash wound around his waist. His sleek dark hair with its premature hint of gray was plaited in the traditional *coleta* and embellished with the *castaña* and a bunch of violet ribbons. He had saturated his hair and skin with some bitter salve that smelled like gentian which contrasted strongly with the subtle cologne, no doubt from France too, with which the Count had liberally doused himself. Different still was the smell of Francisco's familiar pomade and whenever the Duchess caught a whiff of it she was transported to their afternoons in her bedchamber and felt faint and had to close her eyes.

Goya sat close to her sealed off by his deafness from the chatter and banter kept up by Miguel and Pedro. Beside the dishes of anchovies and sweetmeats lay an unopened sketchbook, his pencils and crayons beside it. In between selecting a salted almond or a praline he sat with folded hands, his elbows on the table, his jaws moving slowly, studying the faces of his table companions as if he were trying to follow what they were saying. She was glad to see the ragged and bloody bandage on his hand had been replaced with a clean one. She had wanted to tend it and bind it up herself and wondered whether he had spent this long and anxious day as restlessly as she had. As her gaze settled on Francisco, her hand stole to her throat as she remembered again the ferocity with which he had ripped the miniature from her neck and torn up Miguel's letters. And she once more reminded herself that he might well be aware of the widespread gossip that connected her to the engaging Pedro Romero....

What was he thinking? So near to her and yet so far apart. How much had be recovered from the jarring effects of the last storm-filled night? She ached to know but was careful not to stare at him too openly, anxious not to betray her feelings.

She had selected her costume for the evening after much earnest debate. She wanted to wear something that would show respect for Miguel as a grandee of the realm without suggesting to Francisco that she was unduly attracted to him. Accordingly she had chosen a simple white silk blouse with a pink sash that she knew would remind Francisco of the *maja* costume in which she was posing for him. She had painted the round black beauty spot of the *maja* beside her temple, but had made it small and discreet so that Miguel would not take it for a secret encouragement. Perhaps after the strain of the previous night she had laid on the perfume of Parma violets and the rouge and powder a little too lavishly. She was sure that Pedro would be recalling the flamboyant carriage rides they took together in Madrid where he and the onlookers were accustomed to see her in her *maja* costume. But she was concerned only with Francisco. Somehow she must implore him, if he had not already done so, to lock securely away the explicit drawings he had done of her during their love-making sessions.

"My Duchess!"

She returned Miguel's salutation with a polite and unencouraging half-smile. The wine in the glass in his hand glowed in the candlelight with a purplish color reminiscent of last night's dark stain on her robe. Pedro raised his glass, spilling a few drops of wine on his sleeve as he did so. He gave a foolish giggle, put the glass uncertainly to his lips and stared down at the spatter of crimson on his sleeve with a stupefied look, as if he thought the drops were real blood. Goya alone had not raised his glass to toast her. He sat there, his square blunt hands folded on the table in front of him, looking steadily at each of them in turn without joining in the general mood of levity. She fancied his look rested on her face for a shorter time than it rested on the others. He sat like a stone, his wine untouched. If only she had had a chance to explain to him that it was an accident that Miguel had arrived in Sanlúcar that morning, a mistake that he had arrived at all. Tomorrow she would send Esteban to Cádiz to bring her some stronger medicine from Dr. Arrieta. And she would ask the doctor for some medicine for Francisco too. After the strain of the previous night she feared he might now be passing from sanity to madness, from the hopes of these enchanted weeks with her into what threatened to be a fresh onset of disease and despair. Could Doctor Arrieta prescribe a physic to help stave off the ruin of this noble mind? Now her strength was failing, what could she do—how to prolong the light and postpone the darkness…?

She emerged from her self-absorption with a start and realized that Miguel was now addressing Goya. She could see the younger man's face only in profile but could make out that he had assumed a bright false smile and seemed to be making fun of the older man. Carulli had obviously previously informed him about his deafness. Miguel was grinning and nodding at Goya as if he were making pleasant conversation.

"Why so gloomy, old fellow? Why so glum? Why so dismal, my poor old specter at the feast?"

Goya stared at him, stolid and uncomprehending. It now seemed fortunate he had not made more progress with his lip reading, and that although he could read the Duchess's lips quite well, he could seldom read anyone else's. Miguel was making sport of the painter's condition, assuming it would amuse the Duchess and Romero. Romero, patently unused to drink and by now seriously intoxicated, thought it capital entertainment and flung himself backwards and forwards in his chair guffawing and slurping his wine.

The Duchess felt disgusted with them both and found herself at a loss as to how to stop their behavior before it got out of hand. She leaned over to Miguel, who was leaning towards Goya, and laid a hand on his arm, suddenly acutely aware of the contrast between the young Count and the ageing artist. There was only a difference of twenty years between them, but she had to admit that beside the arrogant and youthful aristocrat in his resplendent clothes, her provincial lover made an indifferent showing. Goya was no stranger to court circles, and maintained a substantial establishment and his own horses and carriages, but he would never acquire the easy patrician manner of a man like the Count. With his round head, his fleshy nose and small deep-set eyes, he carried with him the stamp of his origins in a poverty-stricken hamlet a fortnight's journey from the capital. And he was not ageing well, the marks of illness and overwork only too evident in his thickening features. Studying him in the unflattering light of the sconces, she thought she could detect additional ravages inflicted by the night before, traces of which she feared must be visible on her features too. She was seated so close to Miguel she was almost touching him. She could smell the seductive odor given off by his person. She stole a look at him. To be truthful, the miniature in the locket which Francisco had wrenched from her throat did not do him justice. For a brief moment she was tempted to bury her face in the rich blond ringlets falling onto his shoulders. What kind of lover, she couldn't help asking herself, might this exquisite young nobleman prove to be? Better than Francisco? No. No. *Solo Goya...*! How could that perfumed and conceited young man, however scintillating his outer appearance, possibly rouse her to the pitch of pleasure she had known with Francisco in those long and blissful afternoons? Francisco was a better lover, and he was a better man. How could she begin to compare the force and brilliance of a man like Francisco with a trifler like Miguel, whose chief claim to fame was that he sometimes gambled at cards with the dim-witted King? Better by far to ride out the nightmare with Francisco than wile away the hours with a languid exquisite like Miguel!

The Count, now primed with wine, was starting to bait Goya in earnest. With an increasingly inebriated smile plastered on his face, he had begun to raise his voice until it was almost a shout.

"**How are we getting on then? Still scrubbing and scribbling at our little pictures, are we?**"

He bent forward and gave the closed sketchbook that lay between him and Goya an impudent shove in the artist's direction.

"**How about scrawling a few lines for us, then?**"

The Duchess blushed and laid a hand on his sleeve. He shook it off.

"**Hey, you miserable old thing. What's up? You won't dash off a daub unless it's paid for, is that it? All right then! What's the going rate?**"

He thrust his hand into the inner pocket of his silk jacket and took out a silk purse and threw it on the table.

Her face burned. Carulli stood smirking in the shadows. The

footmen standing around the walls were exchanging enquiring looks. She was ashamed such a display was taking place in front of the servants. From somewhere behind her María Luz had advanced and stood nervously behind her.

The Count suddenly realized that he was talking to a deaf man and shouted even louder.

"**Yes, you, you old clod, you old booby! I'm talking to you. Cash on the barrelhead, will that do you? How much will it take to get the monkey to perform?**"

The Duchess reached over and dug her nails into his wrist.

He swung around to face her and she saw that his drunken smile had disappeared and that it had been replaced by a look of the purest hatred.

So he knew. Carulli had been keeping him informed! The Count was furious. The woman he had been grooming as his wife had given herself to a fellow he considered no better than a tradesman. She could read it in his face. Suddenly she saw him for what he was. A man who had been counting on her to salvage his bankrupt estates and bail him out of debt. She shuddered and swayed away from him. How could she ever have thought of yielding herself to this glittering snake of a creature?

Francisco, she saw, had scraped back his chair and was now standing and staring at his tormentor. During the first few minutes of the Count's attack on him he had remained passive, his expression puzzled. Once he had even smiled fleetingly, uncertain as to how to respond. He had even nodded a little, as if he understood and even agreed with what was being said. It had been some time before he had realized the Count was mocking him.

He did not show his anger but his whole body seemed to tighten and his head lowered. He stood quite still, looking down and across at the Count, his hands hanging at his sides and his fists slowly clenching and unclenching. His bulk was formidable in contrast with the silken sleekness of his antagonist. The Duchess was pleased to see no sign of his pistol or his knife, since this was a man who had been used to settling his own scores in myriad taverns. The stories of his earlier life testified that he was no stranger to violence. She knew if he made a move she would have to call for the footmen who were already whispering among themselves. Carulli, white-faced, was shrinking into the background. Were they all on the point of getting embroiled in one of those terrible scenes of which Goya was so fond of depicting? She felt an awful constriction in her chest. She wished she had stayed in her bed. She wished this dreadful meal were at an end so she could run there now.

Her nails were still digging into Miguel's wrist. Francisco was staring at their joined hands. She saw what conclusion he was drawing and snatched her hand away. She gave a small groan and moved back as far from Miguel as she could. She saw Francisco lean forward and plant both fists on the table, regarding the pair of them with a dull gleam in his eyes. Miguel held the painter's gaze with his own and went on staring insolently up at him.

Carulli was beckoning to the footmen,

There was a sudden tremendous crash.

Pedro Romero, who had been laughing and giggling, had given a final stupid yell and had fallen backwards out of his chair, bringing it down on top of him.

He hit the floor with another peal of laughter but then bounded to his feet even before the footmen had reached him. He sprung up in a single smooth movement still laughing, his body arching like an acrobat's. It was a movement he had executed scores of times in the ring after a *percance*, a tossing by the bull.

Pedro's laugh was intended to cover his loss of face. When the footmen righted the chair he promptly shrugged off their attempts to help him and sank back into his chair. Beneath his smile the Duchess could see he was nevertheless shaken. Again, she asked herself what it was that was making him act so uncharacteristically…?

There was a general perturbation while the servants were

sorting out the mess he had made after grabbing at the edge of the table and pulling down a huge welter of cutlery and glass. Only Goya remained unperturbed, sitting himself down slowly and deliberately as if he had not been taken by surprise and was used to events of this kind. As he watched the servants putting the room to rights, he sat with a half smile on his otherwise somber face.

The Duchess, striving to overcome a feeling of queasiness deep inside her, felt her heart fluttering. Right from the start the whole night had been a disaster. She was about to signal the end of the proceedings but Miguel put a hand on her arm and, as she tried to rise, pressed down firmly as he spoke.

"My Duchess." (That infernal address again!). "My Duchess, I am sure Pedro will not take it amiss if I venture to apologize for him?"

His grip on her arm tightened.

"In these past three weeks, since the end of the season, Pedro has been a little out of sorts. Perhaps my Duchess will allow me to explain. It is an interesting story and although Pedro is a great matador, he is by nature a man of action not of words. He would find it difficult to relate the story himself."

She knew that was true. Except when the conversation was about bulls, Pedro was virtually inarticulate. But there was a sweetness and shyness about him, together with his boyish good looks, that made him so attractive to women.

Miguel was keeping his hand on her arm. He was speaking quietly and had grown calmer. His friend's dramatic tumble had obviously sobered him up. He had perhaps realized that his behavior had not been acceptable for someone of his rank and standing and that he was in danger of jeopardizing whatever chance he might have of mending his fortunes by winning the Duchess's hand. He therefore performed a complete turnaround, attempting to put matters on a decorous footing by relating Pedro's story. He knew he could tell it well and was cheered by the thought that his subject had been behaving even more badly than himself.

What could the Duchess do? To leave the table now would only add to the uncomfortable scene in which they were all involved, including the servants. There would already be too much gossip about it that would eventually reach the court. Carulli would see to that. More scandalous goings-on in the Duchess of Alba's secret hideaway in Andalucía!

Besides which, the Count was subjecting her to the full force of his considerable charm, and she realized that he too would like the evening's proceedings to be brought to something resembling a dignified conclusion.

The Count had his hand on her arm still. Goya was looking at it with that same cold expression on his face. She glanced at him pleadingly. His mouth was set straight and hard, the sharp eyes unforgiving. When Miguel started to speak his attitude was withdrawn. Even if he had been able to speak, it seemed he didn't care to. And Pedro Romero could hardly participate in the conversation either. Spreadeagled in his chair, dazed and rumpled, he seemed as much out of things as the painter although, even in his intoxicated state, he still presented a somewhat graceful figure. At intervals he signaled to the footmen, knocking back wine with a hand that was noticeably trembling.

"You will have noticed, Duchess, that our friend here, to put it mildly, is scarcely himself this evening?" Miguel began.

He looked at the matador, whose eyes were glazed and whose tongue was lolling, and gave a shake of his head.

"As I have said, our poor Pedro has been in a sad state for about a month. He hasn't been the same since the death of his great friend Joaquín."

As he spoke the name, the man beside him lurched forward in his chair and his arms and legs twitched like a puppet whose strings have suddenly been pulled.

"My Duchess," asked the Count. "I take it that you have heard of the death of Joaquín Rodríguez?"

Yes. Yes she had. Everyone had. The news had rippled rapidly through the whole of Spain and had reached even a remote spot like Sanlúcar in a matter of hours. The Duchess had seen him fight many times in the ring and had come to think of him as being almost invulnerable. He and Pedro had been legendary both as rivals and friends. Pedro, latest in an ancient family of *toreros*, had been the champion of the school of Ronda, grave and stately and restrained, distinguished by its air of purity, while Joaquín had been the champion of the Seville school, flashy, showy, swaggering and given to extravagant flourishes and *adornos*. Everyone here at Sanlúcar had assumed that Joaquín Rodríguez had met his death while trying to execute one of his tricky flamboyant passes.

They had been wrong. It had not been like that at all, or Pedro would not have been so affected. He had suffered the loss of more than one of his friends to the bulls at one time or another, and even though he and Joaquín had been especially close, he was used to it.

Miguel explained.

"You see, it was an accident. The most foolish and simple kind you can imagine. That is what has shaken Pedro and everyone else who witnessed it."

An accident? Surely, thought the Duchess, every death in the ring was an accident? No bullfighter lets himself be gored deliberately. Then what was it about this particular accident that had proved so unnerving?

The Count read the puzzled expression on her face and continued.

"It was the last half of the corrida. Joaquín was on the bill with Domingo Carmona and with Pedro. Carmona led off, then Pedro, followed by Joaquín who was six months younger than Pedro. It had been a good afternoon, with bulls of Espinosa y Zapata, which are always excellent. Old Carmona, the veteran, took an ear with each of his bulls and Pedro was in great form and cut two ears with each of his. When Joaquín stepped forward to face the sixth and final bull, the spectators were looking forward to a truly exceptional ending to the day, as Joaquín had outshone even their outstanding efforts with an even more brilliant performance with his first animal. This was the Real Maestranza, after all, and Joaquín was the darling of Seville. With his first bull he had been awarded not just the ears but the hoofs and tail as well. The crowd was wild. When he dedicated the bull to the Countess of Orgiva, turning and slowly saluting the packed seats and speaking a few words, his voice was drowned out by the stamping and whistling and clapping and cheering. It sounded like thunder. All day rumors had been flying that the afternoon would end with something extraordinary. The spectators didn't know what it was, but the matadors and their crews and some of their friends did, and so did the people whose business it was to transport the bulls and keep them in the pen. They had been sworn to secrecy so as not to spoil the surprise. While he stood waiting for the bull to come out, Joaquín was smiling and positively licking his lips. Pedro and Domingo stood behind him with envious looks on their faces. Joaquín had been the lucky one, for at the sorting and the pairing he had drawn the special bull. A bull called Huérfano.

The Count broke off. He turned and faced the Duchess. Almost against her will, as her own overriding desire was to put an end to this painful affair as soon as possible, she had been drawn into the Count's recital. So were her servants hovering in the background, straining their ears to catch every word of the first-hand account of the death of the great Joaquín Rodríguez. She had to admit that Miguel told the story well, as she would expect from a man who was an intimate of *toreros*. He spoke to her with his back turned to Goya in an attitude that closely resembled contempt while the recumbent Pedro had only responded with a heave and a hiccup when the word Huérfano finally penetrated his fuddled brain.

"And then the double gates swung wide and the bull Huérfano came trotting out and took a few steps into the ring, then stopped and lifted his head and stood there majestically, gazing around proudly at the crowded stands. And the whole tremendous clamor in which the crowd had been indulging was suddenly cut off as if all the throats of the spectators had been sliced through with a gigantic stroke of a knife. At the sight of the bull, everyone froze, including the three matadors themselves."

He paused for effect.

"Tell me, Duchess, I know you will have heard of it—but have you ever actually *seen* a bull that is called a *jabonero*?"

She blinked and lifted her chin.

"I am sure you have heard of a *jabonero*, Duchess? Of course it is a very rare animal. Have you ever seen a real, a genuine *jabonero*?"

She gave a stiff reluctant nod, to signify that of course she had heard of it. She was not feeling well and seemed to be having some difficulty in thinking clearly. She seemed to remember seeing a *jabonero* in the ring several years ago. Was it at Chinchón, perhaps, or Aranjuez, or Segovia? Her head was beginning to ache.

Miguel was relishing the concentrated attention of everyone in the dining room, Pedro and Goya excepted. The latter was gazing around him, helpless and smoldering, trying to gauge the listener's reactions and glean some hint of what was going on.

"Well, Duchess, Huérfano was a *jabonero*—a soapstone, not a black bull, but one of a pale color. Sometimes they have a pinkish tinge, like a shade of peach or *melocotón*, not many are white. But Huérfano was, he was a dazzling white. The personification of white. The quintessence of white."

The Count was pleased with the Duchess's reaction. She sat upright in her seat, her back straight, her hands clasping the arms of the chair. She was staring at him with a startled expression, her mouth slightly open in a way that suggested she was not looking at him but at something an immense distance away, something lost in space and time. He stared back at her wondering what she could possibly be thinking....

White bull... White bull... White bull of her dream...

He cleared his throat. His tone became softer and quieter as if he didn't want to disturb her trance.

"The eyes of every single person in the Maestranza were fastened on that bull. For a moment there was an utter hush. And then came an extraordinary kind of concerted sob or groan. It was impossible to describe. Everyone was transfixed. When that magnificent creature began a slow trot around the ring no one moved, not even the matadors down on the sand. He circled the ring until he found his *querencia*, the place he wanted to be and had marked as his own, and he gave a little snort and stood there with his head raised. He stood there like a statue, Duchess, a statue carved out of flawless ivory. I can only repeat that he was perfection. He was everything a bull should be, from the shining points of his silvery horns to the pearly tip of his tail. A bull of bulls! If ever a bull deserved to be granted the *indulto,* the pardon, and be led from the ring, that bull was Huérfano, the bull of Espinosa y Zapata."

White bull… White bull… White bull of her dream…

Miguel had to clear his throat. He seemed subdued by the solemnity of his story as he prepared to launch into its climax.

"Nobody moved. Nobody even breathed. Joaquín remained as motionless as the rest of us as the bull made its royal progress around the ring. Huérfano did not so much as acknowledge him with a roll of the eye or a flick of the horn as he passed him, nor did he or any of his crew take a single step forward and flirt a cloth at him."

He took a long sip of his Valdepeñas.

"I managed to tear my eyes away from that majestic animal in order to take another look at Joaquín. Huérfano was his bull. He must rouse himself. He finally gathered himself together and fiddled with his cape, shaking it out and forcing himself to walk out towards the bull like a man in a daze or a sleepwalker. The bull did not move but deigned to turn its head to watch him approach. The crowd stirred and gave a collective sigh."

He took another long sip of his wine.

"None of us could account for what happened next. It all took place too fast. In a kind of blur. I remember Joaquín halting a few paces from the bull, still fiddling with the cape. The bull still watched him. Joaquín got a good grip on the cape and stepped forward, preparing to make the first pass."

The Count stopped talking. His hands were clasped in his lap and he looked down at them for a moment. He raised his head and continued.

"It is hard to describe what took place next. I doubt if anyone who was there that afternoon in the Maestranza could. It all happened in a flash. Joaquín took one or perhaps two paces forward and I think I heard him call out to the bull and stamp his foot. Then all at once he pitched sideways and I saw the cape flapping as he went down and in a second the bull was on him. What made him trip and fall? Perhaps the sand was slippery, slick with the blood of the previous five bulls. Perhaps it was uneven, carelessly raked after being dampened with water after each fight. In the first minutes of a charge a fighting bull gets off the mark quicker than a racehorse. Joaquín had just got down on one knee when a gleaming horn was in under his ribs on the left side. He had his back to me but I saw his body being lifted high into the air and suspended before it wheeled sickeningly around to the right. The horn had taken him under his heart. The glittering figure in its tobacco and gold embroidery hung onto the horn and turned there, twisting on the horn until it was flung off onto the sand. In that awful stillness we could hear a dull thump as it hit the ground."

The Duchess had leaned back weakly in her chair. She closed her eyes.

Francisco's sketchbook... The dead man slumped and slack and upside down on the horn....

She heard the Count's voice once more. "Confusion, Duchess. Stupefaction. All I can remember was Pedro coming to himself and rushing with his cloth toward the fallen man. His sword-handler acted swiftly too. He thrust out a sword and a cloth to Pedro and Pedro dropped the cape and grabbed the cloth and withdrew the sword from the leather scabbard with a hissing sound we could hear in the stands. Never have I seen a man run so fast. When he reached Joaquín I saw him pause for a second and duck down onto one knee and look at him. He told me afterwards that although blood was spurting from Joaquín's chest the wound itself was surprisingly small. The entry wound from a horn is only a small round puncture. As you know, the damage is all internal as the matador pivots on the horn. Pedro needed only a glance to know that Joaquín was dead."

The footmen and servants had been softly advancing and now stood around the Count's chair as he picked up his glass and took a sip of wine. He set the glass down again.

"Pedro then did something that only Pedro could do. He bounced back from his kneeling position and hurled himself at the bull. Once a bull has tasted blood it must be got rid of immediately, *jabonero* or not. How Pedro came up with the sword and cloth so fast I cannot fathom, but he was on Huérfano in a single movement. He didn't line the bull up with its hoofs together and its shoulder blades open, and I didn't see him aim or profile or cross with the cloth. All I saw was a crimson whirl of the cloth and the glint of the sword and Pedro flinging himself over the bloody horn and the blade plunging home. For a terrible moment I expected to see him cartwheel into the sky like Joaquín but all I saw was his arm flying up as he let go of the sword and then the *jabonero* staggered to its knees and toppled over as if it had been killed by a shot from a musket."

My bull...! My white bull!

The Duchess had not opened her eyes although the tears were coursing down her cheeks. She did not raise a hand to staunch them. It was María Luz who came forward and gently began to dab the moisture away from her mistress's eyes and cheeks. The bystanders would have thought that the Duchess, weeping, her breasts rising and falling as she strove to suppress a sob, had been overwhelmed by the tragic death of the valiant Joaquín Rodríguez.

Some of the female servants could be heard crying softly. But it was not so. The Duchess was weeping for the death of Huérfano. She was picturing the dying throes of the beautiful creature, the blood streaming from its mouth, sullying its white shining breast, seeping around the hilt of the sword buried in its neck and soiling the snowy flesh. It seemed to her that in some unfathomable way, something precious, something vital, something that was Cayetana de Alba herself, was ebbing away with the blood of the stricken beast.

She sat there, her eyes closed, locked in with her vision of wounds and whiteness. She did not know how long it was before she seemed to hear Miguel's voice from far away echoing in the hushed and shadowed hall.

"Then everybody came to life simultaneously. A score of men began to sprint towards—"

The Count's monologue was suddenly interrupted by a tremendous crash.

Pedro's glass had fallen from his hand and smashed on the floor. No one had been taking any notice of him as he slouched on his chair, occasionally nodding and muttering to himself. Jolted into action by the noise, he suddenly stepped onto his chair and with a single bound landed on the table before everyone's astonished eyes. One moment he was drooping and palsied and the next straight-backed and towering over them, his eyes bright and brimming with excitement. In one swift movement he stooped to snatch up a damask napkin and began to use it in imaginary combat with a phantom bull, perhaps the *jabonero* of the Count's recent tale.

They all gazed at him in astonishment as he began to caper up and down the dining table, citing with the napkin, stamping his feet, flapping the makeshift cloth and uttering imperious cries of "*Toro! Toro! Toro!*"

He was swaying slightly, coming perilously close to the edge of the table before righting himself. Then, given his condition, he proceeded to give a masterly imitation of the fighting styles and mannerisms of the aforementioned two matadors.

First he impersonated old Vincente Carmona. In a wicked parody he went mincing up and down the table, making a series of finicking passes and rounding them off with one of the elderly matador's favorite tricks—waiting until the animal was thoroughly bemused and exhausted and then sinking down on an arthritic knee to kiss its muzzle.

Then it was the turn of Joaquín Rodríguez. A gem of affectionate mockery, an ironic illustration of the clever way in which Joaquín used to hoodwink the crowd with a smooth successions of showy passes that actually looked more hazardous than they really were.

At this point Goya suddenly came alive. Excluded by his deafness from the earlier verbal part of the proceedings, he was now aroused at the sight of Pedro's lively performance and broke the silence by loudly clapping his hands in appreciation. He had obviously recognized Pedro's clever simulation of the individual styles of Carmona and Rodríguez and was delighted. He pulled one of the candelabra towards him, arranging its light to suit him, picked up a pencil, opened his sketchbook and began to make rapid impressions of Pedro's droll performance.

Pedro had definitely relieved the tension. Miguel was now laughing, María Luz giggling and even Carulli had began tapping together the fingertips of his white-gloved hands. The clapping was taken up by some of the servants and then by others, and after a while even the Duchess relaxed a little and lay back in her chair, glad to see Francisco was finally unbending and that he had dragged his prolonged flinty gaze away from the Count. He was tracing his lines freely and lightly across the pages of his book, working rapidly in order to capture the cunning details of Pedro's little pantomime. The act of drawing seemed to unfreeze him, to rid him of the vestiges of the lethargy that had gripped him since his recent collapse into despair.

The Duchess, as always, was fascinated by the way his hand sped so surely across the paper, dashing off a delicate line here or a thick bold line there. She knew from the many times she had watched him drawing how the lines he was making would be spaced out in an apparently meaningless fashion until some quick stroke with the pencil or dexterous smear with the thumb or forefinger would fuse them together and make the whole conception leap off the page. She never lost her amazement at the wizardry of it. There was something of the magician about it, sometimes a benevolent magic, sometimes a malevolent one, with shapes like his *garabatos* on the whitewashed wall outside the chapel being conjured out of nothing, plucked out of the air, merging into each other so that what looked as if it could have been a bull might, with a slash of his pencil, turn out to be a boulder, a tree, a star, a giant or a bowl of flowers. She guessed that these undulations of his hand would now be conjuring into existence the whole panoply of the bullfight. She could see his lips pursed in his familiar way as he worked. And when the noise in the hall quietened from time to time she fancied she could hear his soft melodious whistle. With a catch in her throat she asked herself what scrap of song it was. Was it the song she had heard in her first happy dream, the dream in which her heart first melted?

> *Guadalquivir*
> *Beautiful river*
> *White ships sailing*
> *Branches of green*

Watching him and feeling again a threat of tears, she realized that in some uncanny way he was recapturing each step of the drama of Joaquín's death as Pedro, his movements now more solemn, began to enact it. She searched Goya's face, her mind in a turmoil, fervently wishing he would raise his eyes to hers. Surely, if he could forgive her over the incident of the dog, he could forgive her over the presence of Miguel? But no, Goya looked only at the matador, now performing his fantastic dance on the table, the black eyes flicking up and down again at the paper with the withdrawn and almost nonchalant concentration of the artist, seemingly scarcely conscious of the markings his hand was making on the page.

She shut her eyes and lowered her head, giving up the hope that he would look at her. She was suddenly filled with a violent sense of pity—for herself, for Francisco, for the white bull. She had a strange hollow feeling of being outside herself, of being apart from all the hurly-burly. A sharp salty taste rose from her gullet.

If only Francisco would look at her! But what was Pedro doing now? And what was Miguel saying? Why had the clapping and laughter and the encouraging cries of the servants stopped?

Pedro was no longer prancing and gyrating but was now mimicking the moment when Joaquín Rodríguez was approaching the *jabonero* and adjusting his cape. Pedro dipped sideways, and fluttering the napkin in his hand, he slipped on the polished table with everyone gasping as he mimed the bull charging at his unshielded body. Then with a dazzling balletic move he seemed to soar into the air and hang there for a moment before pitching back onto the table.

Then, inspired by a remarkable flight of fancy, he surpassed himself. Flat on his back on the polished surface, limbs spread-eagled, he slid with an incredible swiftness and smoothness along the whole length of the long table, scattering glass and silverware as he went. He propelled himself along by gripping the edges of the table with his fingertips and levering his body with his arms like a man in a rowboat, all done so expertly that the onlookers could only marvel. Not content with this feat, he lay inert and seemingly lifeless for a few seconds and then suddenly hunched himself and shot back again to the head of the table. He paused a further few seconds and concluded the performance by straightening out his limbs and projecting himself backwards in a prodigious back-flip like a circus acrobat, finally landing on his feet beside his chair.

The clapping was now renewed and Pedro, sobered by his reenactment of the death of his friend, acknowledged the applause with a slight inclination of his head and then, seemingly exhausted, flopped back into his chair. When a servant stepped forward to refill his glass, he dismissed him with a curt wave of his hand.

Goya had not joined in the applause, still busy with his sketchbook. The Duchess too had not participated, feeling it was time to assert her authority and put an end to this interminable and strange evening. She needed to regain the sanctuary of her bedchamber. She felt unwell and needed to regain control of the conflicting emotions now sweeping over her. She felt stifled by a sensation of grief, a sensation of piercing sorrows, of profounder and more imminent deaths, the death of joy and hope, of a love that seemed minute by minute to be ineluctably seeping away.

She rose, looking around for her butler and preparing to issue orders for the company to disband. She was startled to feel a hand steal out and catch her left hand in an iron grip She caught her breath. She did not look down. She tried to give the offending hand a vigorous shake to discreetly free herself without alerting everyone's attention. Fortunately the Count had at least had enough good sense to grab the Duchess's hand under the table where it couldn't be seen. She forced a smile and gave her hand an even more vigorous shake but the Count's grip became even more proprietary. When she risked glancing down at him she saw he was smiling. But not at her. His mocking smile was directed at Goya. He lifted the Duchess's hand slightly and then dropped it ostentatiously, making sure Goya had got a clear sight of it.

Again the Duchess sought to loosen the Count's fingers. Again they tightened around her wrist. She looked over at Goya giving a little helpless shake of her head, half appeal, half apology. She was uncertain whether she wanted Goya's help, or whether she was afraid of it. The pistol, the tearing up of the letters, the knife, the smashing of the guitar and the miniature all came swimming into her mind. Would he come storming around the table, trying to knock his rival down? She gave another supplicatory shake of her head. At the very least she was trying to convey her surprise and disgust at the behavior of the man beside her. Yet she was indignant to see Goya just sitting there regarding this play between her and the Count and remaining so impassive and aloof.

Trembling she allowed Miguel to draw her back into her seat again. She stared at Goya uncomprehendingly. Did he feel nothing after what they had meant to each other? Was he deliberately choosing to misunderstand? Miguel was now smirking and was obviously very pleased with himself. The Duchess felt that if she were in better control of her emotions and could summon up sufficient strength, she would have liked to have slapped his silly face....

What was Francisco doing now? Why had he pushed his pencils and crayons aside? Why was he tearing pages out of his sketchbook? He was placing several pages on the table in front of Pedro, at the same time giving him a friendly pat on the back. Pedro had slipped into his earlier torpid condition and did not react.

Goya ripped out another sheaf of papers, glanced at them briefly, and then with a little flip of his wrist, he sent them skimming along the polished surface of the table towards the Count and the Duchess. They skidded and struck the Count's embroidered sleeve and then dropped into his lap. He had to disengage the Duchess's hand to stop them falling onto onto the floor. The Count shuffled them together, shrugged his shoulders and shot Goya an indulgent and contemptuous smile. He laid the sketches out on the table in front of him. The Duchess, anxious now and trembling, leaned over the Count's shoulder to look at them.

There were three sketches. The Count inspected them piece by piece.

The first was of the Count. At first glance the sketch looked unexceptional. It depicted an outstandingly handsome, indeed a beautiful young man, leaning back in his chair with his limbs disposed in an elegant pose. His golden ringlets, highlighted in yellow crayon, flowed down over the shoulders of his stylish jacket. The Duchess peered closer. It seemed the young man seemed far too beautiful, his relaxed pose affable but bordering on the effete. The portrait was the speaking likeness of that glistening snake whose image had flashed through her mind a few minutes ago.

Miguel had finished with the first sketch and slid it under the next. The Duchess saw it was a portrait of her. For a moment she swayed, hesitant and fearful. It took a moment before she could bring herself to peer at it again, afraid she would see a subtle caricature, like the sketch of Miguel. She felt relief. There was nothing satirical in the image of the woman shown head and shoulders in the drawing. This woman was beautiful, irrefutably exquisite, a woman of delicate loveliness. It brought the tears to her eyes and she looked over at Goya who was busy gathering up his materials and shutting his sketchbook. She wanted so badly to tell him how touched she was, how overwhelmed by pride and gratitude. She was too overwhelmed to take in the third drawing Miguel was now placing on top of the pile.

It was a brutal awakening.

Miguel had reached across to bring one of the candles closer in order to view it more clearly. She saw a full length double portrait of her and the Count. If Miguel had failed to see the satire of the first sketch of him, he could hardly fail to do so now. He had regarded the first image with a complacent smile, preening himself and tilting himself back in his chair so as to better admire it.

The Count stared and then brought his chair up with a bang. The Duchess cowered in her seat.

Goya had depicted the Count as how he might appear in another ten or fifteen years—balding, his features swollen and puffy, the golden years long past. He was sitting at a card table, a losing hand of cards scattered in disorder on the baize table in front of him, the top button of his trousers loosened over his bloated belly, his pockets inside out to show they were empty of money. On his fat and pendulous face was a foolish simper, and his blubbery body and fleshy features bore an unmistakable resemblance to one of the hogs the Duchess had seen repeatedly depicted in his sketchbooks.

But more merciless and cruel was the drawing of the Duchess.

She and the Count were depicted as a hideous couple, a truly gruesome pair. Goya had drawn her sitting beside Miguel at the gaming table, gazing up adoringly into his piggy face with an arm linked through his. He had not made her porcine but had done something even worse. He had turned her into one of his ill-favored witches, withered and scrawny to the point of emaciation. More horrible still, not only had he portrayed her as a witch, but she seemed to bear a distinct resemblance to the woman she most feared and detested, Queen María Luisa. She gazed with horror at the image of the middle-aged wreck of a couple, the Count as vacuous and self-centered as the King, the Duchess as chop-fallen and as repulsive as María Luisa, embracing her swinish consort with a stick-like arm.

She sat rigid, unable to move.

Even the vainglorious Count had caught the artist's drift. He rose very slowly and very deliberately to his feet. He bent forward and picked up the nearest decanter and filled his wine glass to the brim. He stared at Goya, raising the glass as if in a toast.

Goya too had risen. He stood staring back at the Count with the same stony expression he had worn all night.

The Count, without taking his eyes from Goya, pushed the drawings away from him. He tilted his glass. He tipped it over and poured the wine over the drawings.

Goya's expression did not change.

The Count took up the crystal decanter and again filled his glass. Again he tilted it. A rush of scarlet liquid poured onto the table engulfing Goya and the sketchbook and the artist's materials lying on the table around it.

Goya showed no reaction. He calmly lifted the sketchbook out of the crimson pool and gave it a shake. His eyes never wavered from the Count's face as he gave him a long and ceremonious bow.

A hush had descended on the hall. The servants stood rapt, dumfounded by the scene being played out at the table.

Goya turned to the Duchess and bowed again, slowly, bowing ever lower. The Duchess lifted a tremulous hand to her mouth. She felt herself growing pale, and paler still. As pale and white as the poor *jabonero*. She felt as if the sword that had killed Huérfano had been thrust straight through her heart too.

Then he turned, ignoring the wine-soaked mess on the table in front of him. He tucked his wine-soaked sketchbook beneath his arm and, thrusting back his shoulders, he began to cleave his way through the crowd of agitated servants.

In the silence, the Duchess gave out an anguished little cry.

Goya would not have heard it. He would not have heard it, nor would he have seen the Duchess lay her head on the table and begin to weep.

Nor did he see the flow of blood that surged from her throat and spread in a scarlet flood across the table, mingling with the crimson pool of wine.

For Goya was gone.

A CAVALCADE OF three coaches lumbered through the straggle of the suburbs and entered the huddle of narrow streets that would bring it to the heart of the city. With many halts and wrong turns it made its way through the rain and darkness towards its goal in the Street of Disillusion.

Número Uno, Calle del Desengaño. Or what could be seen of it, that is, as the untidy procession swayed and bumped around the last corner and drew to a halt outside the dark and forbidding building at the end of the row. The only light that came trickling through the murk was the watery glow of candles from the windows of the few houses whose inhabitants had not yet gone to bed, together with the sputtering illumination of the street lamps which stank and smoldered and gave off a continuous oily smell and a drift of sticky flakes.

The leading coach creaked to a halt and the others bunched up behind it. The horses were exhausted. They stood inert. They no longer had the strength to raise their drooping heads or stamp their hoofs. The rain streamed off their matted manes and clotted flanks. A coating of mud clung to their legs and bellies from their four-day journey from Andalucía. It clung to the hats and cloaks of the drivers and grooms whose task it was to ride on the outside of the coaches. Men, animals and vehicles, all were plastered with the muck of the roads. The coat of arms painted on the doors of the large coach at the head of the line were obliterated. For the moment the doors of all three coaches remained shut. The coachmen were too stiff to stumble to the ground. They sat motionless, chilled to the bone.

After a numbed interval, the coachman on the box of the leading coach succeeded in summoning up enough energy to lower himself to the ground and stood leaning against the wheel. It is due to the exertions of this small wiry man that the caravan has reached its destination. For four full days he had flogged it on for eight to ten hours at a stretch, taking advantage of every minute of the short winter day, refusing to be deterred by the need to change a broken wheel or mend a snapped harness or fix a splintered axle. He had dragged fallen horses back on their feet, tugged them out of ditches, coaxed them across frozen puddles. It was his unflagging zeal that had brought them up the Avenida de Portugal and the Calle de Extremadura to the Calle Mayor, then past the Puerta del Sol for a final push into the tangle of streets leading to the Calle del Desengaño.

He braced himself and stood swaying on the slick cobblestones as if on the heaving deck of a ship. He took a deep breath and started to bellow in a resonant bass that seemed startling for so small a man:

"*Leap to it! All out! Look lively! Stir yourselves!*"

His voice acted on the sleepy occupants of the coaches like the call of a trumpet. Doors of coaches slowly opened. Servants began to pour out into the street and stand dazed, knuckling their eyes. Grooms toppled off their boxes and tottered about, lunging for the heads of the horses as the roaring of the little coachman roused them from their torpor and set the harnesses jingling.

There was an exception to the general bustle. There was no sign of life from the large coach. It remained still and silent. Servants ran to let down the steps but in spite of the stir and hustle the door stayed obstinately closed.

The servants milled around in the roadway, trying to dodge the filthy streams that spilled over from the gutters. Some of them attempted to light torches which were immediately extinguished by the rain. The gutters swirled with the muck of the capital, where the trash was thrown into the common drain. Dead cats, the contents of chamber pots, the offal from fruit and vegetable stalls and butcher shops came flooding down. Accustomed to clean sweet air after their weeks in the country, the servants held their noses to ward off the stench.

The chaos was brought to an end by an appearance at the door of the second coach of a middle-aged man, lean and of only moderate height but of an obvious authority and commanding manner. This person of consequence was still fresh looking in spite of the long and fatiguing journey, immaculate in a livery of gold braid and bottle green. His wig beneath the three-cornered hat was neatly combed and powdered. He stood at the door of the coach donning a pair of white gloves and then, with a flick of his ebony silver-mounted cane, he motioned for a servant to hurry forward with a capacious oiled silk umbrella. Only then did he fully descend from the coach, directing the bearer of the umbrella to keep his person well covered. He paused for a moment at the edge of the gutter, then stepped across it fastidiously in his white knee breeches and soft leather pumps with silver buckles. With careful deliberation he ascended the three steps leading to the massive front door. He halted and rapped in a slow and ceremonious manner on the panels with the silver-headed handle of his cane.

No answer. He rapped again. No answer. He rapped a third time. Still no response.

He shrugged, turned, and descended the steps, signaling to the servant with the umbrella to hold it closer to him. He picked his way back across the gutter and approached the large coach emblazoned with the coat of arms. Its iron steps were still raised. The handle of the door was above the level of his head so it was necessary for him to reach up in order to give a respectful tap on the window with his cane.

At once the window lowered as if the occupants of the coach had been waiting for his signal. The bare head of a young woman emerged from the window. When she leaned out she felt the full force of the rain and ducked her head back in, poking it out again after swathing herself in a woolen scarf. She was a pretty woman, her black skin indicating her African origin. Most of the people gathered in their nightshirts or in various stages of undress watching the scene from the windows of their houses or the shelter of their doorways were familiar with her appearance. They had often seen the young black woman accompanying her mistress through the streets of the capital and her appearance suggested that the principal occupant of the carriage standing in the street may be no other than the beautiful and beguiling Duchess of Alba.

The African woman and the man with the cane exchanged words. The spectators who were close enough heard the man speaking in a foreign accent. Some thought it might be Portuguese or French but others recognized it as Italian. The girl hesitated for a moment and then pulled her head back into the carriage. The man stepped back under the protection of the umbrella, the holder of which was now thoroughly drenched. He flicked a drop of rain from the gold braid on the front of his jacket.

A ripple of excitement went through the crowd as the African woman made ready to leave the coach. A groom ran forward to lower the steps and the woman turned around and descended backwards, quick and nimble. Another umbrella was quickly brought forward and she stationed herself at the bottom of the steps plucking at her scarf and looking up anxiously at the open door of the coach. She lifted her arms in a supplicatory manner towards the top of the steps, concerned for the safety of the woman who now appeared.

When it caught sight of her, the crowd uttered another louder murmur. The leading actress in this nocturnal drama was about to make her entrance. Although the woman's face was heavily veiled, they could tell from her bearing that it was indeed the Duchess of Alba. The throng who had now advanced into the street craned forward. The man in the green livery gestured with his cane and the servants formed a barrier around the coach. The whole scene had suddenly brightened, thanks to the lighting of additional lanterns. It was as if footlights had been turned up to lighten the effect. And indeed there was something of the classical heroine about the woman who now stepped onto the topmost step of the carriage.

The jostling ceased. The chatter died away. The crowd stood quiet. The leathery little groom wrestled with his horses and hushed them. The dapper man in the green and gold drew himself up and called for silence by striking the ground with his cane. The African woman stood like a statue, her arms still raised.

The woman in the door of the coach was not aware of any of this. She was conscious only of the house across the street, stony and lightless. She was clad in black from head to toe. The black dress added to the impression of the tragic heroine. With a deliberate movement she drew aside the black scarf and the traveling mask that covered her mouth and throat. She raised a black handkerchief to her mouth, her lungs assailed by the rank fumes of the smoldering street lamps. She stooped a little and a cough could clearly be heard echoing off the flinty façade of the house across the street.

She straightened. The crowd noted the pallor of her face, the blanched face of a woman not as young as the African woman but not so many years older. She stood upright, looking very fragile in the sulky glare of the lanterns.

The lanterns lifted as she descended from the carriage. She moved slowly, the handkerchief pressed to her lips, holding her black skirt away from her body. The African woman gave a little cry and ran forward with her arms extended. A pair of servants darted forward opening their umbrellas. She was heedless of the swollen gutters, or the rain that was already saturating her clothing and dripping from her cheeks and forehead, from her shoulders and her gleaming black hair.

Looking neither to left or right but directly ahead she made her way between the line of servants who were linking their arms to provide her with passage. She moved like a sleepwalker unaware of anything but the wide dark doorway of the silent house ahead of her. It seemed to draw her to it. Only when the man in the green livery stepped forward, bobbing and bowing, did she become conscious of the presence of another person. With a fulsome gesture he offered her his arm to lean on. She turned her head momentarily and threw him a glare of unmistakable scorn and dislike. Abruptly she shook him away.

She mounted the three steps leading to the door, her chin raised and her shoulders rigid. She looked like a queen mounting a scaffold.

She reached the door.

Did she not realize the house might be empty? Why was she raising a small fist to knock on the thick panels of the door? Or if the house were not occupied, did she imagine that its owner was lurking within its shrouded depths? Did she believe that if the rapping of the silver-mounted cane produced no answer, that the tapping of her little hand could be heard?

She could not accept that the house was locked and barred against her. She lowered her head and placed a cheek against the cold wet oak surface of the door.

She called out.

"*Francisco.*"

She pressed her palm against the door.

"*Francisco.*"

The crowd shuffled forward to eavesdrop and was held back by the servants, wondering why she was calling out to a man whom they all knew to be deaf. And why was she calling in such a low and broken voice as if she couldn't help herself?

"*Francisco!*"

Such a distance and so many days to arrive at the dead of night and in the rain to find this house deserted....

María Luz and two or three of the servants who were huddled under umbrellas and who were closest to her watched as she slowly and painfully straightened her back. Although her back was towards them they could see her hand as it reached in to the bosom of the black dress and took out an object which she held for a moment in her hand.

María Luz, peering sideways, saw it was a letter, a letter much dampened by the rain, the inscription blurred and streaked.

There was no aperture in the door through which to put it. The woman's hand wavered. Then María Luz saw her work it into the space between the door and the jamb and wedge it there as firmly as her strength permitted.

"*Francisco!*"

A whisper this time.

She swayed and tottered. With a cry María Luz ran up the steps towards her. She took the woman in her arms and turned her and led her gently back towards the coach.

She let herself be led. The crowd and servants fell back. Then, at the foot of the step of the carriage, she halted. She removed the black girl's encircling arm.

The Duchess of Alba mounted the steps and entered her coach.

The grooms and servants quickly took their places.

The weary horses started up and the little cavalcade moved off, away from the Calle del Desengaño and towards the Alba palace at Moncloa.

The crowd broke up and slowly drifted away. The householders returned to their houses. The letter stuck in the side of the door remained there unnoticed until the owner of the house next door, clad in a nightshirt and nightcap, caught sight of the pale square of damp paper hanging precariously from the crack in the door.

Consumed with curiosity, he gave a stealthy glance around, made sure that the street was rapidly emptying, stalked up the steps and put out a hand to take it.

As he did so the door swung abruptly open. The letter fell to the ground. He was dealt a violent shove in the chest. Staggering down the steps, he scampered as fast as his legs would carry him into the safety of his house, banging the door behind him.

A dark broad-shouldered figure in shirt sleeves stood in the shrouded doorway. He stepped onto the top step and looked up the road in the direction in which the Duchess's coach had disappeared.

A large stray dog with a matted coat trotted down the street towards him, sidled up the steps, and sniffed at the fallen letter with a blunt snout. The man bent down as if to stroke the dog and pull its ears, seeming to want to give it shelter, but the big dog took fright and trotted away and disappeared around the corner.

The man straightened up, preparing to retire inside and close the door when he saw the letter.

His paint-smeared hand reached down and picked it up.

...AND SO TONIGHT, *six years later, laying down his palette and brush, he wanders across his studio to a table on which lies an untidy stack of letters. There must be a score of them. He shuffles them together and takes them up and flips through them with his thumb. They are all unopened. He throws the stack down, then hesitates and picks one out at random. He turns it over, starts to slit it open with a thumbnail, then shrugs and lets it fall back onto the table with the others.*

His mood is as distracted tonight as it was that night in Sanlúcar six years ago. He moves to a chest of drawers and blows again on his cold cramped mittened fingers and pours himself another glass of aguardiente *and tosses it back. The raw taste burns his throat. He chokes a little. This morning he has been brought the news of the death of Cayetana de Alba. His assistant, Asensio Juliá, has come running up the stairs, seized the notebook in which he writes his messages for his employer, who still has not mastered the art of lip reading, and scrawled down a single sentence. The young man shrinks back, staring with a kind of terror at the expression on his master's face as he reads the message, then spins around and flees downstairs and out of the door and away from the house.*

Cayetana. Dead. Last night at Buenavista. The notebook drops to the floor. It will not be until the afternoon of the next day that he will emerge from the house and walk to the local coffee house to read the newspapers. There in a corner, among the nods and nudges and knowing whispers coming from the other tables, he will soak up the rumors and innuendoes that are circulating around the capital. The papers will hint that the Duchess had been poisoned by the Queen who, with the Prince of Peace, has lost no time in seizing the Duchess's jewels and paintings. Her death, the journalists intimate, was long-drawn-out and agonizing. He will throw down the newspapers and with a stony look on his face stalk out of the coffee house, ignoring the sidelong smiles and smirks of his fellow coffee drinkers.

But tonight he goes back to the chest of drawers and pours himself another glass of aguardiente. *Several times in the past months he had galloped in his carriage past the site of her unfinished palace of Buenavista, noting its grandiose size and its opulent extravagance. For some years now the Duchess had been giving way increasingly to excess and lack of restraint. Her behaviour had been growing steadily more careless, her costumes more outlandish, the paint on her face more garish. Her reckless expenditures on Buenavista and her other palaces and follies had drained even the deep purse of the Albas.*

All this he knows. All this he sees for himself. From time to time their paths have crossed, at court or when he had been working at some great house where she had been a guest. Conscious of the gossip and tittle-tattle about their intimacy during those few short weeks at Sanlúcar, they merely exchanged brief looks and went about their separate ways. It would not have been politic for either of them to have made the details of their intimacy more public than they already were. Yet those brief looks had been filled by them both with questioning and with reproach, with sudden and swiftly supressed flares of hurt and anger, with a baffled hint of something like regret. And how, hurrying past her in some passageway, could he fail to notice how pale and fragile she seemed, how she moved increasingly slowly, increasingly painfully, her features ever more pinched and drawn? Once he had turned a corner into one of the larger reception rooms and come upon her where she sat slumped, her eyes closed, on a padded bench, as if her duties as the Queen's lady-in-waiting had thoroughly exhausted her. Another time he had entered a small antechamber and found her leaning back against a wall, her eyes shut and a handkerchief soaked in cologne pressed to her temples, her head resting on María Luz's shoulder. What an expression of silent reproof, even contempt, there had been in the dark eyes of the Arab woman as they followed him as he strode quickly by! Yes, it was not as if he had not had plenty of opportunities to see how ill she had become, but he had choked down any pity or concern. The bitter memory of that last evening at Sanlúcar had still proved too strong. He had hardened his heart, and passed on.

And yet, even so, in all these years her letters had never ceased to arrive. They had been furtively handed to him in the most unlikely places by Esteban and, after the old coachman's death, by Pascual. He has found them slipped into the pockets of his jacket while he was busy working at court, probably by María Luz. He would have liked to have stopped to talk to Esteban or Pascual, his comrades on the wild ride where he had lost Baltasar. But the two men, obeying their orders, had simply pushed the letters into his hand and hurried past. María Luz had done the same, thrusting a letter at him before ducking her dark head and hastening on, her eyes brimming with perplexity and silent rebuke. This would strike him to the heart, filling him with a fierce sense of injury and indignation. Each letter has been summarily dismissed, tossed on the heap with the rest. Yet, as he stands there in his darkened studio, gulping down his brandy and poking the letters about with frozen fingers, he has to ask himself why he has never destroyed them, why he has not torn them to pieces as he had long ago torn up the letters of Miguel de Altolaguirre?

More aguardiente. *Another cigar. Why not? She had not liked him drinking and had wrinkled her nose up at his cigars. How finicky that woman could prove herself at times! He pours another glass of the* aguardiente, *a much larger one, and selects another cigar, lighting it from one of the candles and puffing out a long defiant stream of smoke.*

He feels himself shivering in spite of the thick padding of his overcoat and the woolen scarf wound tightly around his neck and chest. He stamps and shuffles his numbed feet. It must be chillier tonight than he thought. He must try not to keep himself cooped up in his house and studio so much. Both Doctor Arrieta and Doctor Bonells have advised him that he must get out more into the fresh air.

Another shiver. The atmosphere in the studio is growing ever more stale and oppressive. He misses Josefa. He misses Javier. He misses the familiar commotion of the servants who have gone to Zaragoza to escape the threat of yet another outbreak of yellow fever. Josefa, bless her kind soul, had not wanted to leave him. He had insisted. How could he risk the death of his wife and son? Thank God, if God there be, that one son, at least, had been spared to him....

Carrying his glass of aguardiente *and smoking his cigar, he wanders* back to his easel and thinks half-heartedly about resuming work. Work. Work. There is always work. He tries to drive from his mind all thoughts of Cayetana and the summer days at Sanlúcar. As he won't accept that he missed Cayetana, he cannot admit that he misses all of that lively company. What will happen to that happy band of men and women he remembered from the servants' hall now that the Alba household is destined to be broken up? The Neapolitan queen won't lose any time in turning them out. María Luz and her daughter, where will they go? Will they find some ship to carry them back to Africa? May God be good to them all....

He turns away from his easel and approaches a small table on which stands a tall stack of his sketchbooks. He lays down his glass and his cigar and locates a particular sketchbook and eases it out of the stack. Even though he has resolved to put all this behind him, surely he can be permitted one final sentimental moment? He moves the book closer to the candles and begins to turn the pages. Yes, there they are. There are the pretty wenches, disporting themselves in the stream and hanging out the washing. There they are. There are the grooms currying the horses and polishing the harnesses. There are the whole of the lighthearted throng, dancing and singing and playing their instruments on the bank of the little river with the herd of bulls grazing on the bank beyond. Lightly he runs a tip of a finger over the surface of the pages. He sighs.

But then he scowls, fluttering through the next dozen pages rapidly. Those he doesn't want to look at. This is the place in the book where he ripped out the three drawings he made during the course of that mad dinner where Pepe Romero capered on the table and the Count de Altolaguirre chose to mock him, the drawings that he sent skittering down the table. He runs a nail along the ragged edges in the spine where the pages are missing, feeling the bile surging in his throat, like the blood that had come flooding, he had been told, from the mouth of Cayetana.

But how can he resist? How can he stop himself from turning back with cold and clammy fingers to those pages in the sketchbook he had hurried past? He closes his eyes, seized with a sudden stab of pain. For there she is. There is his Duchess, his Cayetana. An atrocious death, *tomorrow's newspapers will say—but here tonight in his drawings she is still alive and entirely beautiful. In this sketch she is being divested by María Luz of her orange blouse and black lace skirt. In another she is standing beside her dressing table in her petticoat, awaiting his breathless arrival from the music room. And here she is in a silken wrapper, beckoning to him as he slips into her bedchamber. And this one? In this one she stands turning her head and smiling over her shoulder, hoisting up her petticoats with the provocative gesture of a true* maja *to reveal her bare backside.*

He presses down hard on the next page with the flat of his hand. He lets a long minute pass before he removes it and looks down.

Cayetana in the full glory of her nakedness, offering herself frankly and without affectation. Not the Duchess of Alba. A woman, simply.

Again he turns a page and conceals it with his hand. Another long moment. He uncovers it.

Cayetana naked on the bed, her disheveled hair hanging in a thick braid down her back.

Slowly and gently he closes the sketchbook and lays it softly down on top of the pile. Beside the sketchbooks lies a thick folio, its boards bound with black ribbon. He frowns and hesitates, pinching his lip, then unties the ribbon.

The folder contains several dozen aquatints printed on copper plates, a series on which he embarked soon after his departure from Andalucía. The preliminary sketches for many of them were already in the sketchbooks that so dismayed Cayetana when she happened upon them that first morning in the music room at Sanlúcar. These are the plates of his Caprichos, his whims and fancies, dredged from the darkest corner of a darkening mind.

He leafs through them. Yes, here are the so-called perversions, together with the whole panoply of demons that wing their way nightly through his dreams. And witches. Witches. Plate after plate of witches. And why not? Since childhood, since babyhood, since his days in the cradle, he has been haunted and hunted by witches. His mother, his grandmother, all his aunts have stuffed him full of tales of the witches that swarmed around the houses in the village and teemed in the countryside around it. Hasn't he always had to take precautions? Hasn't he always had to guard himself against these carriers of contagion who, since his illness in Cádiz, have taken advantage of his deafness to throng ever more closely around him, defying his efforts to beat them off? Can't he feel them now, at this moment, sneaking around outside the house, pressing their faces against the window panes and leering at him? They are always there. Why were the people at Cádiz and Sanlúcar so alarmed and surprised when he tried to scare them away and protect them all by firing his pistol and his hunting gun out of the windows? Didn't they understand? Didn't any of them notice the words written at the bottom of one of the plates? **Where is this infernal swarm heading, howling through the shadows of the night? By day you can bring them down with a single gun shot, but by night it is a different story.** *He shudders and casts a fearful glance at the windows of the studio and reaches for his drink. No use. Gunshot or no gunshot, they will never let him be. What better victim can they find to torment than a wretched man who is deaf? What can he do but try to use his brush and his burin as weapons to hold them at bay and try to warn the world about them? Yet what good will it do? The forces of evil have been hovering around him since he was a helpless infant, fluttering around mankind since the beginning of the world. How can he use his poor gifts except to render them more visible...?*

Ah yes, but what about that most malevolent class of witches, the most dangerous, those witches that come in the prettiest guises? He starts to flip through the plates. Take this one. Take this beautiful maja *with her streaming mane of black hair. Whom does she resemble? Whom does she bring to mind? Surely the words at the foot of the page make it crystal clear?* **Ah, what bitterness and heartache afflicts the man who comes anywhere near her!** *And what about this one, this pretty* maja *smiling behind her mask, surrounded by a mob of men who are clowns and harlequins?* **The world is a masquerade. The faces and the costumes and the voices, all of them are false.** *Or this one.* **It had to happen. It couldn't have ended in any other way.**

Bitterness and heartache. Oh how he felt them then, oh, how he feels them now, keeping his vigil on the night after her death. He starts to close the folio. He hesitates. One other plate. One he doesn't want to look at. One he has been deliberately avoiding. Yet look at it he must, his fingers shaking as he turns the pages. He had placed it near the end, though it was the first one that he executed and the one that cost him the most pain.

He moves the candles on the table further back. With a trembling fingernail he scores a line beneath a single word at the bottom of the picture. **Volaverunt.** *The only title in the entire collection that is not in Spanish, as if its significance is too solemn and too poignant to be entrusted to his native tongue.*

Volaverunt.

They have flown away.

The light from the candles flickers over the page giving the figure in the center the sensation of flying.

His Maja. *His Duchess. His Cayetana. Flying. Flying away.*

He takes a candlestick and moves it backwards and forwards over the page.

Flying… Flying….

He moves the candle closer to read the inscription:

This band of witches provides a pedestal for our charmer, though serving for ornament rather than for use. In fact the heads of these witches are so inflated with gas that it requires neither balloons nor witches to enable her to fly.

Gasbags. Windbags. Three male witches hovering with daft grins on their ugly visages, witches who can readily be recognized as being the three leading toreros in Spain. These gasbags like hotter-than-air balloons, floating on fighting capes inflated with their own wind. How they gape and how they strain, their bullfighter's pigtail sticking out in the empty air behind them.

Costillares. Pepe-Hillo. Pedro Romero. Looking down at them he can't help feeling a little regretful, now, at having portrayed them in this way, since Costillares and Pepe-Hillo have both died since he engraved the plate. At least old Costillares died peaceably in his bed, whereas Pepe-Hillo, who used to boast of his twenty-five gorings, was snuffed out in the prime of life by a bull of Peñaranda in the ring here at Madrid. Still, it had been exasperating to see them lolling back on the cushions of Cayetana's carriage, watching them preen their silly selves and pretending to be her lovers. He had picked up his burin and used it like a banderilla to skewer them. Yet all the same, staring down at his parody of Pedro Romero's handsome features, the lips and the jaw thrust out in the way they'd been thrust out that night when he had been strutting around on Cayetana's dining table, he can't help feeling a pang of regret. After all, Pedro had tried to make amends for clowning around. Only a week or two later he had turned up here in his studio with an apologetic grin on his face and had apologised for his and the Count's behavior. He wouldn't for the world have intended to offend a person as distinguished as Don Francisco! Would he be allowed to make amends by commissioning Don Francisco to paint his portrait, for which he would pay any fee that Don Francisco would be pleased to accept? How had it been possible to resist that famous charm? Of course Don Francisco would paint Pedro Romero's portrait. And of course there would be no mention of a fee.

Yet what of Pedro's insufferable comrade, the Count of Altolaguirre? What news of the egregious Miguel, during the course of these intervening years? A pleasure to reflect that, where the Count is concerned, matters have not gone well. They may even be said to have gone from bad to worse. Unlike Pedro's, the Count's fortunes have gone steadily downhill. Drinking and dissipation have bloated his face and thickened his body. They have thinned his fair hair and reddened the veins in the blue eyes. Gambling has eaten up the revenues from those barren estates in distant Galicia. Bankrupt and discredited, his features sallowed by his damaged liver, he is still occasionally to be seen creeping about the fringes of the court, trying to touch for a loan spongers and scroungers as disreputable as himself. And it is an additional satisfaction to know that he is now habitually accompanied by that weaselly creature, Cayetana's former butler. No longer is Carulli the trim figure in green and gold, but is now unkempt and down at heel, in a frowzy wig, with a tarnished cane, cracked pumps and stockings with holes in them, skulking about the court at the heels of his new master, the Count of Altolaguirre. The word around court is that within an hour of returning from Andalucía to her palace at Moncloa, Cayetana had sent him packing. It was said that he had expected, as a reward for his services as a spy at Sanlúcar, to be taken back into service by the Prince of Peace, or even by the Queen herself. But how could even that slippery couple find such a man trustworthy? He had served his purpose. Only someone as shady as Altolaguirre had been willing to take him on, and now he is reduced to tottering around Madrid after his master, as the Count goes about cadging drinks and dodging creditors and trying to scrape up a few paltrey reales *to squander at the gaming table. A pretty pair!*

Why, why had she ever taken up with a scoundrel like Altolaguirre? What could she have seen in such a coxcomb? The locket with the miniature. The love letters tied with a velvet cord. Dear God, how he had hated that man! Dear God, how he had hated HER. But at least she hadn't degenerated into the kind of travesty the Count had become, ending up as the sort of figure portrayed in the second of the two sketches he had done at Sanlúcar. He forces himself to gaze down at the figure in the print, soaring above her cluster of gaseous toreros. Yes, she had retained her beauty to the end. That was how she'd looked on those mortifying moments when they'd brushed up against one another in some passageway at court, or when they'd ridden past each other in the street, she in her carriage, he in his. Beautiful. Beautiful to the end.

There she is, the only character in that aerial quartet who has been drawn with love. Every one of the thousands of lines on the black shirt and black shawl, on the jacket and the sash and the embroidered armlets, had been graven with slow and loving care. Where is she sailing, his maja, *his lovely witch, sailing with naked feet with her hair streaming out behind her? Why has he made her look so serene and yet so sorrowful? And crowned her head with that gigantic moth with its wide-spread wings? The moth, a creature of the night, a fitting companion for a beautiful witch, the sign of inconsistency and infidelity.*

Yet surely also a creature fragile and mysterious, destined to live only a brief and brilliant life? And why has he placed his maja *so high up in the heavens, floating there at the hour of sunset, not surrounded by the black vapors of the night encompassing his witches in the other pictures in the folio? That pale proud face. Does it express resignation? Does it express regret? Was it regret and resignation he had himself felt, after his flight from Sanlúcar...?*

He closes the folio. Slowly. Softly. He stands irresolute. What has prompted him to strip away the bandage from the wound? He takes a deep breath. He sways on his feet. It is late. He is tired. It has been a hard day. The candles are guttering down. It is time for him to seek his cold and lonely bed....

But all at once he is seized with a fresh idea. He tries to resist it, as he tried to resist looking at the print in his Caprichos. *No use. He finds himself stepping away from the table and dragging himself across the studio. He doesn't take a candle with him—why should he expose himself to even more distress?*

Behind the easel canvases are stacked rank upon rank against the wall. The two pictures he is looking for are placed together. He cannot fool himself that he doesn't know where they are. He pauses, draws himself up, squares his shoulders, shuts his eyes and stands motionless with his head thrown back. He places a hand over his beating heart. He can feel the pulses trembling in his wrists and temples.

He has to take another deep breath before he can open his eyes and reach out a hand towards the two oblong canvases at the rear of one of the stacks. He grasps one of the frames but then stops and draws back his hand.

Why look at them? He hasn't looked at them since he painted them. Why subject himself to fresh pain?

Paintings of his Maja. *Paintings of Cayetana. Neither painting wholly completed. The heads still lacking. The faces still empty ovals.*

Why had he painted her like that? What witchery possessed him? Was it rage? Was it revenge? What greater revenge than to hold the Duchess of Alba up to ridicule? What greater revenge than to stealthily circulate pictures that showed her both in her frivolous finery and as the most wanton maja *of them all, the* maja *as naked harlot, the* maja *as a naked whore...?*

Naked. Stark naked. Thus could he make her smart for the pain she had made him suffer, she and her Miguel, on that last night in Sanlúcar...!

But something had happened. His hand would not obey him. His brush had refused to delineate her with the slashing strokes he intended. The hand that had caressed that flesh could not break faith with it. Just as he had not been able to damage her image in Volaverunt, *he could not violate her image now. No, he could not deny or betray the supreme sweetness of those weeks in Sanlúcar....*

And as he has not been able to forget that flesh, and play false with those memories, he had not been able to paint in her face. At the last minute he had shrunk from it. If people wanted to believe he had merely intended to paint a dirty picture, a portrait of some whore he had picked up in the streets, then so be it. Let them think what they liked....

It was when he had started on the second painting, the one where he had shown her tarted up in her maja *finery, that he began to feel some of his rage and resentment draining away. But not all. Not completely. Not quite. Even when he was painting the second one, he'd been afflicted with those terrible moments, moments when he'd been shaken as if with ague brought on by yellow fever. The miniature. The bundle of letters in the drawer of the dressing table....*

He pushes himself away from the wall and stands upright. He flings out a hand and reaches for the other painting, the second one, the one painted after the picture of her naked. But again he draws his hand back. He can see in his mind's eye this image of the woman sharpened by the darkness and by his deafness, as now are all his pictures. He draws his hand back as abruptly as he drew it back from the other one, afraid that seeing it flaming too vividly against the dark will cause him greater anguish than the earlier one....

He visualizes her lying resplendent on her gray silk sheets, wearing the pearly tight-fitting shift and the black and gold jacket. Around her waist is the scarlet sash, and on her tiny witch's feet are the jeweled Turkish slippers. He has seen her thus a hundred times, reclining on her pillow, her arms raised above her head as she waits for him to enter the bedchamber....

He feels as if a hand of ice is fastened around his heart, gripping it and squeezing it. He can scarcely breathe. Those soft arms are raised invitingly, but yet again there is only a blank where the face should be. He shivers. Sooner or later he will have to paint in those two blank faces. But whose, since he can't bear to destroy the pictures and can't bear to put in hers? Whose then? Easy to dabble something in. But whose? How about good old La Tirana, who has been so mystified by his neglect since his return from Andalucía? But how to fit those florid features onto that delicate body? Then, if not La Tirana, what about one or other of his other singers and dancers. Rita Luna, perhaps? Or Narcisa Zárate? But no, in the end he'll probably have to settle for the features of some real maja, one of the brassy girls he can find any evening in the local taverns.

Yet why is he racking his brains about it now, at this time of night, at the witching hour? Maybe the best solution would be simply to burn the wretched things, get rid of them to avoid the risk of them falling into the wrong hands....

Burn them! Burn them! For how many weary years had he got to go on wrestling with the fear that he had lost her through his own pigheadedness? Lost her because of the violent temper to which he has all too often given way? Lost her because of his own stubborness and because he could not control his feelings? Of course she should never have ordered the dog to be shot, but how could she have known that Baltasar had been the pet and playmate of his dead sons? Lost her because of a senseless fit of jealousy over a stuck-up popinjay like Altolaguirre! Perhaps she hadn't really meant to invite Altolaguirre to Sanlúcar in the first place? Perhaps he and Pepe had simply foisted themselves off on her unannounced? That creepy butler of his, what was his name? He had always suspected that that nasty little fellow may have had something to do with it....

What was it he had written on one of the plates, the plate he'd originally intended to put first in the folio? **The Sleep of Reason brings forth Monsters.** *Couldn't that apply as much as to the nightmares and imaginings of his own mind, to what had happened in Andalucía? That night in Sanlúcar, hadn't his own reason been asleep, and hadn't his reason let the monsters loose? Perhaps by letting his reason sleep he had lost Cayetana, a woman who had loved him, a woman who had tried to alleviate his sickness, to coax him out of his deafness, who had tried to dispel the darkness and to banish the monsters....*

How could he measure the sum of what he had thrown away? He covers his face with his hands. For the first time in his life he is revolted by the smell of paint on his fingers....

What is he to do? How is he to live? What chance can there now be of keeping the monsters at bay...?

He shakes himself. He lifts his left hand and stares at the back of it, twisting it this way and that in the candlelight. The marks made by Baltasar's teeth have long since vanished. Foolishly he tells himself that he wishes his hand hadn't healed, that he still had something personal and painful to remember her by. But there is nothing. He rouses himself and mutters to himself, "All the same, she shouldn't have tried to kill my dog." Then with a sort of desperation he reaches for a tall canvas that stands by itself against the wall. He lifts it up and holds his arms out at full length, then brings it close to his face, squinting at it in the fitful candlelight. He utters a sound between a groan and a sob.

He takes a rapid step and plants himself in front of the easel. He plucks the canvas on which he had been working from the easel and throws it into a corner and puts the other one in its place. It slips sideways and he makes a grab for it to prevent it from falling. Fortunately the paint on it has long been dry. He rights it with trembling fingers.

He averts his eyes, as if afraid to confront it. He gives himself another shake and takes a deeper breath and turns his back on it and begins to move around the studio. He pours another aguardiente, *his fingers awkward in their leathern mittens. He starts to open drawers, searching for fresh candles. He takes his time lighting them from the* flickering wicks of the candles in the candlesticks, screwing them into the congealing pools of wax.

When he feels he is ready, he returns to the easel. He stands in front of it, his head lowered, his hands hanging by his sides, his fingers clenching and unclenching. He slowly raises his head.

Burnt orange blouse. Crimson and gold armlets. Long black skirt with its apron of Mechlin lace. Broad scarlet sash. Shawl with a high jeweled comb foaming about the shoulders and bosom....

The brightening gleams of the candles ripple across the surface, bringing the woman to life.

He raises his hands and strokes the face with a knuckle.

He strokes the brows he had once blackened with his thumb. He strokes the cheeks he had once rouged. He strokes the legs in the white stockings and the feet in the embroidered slippers.

All finished. The picture finished. The woman dead.

He takes hold of the edge of the easel and lets himself sink slowly to his knees.

Mind empty, head thrown back, he stares up vacantly at the canvas. It seems to him the woman is hovering above him, floating up and away from him.

Flying. Flying.

He sinks down further.

The slim and tapering forefinger of the receding woman is pointed downwards directly at him. Inscribed on the great pearl ring on her middle finger is the name of the august and ancient house to which she belongs:

ALBA

On the smaller gold and enamel ring on her forefinger is incised another name:

GOYA

His eyes travel slowly down to the sandy ground beneath her feet.
Where are the words that were once written so large and so lovingly on the sandy soil beneath the jeweled slipper?

SOLO GOYA

Where are they?
Brushed out.
Obliterated.
He stares at the empty strip of sandy soil as if staring at it could restore the words he wiped out six years ago with three strokes of his brush.
He feels numb and hollow.
He moves his cold stiff limbs and tries to rise.
The ring with his own name. GOYA. That at least it had been necessary to spare. How could he bear to expunge every trace, every last memory of those bittersweet months at Sanlúcar…?
He has risen halfway to his feet when suddenly, without any warning, as if snuffed by some invisible agency, all the candles in the studio are extinguished.
He utters a stifled frightened sound, his arms flailing in the darkness. His head strikes the leg of the easel as he tries to grip the ledge to haul himself up. The easel rocks and almost brings the portrait down on him. Just in time he relinquishes it and lies down on the floor, panting.

SOLO GOYA
GOYA SOLO
ONLY GOYA
GOYA ALONE

He heaves himself up one on knee and stays there crouching. His eyes rake the darkness. What are those shapes in the corner, blacker than black? What are those shifting shadows sidling along beside the wall, darker than the darkness?

Witches and warlocks. Circling. Creeping nearer. Closing in.

He utters a cry, there is no one to hear, a cry he cannot hear himself. He claps his hands over his ears.

Deafness cannot protect him. Guns and pistols cannot help him. The witches and warlocks and all of their devilish troops will find a way to get into his head, they and their infernal clamor will find a way to get into his skull and lodge themselves inside it....

He squeezes his eyes tightly shut and presses his hands harder over his ears.

He can feel them now. They are entering him. Invading him. In spite of his deafness he can hear their hellish twitterings, their obscene rustlings, their filthy whisperings. They will never leave him now.

He rocks back and forth. He has a vision of Baltasar, jaws agape, eyes glazed, shivering and resigned to his fate as he disappears slowly, slowly into the quicksand.

He too feels himself being drawn down.

Slowly, slowly.

He is locked in with his monsters now. Shut in with them forever.

GOYA ALONE.

In 1901 Goya's remains were disinterred from his tomb in Bordeaux, where he had died in 1826 at the age of 81, for eventual reburial in the Church of San Antonio de la Florida in Madrid.

The skeleton was found to be missing its skull, a suitably mysterious and macabre final touch to what had been a steadily darkening existence.

The Duchess of Alba died in Madrid in 1802 at the age of 40, and in 1945 an autopsy was performed on her remains.

The feet of the corpse were discovered to have been chopped off. Another mystery. Was she regarded as a witch and her feet removed to prevent her from walking after death?

Notes

Goya really did live at Número Uno Calle del Desengaño, the Street of Disillusion.

And he really did paint the words SOLO GOYA beneath the feet of the Duchess of Alba in her Sanlúcar portrait (now in the Hispanic Society of New York) and subsequently paint them out. Their existence was only revealed when the portrait was cleaned in the late twentieth century.

The Duchess was at Sanlúcar de Barrameda in the late summer of 1796. Goya had fallen seriously ill while staying with his friend Sebastián Martínez in Cádiz and had become totally deaf. A painting by Goya of himself as a patient *in extremis* being tended to by a doctor can be seen in the Minneapolis Institute of Art. He painted his second portrait of the Duchess at Sanlúcar and also drew the lewd sketches of her in his bedchamber in what is now known as the Sanlúcar Notebook, an assemblage of 18 drawings in brush and Indian ink.

Most of the chapters or sections of the novel are based on actual paintings, drawings or etchings by Goya. Queen María Luisa, Sebastián Martínez, Ceán Bermúdez, La Tirana, Narcisa Zárate, Pedro Romero and others were real people, all painted or sketched by Goya. The best source for these portraits is the monumental LIFE AND COMPLETE WORKS OF FRANCISCO GOYA by Pierre Gassier and Juliet Wilson (published in an English version by Raynal/William Morrow in 1971). Therein may also be found the self-portraits by Goya mentioned in the text—the self-portrait in the Bolívar hat in the opening scene with the Duchess in the coach, the self-portrait as viewed by the Duchess from her bedroom window, the self-portrait of the artist wearing his hat with the candles stuck around the rim which he wore when at work in his studio.

Pedro Romero, Costillares and Pepe-Hillo were real and famous bullfighters. The other *toreros* in the bullfighting scene with the *jabonero* are invented, as are Miguel de Altolaguirre, Salvatore Carulli, Esteban and Pascual. So is the name of the mastiff Baltasar whom, for story purposes, I have made the pet of Goya's two infant sons who had died shortly after Goya went to visit Sebastián Martínez. This idea was suggested by a painting by Goya in the Prado depicting a huge brown mastiff attended by two small boys. Also in the Prado can be seen paintings of children playing at soldiers, blowing up balloons, and so forth, and pictures and cartoons of revelers at a picnic flying kites, walking on stilts, tossing one another in a blanket, playing blind man's bluff, playing instruments, etc. The death of Baltasar in the swamp is based, of course, on the famous painting of the drowning dog in the room at the Prado devoted to the so-called "black" Goyas, while the "black" portrayals of witchcraft, of the Inquisition, etc. are all taken from actual sketches and etchings. The image of the Duchess in the guise of a flying witch, the drawing of the teeth from the hanged man and the Sleep of Reason are contained in *Los Caprichos*; the image of the spectator dangling on a bull's horn is from the *Tauromaquia* and the Duchess's dream of the white bull is from the herd of ghostly cattle depicted in a plate entitled *Disparate de Tontos* in the *Disparates o Proverbios* series. The Duchess's nightmare ride on the winged monstrosity has been suggested by a plate called *Disparate Volante* in the same series. Sinister doodling on walls was also a known habit of Goya's.

The Duchess possessed a little bichon frisé which figures in the first portrait Goya painted of her (Alba Collection, Madrid) and that I have named Conchita. Goya was certainly much taken with dogs, cats, birds and other domestic creatures and lost no opportunity of including them in his paintings. The Duchess's previous lovers are all inventions.

María Luz and her daughter Estrellita are a special case. The Duchess had indeed adopted a small black child she called María Luz and who is shown playing on the Duchess's bed in one of the sketches in the Sanlúcar Notebook. Again, I have taken the liberty of making María Luz the girl's mother and naming her daughter Estrellita.

Finally, a word about the *maja* paintings. Goya appeared to have painted the naked *maja* first in 1800 and followed it in 1805 with the clothed *maja*, both paintings that date from the years between Goya's abrupt departure from Sanlúcar and the death of the Duchess. It is not too fanciful to suppose that he painted them as a bittersweet reminder of his weeks at Sanlúcar. The curious thing about them is the contrast, the startling disparity between the beauty of the two bodies and the coarseness of the two heads. The body and the heads seem to belong to different women. Moreover, the heads seem to be awkwardly, indeed unconvincingly, placed on the women's shoulders as if they had been hurriedly and carelessly cobbled on as an afterthought. Therefore I do not believe that I have stretched whatever might be the truth of the matter too far in suggesting in the final pages of my story that the body of the woman in question is the body of the Duchess of Alba and the features those of some *maja* whom Goya had encountered in the streets, or perhaps of some actress or singer with whom he had been intimate.

In the course of time Goya parted with his pair of *maja* paintings. On the other hand, he jealously guarded his final portrait of the Duchess of Alba, keeping it in his possession and only presenting it to his sole remaining son, Javier, after the latter had attained manhood.

Acknowledgments

As principal contributors to the writing of this book, representing as it does, with my biographies of Diego Velázquez and Hernán Cortés, the completion of what may be termed a Spanish Trilogy, I have to thank the sustained support and encouragement of my daughters, both of them adept in the arts and both of them retaining lively recollections of our years together in Spain.

Bronwen, an informed student of painters and of painting, typed out the successive revisions of the novel, while her sister Rhiannon, a designer and maker of jewelry, proved an additional and unflagging source of strength.

Nor must I forget to pay warm tribute to Patricia Zagorski, professor of music and an artist in her own right, who has followed the making of this and others of my books with a close and unstinting attention and who has provided me with many valuable insights and suggestions.

JON MANCHIP WHITE was born in Cardiff, Wales, the son of a shipowner. Educated at Cambridge University, he served during World War II in the Royal Navy and in the Welsh Guards. After acting as the first story editor of BBC TV, he spent four years in the British Foreign Service before resuming his career as screenwriter and story editor, working among other companies for the Bronston Organization in Paris, Rome, and in Madrid, where he spent five years. In 1967 he went to the University of Texas at El Paso to start its creative writing program, and in 1977 he went to the University of Tennessee at Knoxville to initiate a similar program. He retired in 1994 as the holder of the Lindsay Young Chair of English. He is the author of thirty books of fiction, history, travel, archaeology and anthropology in addition to numerous movies and television plays, *Solo Goya*, together with his earlier biographies of Diego Velázquez and Hernán Cortés, concludes what might be termed a Spanish Trilogy.

CPSIA information can be obtained
at www.ICGtesting.com
Printed in the USA
BVHW071224190820
586812BV00001B/119